I0579275

SOME LEGENDS NEVER DIE

Monsters and Mayhem Book Two

E A COMISKEY

Scarsdale Publishing, Ltd

Some Legends Never Die: Book Two Monsters and Mayhem © *2020 by Elizabeth Ann Comiskey*

All rights reserved. No part of this publication may be reproduced, stored in a retrieval system, or transmitted, in any form or by any means without the prior written permission of the author, nor be otherwise circulated in any form of binding or cover other than that in which it is published and without a similar condition being imposed on the subsequent purchaser.

This is a work of fiction. Names, characters, places, and incidents are either the product of the author's imagination or are used fictitiously, and any resemblance to actual persons living or dead, business establishments, events, or locales, is entirely coincidental.

ISBN 13: 9781953100085

Cover design by Dreams2media

First Trade Paperback Printing by Broken Arm Publishing: June 2019

10 9 8 7 6 5 4 3 2

If you purchased this book without a cover, you should be aware that this book is stolen property. It was reposted as "unsold and destroyed" to the publisher, and neither the author nor the publisher has received any payment for this "stripped book."

SP

TRADEMARK ACKNOWLEDGEMENTS

Coca-Cola

Little Anthony and The Imperials

1968 Shelby GT

Paul Anka

John Deere

American Audubon

NASA

To Serve Man (The Twilight Zone)

Tupperware

Whole Foods

Tweeting (Twitter)

Google

Sears

Jeopardy

Dan Brown

Irish Spring

Lord Voldemort/*Harry Potter*

James Dean

Sherlock Holmes

Schwarzenegger

Thing Number One and Thing Number Two (Dr. Seuss)
"Do not pass Go. Do not collect two hundred dollars."
(Monopoly)
Tom Hanks
Chewbacca/Obi Wan Kenobi (Star Wars)
Felix The Cat
Jell-O, Registered trademark of Kraft Foods
Good Housekeeping, a magazine owned by the Hearst
Corporation

For Brian, my twin soul.

CHAPTER ONE

Richard

COBWEBS DANGLED FROM SPLINTERED WINDOWS THAT dotted one side of the rusty trailer. Screams emanated from behind the thin, poorly constructed walls. Near the front door, a tall, thin man in a dark tailcoat shouted above the joyous rumble of the crowd. "Come one, come all. Take a journey through the afterlife. Mingle with spirits, dance with monsters, but don't stay too long or you may forget your way out of the Tomb of the Dead."

Richard rolled his eyes at the carnival barker. Kids spending an hour's income of their parents' wages for the privilege of three minutes of being scared by plastic skeletons and rubber spiders. Little brats had no idea what really peered out at them from the shadows at night. How could they? He hadn't known. For more than seven decades he'd gotten along just fine, more or less, thinking humans ruled the prime spot in Earth's food chain. Then Stan friggin' Kapcheck, his neighbor at the Everest Senior Living Facility, got him mixed up in monster hunting and he hadn't trusted a dark corner since.

Today, though, he clung to his determination to enjoy the moment and ignore the world of monsters. He tuned out the nonsense going on at the carnival "fun house," and focused his attention upon the masterpiece before him. That particular corndog rivaled anything ever created by some over-bred, high-falootin' French chef, and he'd go to the mat to defend that opinion with anyone who dared tell him otherwise. This lumpy, slightly misshapen masterpiece bore no resemblance whatsoever to any factory-made frozen food-like product. He'd watched the kid with purple spiked hair jam a stick in a hotdog and dunk it into a clear plastic tub full of creamy batter before dropping it into the basket of bubbling oil. When it came out, golden crust gleaming like the life-giving sun, Richard knew he'd won the culinary lottery. The kid then proved he was a genius in freak's clothing when he scooped a handful of fried onion petals into a paper basket and laid his creation upon that glorious bed of grease.

Richard asked for a Coke to go with it, paid roughly the same amount as he had for a week's groceries back in his lonely widower days, and shuffled across the blacktop to the picnic table Burke and Stanley had staked a claim to. He had to weave his way through a crowd that included a ten-foot-tall Uncle Sam, two enormous peanuts with legs, and a frazzled-looking woman with a troupe of children bouncing along in her wake like a row of over-sugared ducklings. Finally, he reached the table and set his treasures on the rough wooden tabletop. All the while, the rich, heady aroma of fried cornbread and onions rose from the flimsy basket, teasing him with promises of flavor to come.

Too eager for lunch to care about dignity, he used his right hand to hoist his leg over the bench, plunked down on his bony butt, used both hands to get the left leg up and over, and swiveled into a proper seated position. He neither knew nor cared how he'd ever manage to extricate himself from the table and its attached benches when the time came. That first bite made it all worthwhile—crunchy on the outside, moist and steamy on the inside, with the salty meatiness of the wiener in the middle. He mashed it up between ill-fitted dentures, struggling to stifle a moan. The second bite held more meat and less bread and contained a surprising little burst of delicious grease.

When he lifted the tab on the can of Coca-Cola, it popped with a satisfying hiss and a snap that sent an effervescent spray of icy soda raining down to settle like so many dewdrops upon the white hairs of his forearm. The sweet, tickling liquid sowed a row of cold satisfaction down his throat.

He closed his eyes and sighed in pleasure while Little Anthony and The Imperials sang over the loudspeaker about tears on pillows and someone revved the engine of the 1968 Shelby GT they'd brought to exhibit in the classic car show. When he opened his eyes, he found Burke sitting directly across from him, eyebrows raised just above the rims of her enormous mirrored sunglasses. Her cheeks lifted in a smile that displayed the freckles on her tawny brown skin.

"Why you grinnin' like a possum eatin' a sweet potato?"

She selected a peanut from the cup on the table and used her manicured pink nails to break it open. "I just don't think I've ever seen anyone enjoy a meal so completely."

Richard popped an onion petal into his mouth. The crunchy tang highlighted the other flavors, overwhelming none of them. The culinary lottery, for sure. "Now it's a crime for a man to enjoy his lunch?"

Unaffected by his gruff tone, she ate her peanut and reached for another. "I think it's nice that you are so happy."

"To truly, thoroughly enjoy a meal is considered by some to be a high form of meditation, capable of bringing a man into communion with the gods," Stanley said in his fancy British accent. He sat on the tabletop, his perfectly shined black shoes propped on the bench. He wore slim fit blue jeans and a bright white, starched shirt with the top two buttons open and the sleeves rolled up to the elbow. A newsboy hat protected his bald head from the bright Alabama sun.

"Why can't you sit on the bench like God intended?" Richard asked.

Miss Peanut Festival strode past in impossible, sparkly silver shoes. Her tan legs flexed and stretched beneath a pale-yellow skirt tossed about by the gentle breeze. Golden locks hung in ringlets nearly to her slim waist. Her eyes lingered on Stanley a moment and a smile kissed the dimpled corner of her full, wide mouth.

Stanley tipped his hat in her direction. "The view is delightful from up here, Richard."

Richard harrumphed into his corndog. "I ain't some dirty old man." But he couldn't quite keep his eyes from following the princess's progress as she sashayed around a corner and disappeared.

Paul Anka took over the music and started crooning for his girl to put her head on his shoulder and whisper in his ear. A group of teenage girls on a ride screamed high above their heads. "It ain't a bad little festival," he admitted.

"Indeed," Stanley agreed. "Did you know that most of the carnival companies in America aren't actually operated by humans at all but by—"

"Stop it," Burke said. "I don't want to know. For half a year I've been chasing hide-behinds and fighting shapeshifters. If the ride operators here are all descended from Big Foot, I don't even want to know. For one day, I just want to sit here and eat these peanuts and not worry about what might be looking to eat me."

"They don't eat people. They—"

"Stanley Kapcheck, I swear to God, I will pistol whip you if you try to finish that sentence."

Stanley chuckled. "I don't often see the resemblance

between you and your grandfather, but at moments like this, there is no doubt in my mind." He waved at a troupe of silver-haired cloggers clad in impressively supportive tights and leotards bedecked with all manner of red white and blue spangles and fringe. The taps on their shoes click-clacked against the pavement, creating a ruckus akin to the wheels of a steam engine rattling along a rusty rail. The ladies blushed and waved back.

Richard rolled his eyes and focused on enjoying the last of the corn dog. An unsettling weight pressed against his ribs but another sip of Coca-Cola carried the pressure away on the wind of a long, low belch. Several of the cloggers' smiles turned to dirty looks flashed at him. He shrugged, unapologetic. Everybody burped. If some people wanted to pretend otherwise, well, he couldn't stop anyone from being as uppity as they chose to be.

When the noise from the cloggers died down, the paper basket was emptied, and the peanuts reduced to a pile of empty shells, Stanley said, "You know, at some point, we're going to have to decide whether or not we have the collective courage to face this challenge."

"Stanley," Burke said, a warning in her voice.

Stanley shifted so he could more easily see Burke. "I know you've no desire to discuss the hidden dangers of the world today but, honestly, isn't that why we stopped here? To take some time to evaluate what we know and proceed with prudence."

"You might be the expert hunter in this group," Richard said, "but you don't know about this. Not the way Burke and I know."

"Once you enter her world, it's nearly impossible to get out again," Burke said.

"She'll suck at your soul until you start praying for death," Richard added. He shuddered at the memory of sitting in his room at the nursing home, waiting for his body to realize his life had ended long ago. Those were the days before Stanley had dragged him into the whirlwind of a monster-hunting existence. He'd been blind to the wonders, both good and bad, hidden in plain sight all around him.

"She's protective of her offspring, but she'll turn on them, too, given the slightest provocation," Burke said.

"Then we must be exceedingly careful not to provoke her," Stanley said.

"She draws you in with tears, makes you feel sorry for her, so you aren't expecting when she moves in for the kill," Richard said.

"We shall remain on guard against all forms of emotional trickery," Stanley said.

"She's clever. She'll try to separate us. Divide and conquer," Burke said.

"No one goes in alone. That's just good hunter sense," Stanley said.

"That nest of vampires in California was downright open-minded by comparison," Richard said.

"I cannot force either of you to face this, but the connection between her and you is powerful and I don't believe you'll rest well until this matter is settled. You two will not dissuade me from my opinion. Together, we are strong enough to deal with her," Stanley said.

Burke wrapped the end of one long braid around her finger. "You don't have anything like her in your journal, Stanley."

Richard sucked down the remainder of his Coke. "She's got these pointy little fingernails and they make this noise—"

"It'll destroy you from the inside out," Burke finished for him.

"Surely you both exaggerate. In all this time fighting monsters—"

Burke leaned forward on both elbows. "What will you do if

things go south? We can't defeat her by stabbing her with a silver dagger or shooting her with lead bullets."

"Salt won't keep her away. She thrives on the stuff."

Stanley cocked his head to one side and regarded them in silence for a little while. On the loudspeaker, a low southern voice announced that the greased pig contest would start in thirty minutes. A teen boy walked by lugging a stuffed monkey as large as himself. A banner flapped against the wall of a nearby building. In big red letters on a white background, it announced, "Coleum Corp, where there's space for all." At last he said, "She's your family. Your daughter. Your mother. And since you are the closest thing I have to family, when she calls and asks that we come for an early Thanksgiving, I say we ought to go and eat turkey and pumpkin pie. And no amount of chatter from the two of you will convince me that the woman is some kind of demonic entity."

Burke dropped her head onto her folded arms. "She's going to try to hook me up with someone horrid," she mumbled against the tabletop.

"She'll try to get me back in the nursing home," Richard said. "She thinks I'm old."

"You *are* old, Dick."

Richard scowled. Lord, but he hated being called Dick.

Stanley just chuckled. "Come on, you two sourpusses. It's a festival. Let's enjoy it."

"I *was* enjoying it until you insisted we have this conversation," Richard said. Already, his stomach had begun to send out distress signals, but no matter what came, the delicacy had been worth it.

"There's a greased pig contest," Stanley said, hopping lithely down from the tabletop.

Unnatural. Even if he didn't have aches and pains, which he ought to have at his age—well, technically, he should be dead at his age, but all things considered—he still ought to have the decency to move at a certain accepted and expected pace. To do otherwise served no purpose but to brag. Pompous old peacock.

Richard carefully hoisted himself out of the picnic table with a fine and proper amount of grunting and crunching joints, as befitted a senior citizen.

Burke collected their trash and dropped it in a nearby bin. "What exactly is a greased pig contest and why are we going to see it?"

Stanley strolled through the crowd with his hands in his pockets, face tilted slightly up toward the crystalline sky. "They grease up a pig and set it loose and try to catch it. There's a skill to it. Not everyone can manage."

"No doubt," Burke replied.

"This year, the organizers of the race wanted to get more bang for their buck."

Richard's guts squirmed. After six months with Stan Kapcheck, he understood this sensation had little to do with his gastric worries and more to do with the pending announcement that death and destruction loomed in their near future. With Stan, there was always a pending announcement of death and destruction in the near future. That was Stanley's stock in trade.

"They sought out the fastest, most powerful pig they could find," Stanley said.

Burke's glasses remained pointed straight ahead, her lips pressed into a thin, tight line.

"They selected a real doozy. Not just an average pig, but a saehrimnir."

"One day, Stanley. Just one day of hanging out at a festival," Burke said.

Stanley pulled one hand from his pocket and lifted it in a gesture of surrender. "Festivals are tricky. Like I tried to tell you. More often than not, the carnivals are run by—"

"Just tell us what the devil a saehrimnir is," Richard snapped.

"They are pigs destined for the tables of the Norse gods. If anyone here dares slaughter one, the wrath of the gods could well wipe Dothan, Alabama, right off the map." Stan winked at a redhead in a pair of teeny tiny shorts and a crocheted halter top that served little purpose beyond keeping her just this side of a public indecency citation.

The woman winked back.

Richard burped and immediately felt a little better. "They're just going to catch it though, right? Not like they'll tear it limb from limb."

"Well, that's true," Stanley agreed. "They won't slaughter it right now, but once it's been caught it goes back with the other pigs."

"So?" Burke asked.

"What do you think happened to the little piggy who went to the market fair, my dear?"

"So, we need to steal a pig and set it loose?" she asked.

Stanley nodded. "Precisely, but we need to be quick about it."

"Why's that?"

"Because, as I tried to tell you, the carnival is run by—"

"Forget it," she said, holding up a hand to stop him. "Forget I asked. I seriously don't want to know."

"Great. We save the pig and then we head north to eat turkey," Stanley said. "I can't wait to meet your daughter, Dick."

"Maybe we can just stay here, eating pork chops and bacon, until the gods come to kill us," Richard said.

Stanley laughed. "I love that you're developing a sense of humor, old boy."

Richard harrumphed again. Who said he was joking?

CHAPTER TWO

Burke

THE GREASED PIG CONTEST WAS TO BE HELD IN AN ARENA OF twelve-inch-deep black muck, ringed by a welded steel fence. Spectators gathered around the edges with their tub-size lemon shake-ups and fried food of every sort. Near the gate that led into the circle, two old farmers sat at a table. As each competitor arrived, the men signed him in and gestured for him to pass through the gate into the muddy mess. So far, six young men in cowboy boots, jeans, and tee-shirts with logos advertising beer, cigarettes, and conservative political candidates had progressed through the registration process. They laughed loudly and slapped each other on the back.

Burke crossed her arms. "Now what?"

"The pig is in that little white shed behind the registration table. They'll let it into the ring once everyone is ready to begin," Stanley said.

As if it heard him, the animal let out a snort that Burke felt in her bones. The little plywood shed shuddered.

"Whoever thought this was a good idea must have been nuttier than a squirrel turd," Richard said.

"It's usually a baby pig," Stanley told them.

Burke eyed the shed. It must have been five feet long and four feet across. The structure shifted as another grunt emanated from within. "That's no baby."

Richard shuffled a step or two forward and faced Stanley with a scowl. "How'd you even know about this, anyway?"

"They announced it on the loudspeaker, Dick. Didn't you hear?"

"That ain't what I mean. How'd you know about this pig and all the trouble?"

Stanley nodded toward the registration table where one of the old farmers was now standing, saying something to the crowd around him. "Last call for registrants. Burke, you need to hurry."

A laugh burst out of her before the sneaking suspicion that the old man was serious snuck in. "You're kidding."

"How else will we get the pig?" Stanley asked.

"We could wait until it's over and the thing is tied up again."

"And if it's injured in the contest? Loaded onto the meat packing truck immediately after? Carted off to some unknown location? Then what?"

Burke looked to her grandfather for help but he just shrugged. *I should have taken his sorry butt back to the nursing home when this all started.*

"It won't be so hard, my dear. You've faced far worse monsters than this."

"Not... not..." She gestured vaguely toward the filth. "Not in the mud."

Stanley smiled. "Mud is good for the complexion."

Her nails bit into the flesh of her upper arms. "If it's so fantastic, you go catch the pig."

He laughed. "There is a reason the old men are sitting at the table while the young men compete. They'd never let me in, Burke. I'd be considered a liability."

She glared at him.

"Time is of the essence, Burke."

Perhaps her grandfather would take her side. "Don't you have anything to say about this?"

"It would be a shame to see this pretty little town burned out of existence."

She gritted her teeth and spun away from them. Crazy old men ought to be locked up for their own safety and the safety of others. She stalked to the table and told the men she wanted to catch the blasted pig.

They exchanged a look and burst into laughter.

Burke took a deep breath and fought for control of her rage. "Did I say something funny?"

The guy on the left knocked his John Deere hat askew as he wiped his eyes. "We just don't get many participants of the female persuasion."

The guy on the right mopped his face with a red and white bandana. "There's a quilting bee tonight in the grange building."

She slapped the $10 participation fee on the table. "Take my money. Write my name down. Don't make this difficult."

John Deere's smile faded. "You could get hurt."

"I'd say that's my concern, not yours."

They exchanged another look and a shrug.

"Okay, then," bandana guy said. "Don't say we didn't warn you." He asked her name and wrote it on his clipboard.

The other man leaned forward and whispered. "Watch out for Cletus in the white undershirt. He's downright mean and too darned stupid to know better."

Burke glanced toward the group of men inside the arena. They all stared at her.

The guy in the white shirt stood half a head taller than the rest. His long blond hair was tied back in a sloppy ponytail. He had a tattoo of a cross on his left bicep and a naked woman on his right. He grinned at her, revealing teeth that were at least three short of a full set.

She thanked the old man for the warning and proceeded through the rickety gate. Her feet, clad in boots she'd purchased less than a month earlier, sank into the bog. Each step produced a sucking sound loud enough to be heard above the noise of the crowd—an impressive feat, now that the entire group was hooting and whistling, jeering, and screaming both insults and encouragement.

Cletus jabbed the short, skinny cowboy next to him with his elbow. "Hey, pretty lady. I think maybe you took a wrong turn."

Burke ignored him and took in the rest of the group. They were short and tall, slim and stout, but clearly bonded by a love of belt buckles the size of dessert plates.

"Did Mammy sent you in here to fetch something special for Massa's dinner table?"

Her attention snapped back to the gap-toothed man.

He spit out a yellow glob of nastiness. "You're in the wrong place, girl."

Burke put on her prettiest smile and joined the group. "You boys all here trying to catch this pig because you're unhappy with the sausage God gave you?" She winked at Cletus. "I guess that's why you seem most desperate of all."

His gap-toothed grin melted. "You best be careful, girl. A person could get hurt doing this kind of thing."

She inched closer to him and lowered her voice. "I've felt the blood of monsters twice your size splash across my face. I know what it is to sink a knife into living flesh. You want to hurt me? Bring it, pencil dick."

The little crowd of men backed away.

Cletus blinked at her as if trying to puzzle out the meaning of her threat.

A voice boomed over the loudspeaker, "A great big thank you to Coleum Corporation for sponsoring this here event and most everything else in the great forty-eight these days. Now, y'all ready to rastle some pork?"

Burke searched for her companions.

Her grandfather clung to the railing. He watched her with wide eyes. His wrinkled hands gripped the wire fence, and he pushed his dentures around the inside of his mouth.

Stanley stood with his feet shoulder-width apart and his hands in his pockets. The bright sun reflected on his polished shoes and twinkled in his eyes.

The man in the John Deere hat yanked a cord that pulled the shed door open. A beast easily three times Burke's weight and nearly as long as she was tall burst out in a blur of shiny pink skin and squealed at a pitch that reminded her of the metal-on-metal shriek of locomotive brakes.

The gate to the arena was slammed shut behind the animal and the men leapt into action. Two of them managed to land on the animal's back. One slid straight across. The pig slipped out from under the other, squealing even louder.

Cletus put himself directly in the pig's path and was knocked on his butt in the muck.

Burke watched the men grab, again and again, trying and failing to get a hold on the trunk-like neck. Each time, the pig shot out of their arms like a watermelon seed being spit out. The animal grew wilder and more frantic with each passing moment.

Cletus was tossed in the air and landed next to her.

She gazed down at him.

He glared up at her. "Girl like you belongs on her back." His hand flashed toward her ankle, but before he could pull her down, she hopped and shuffled and felt the satisfying crunch of his hand under her foot. The earth was soft. She didn't think it was broken, but his pained grunt was satisfying, nonetheless.

The pig always turned to the left. It watched over its left shoulder. It tilted its head to the left. Something was wrong with its right ear or eye. It had a weak spot.

"Excuse me." She twisted her toe into the back of his hand as she stepped away.

A cowboy flew through the air past her and landed with a muffled thump on top of Cletus, who let out a grunt not entirely unlike those made by the angry beast.

Burke remembered that pigs' bodies bore striking similarities to human bodies. She knew a fair number of tricks for fighting humans. If the gods wanted their bacon, they'd best grant her wish that her tricks would carry over.

She jogged around the arena, her feet making horrible, squelching, sucking noises with each step, and came up on the pig's right side. Two men tried to leap on it from the left, but it saw them coming and danced out of their way, leaving them in a tangle of filth-covered limbs.

Now or never.

Honing in on the spot on the neck, between the shoulder and the ear, that would instantly incapacitate a human, she threw herself at the beast, arms outstretched like superman.

Bingo!

Her fist struck the exact location she'd been aiming for. The force of punching a five-hundred-pound creature jolted through her hand all the way up into her arm, into the middle of her back, and she landed on her back with a sickening splat.

The pig stopped squealing and thrashing and stared at her with surprisingly human eyes as if to say, "Really, that seemed rather uncalled for." And then, with the slow grace of a Giant Redwood succumbing to a lumberjack's axe, it toppled.

That was the general idea of what she had hoped to accomplish with the maneuver; however, she'd not planned on the creature falling in her direction. Scrambling away through the mud was a lost cause. She only managed a sad, sticky half-revolution before she found her legs pinned under enough pork to feed an entire village of heathens.

The crowd fell silent.

Burke turned her head, wincing at the sensation of slimy goo being rubbed into the back of her scalp. He grandfather's mouth hung open. Stanley gave her a thumbs up.

If she had access to a gun, she might have shot him.

Contest officials, believing the animal had been killed, drove a tractor on tank-like treads into the arena and used chains and the tractor's shovel to lift it and carry it away.

John Deere extended a hand to Burke and she allowed him to help her up. All her parts seemed to be in working order, if a bit numb from being squished so very thoroughly.

"Ain't never seen anything like that in seventy-three years."

She pushed a dirty, wet braid away from her face with a dirty, wet hand. "Life's full of surprises." Her attention stayed on the tractor and the two old men trotting in its wake. "I gotta go."

"I reckon you get a prize," he said, though he seemed unsure if that was true. Probably because she was supposed to catch the pig, not kill it.

Burke couldn't help but ask, "What's the prize?"

"Two free passes to the demolition derby."

"What's a demolition derby?"

He regarded her with the expression of someone gazing upon an oddity that was hard for the mind to accept. "'s a race on a figure eight track. Means the drivers gotta get past each other in the cross."

"People pay to see that?"

"Well, yeah. Runs 'bout six bucks a person."

No way she heard that right. "Six dollars?"

"Yes ma'am. Course, there's a discount for veterans."

She gestured at the mess around them. "People do this for twelve dollars' worth of prizes?"

He scowled. "They're good seats. Right up front."

A yelp near the gate caught her attention. A medic was wrapping Cletus's hand in white tape. Cletus barked obscenities at him.

Burke shook her head, trying to clear the clutter. "Yeah, well. Give them to that guy. He earned it for dealing with Cletus the Assclown."

The tractor and both of her companions disappeared in the distance.

"I've got to go. It's been real."

As she passed, Cletus yelled an unimaginative racial slur at her and then yelped. "Careful!" he shouted.

She peeked over her shoulder in time to see the medic give an unapologetic shrug that made her happy he'd be receiving the free race tickets.

In a field behind the steer barn, Richard stood watching the tractor dump the pig into the back of a semi-trailer. "You weren't supposed to kill it," he said. "That was the whole point."

"It's not dead. I just knocked it out."

"Knocked it out?" he repeated.

"That's right."

"But... You... It..." He blinked slowly. "How?"

She tried to brush some of the mud away. It smeared, giving better coverage than high-quality latex gloss. "Girl tricks."

"Nobody likes a smart alec," he muttered.

She rolled her eyes.

The trailer door slammed shut and the guy drove away on his tractor, passing a long red Cadillac on the way. Stanley parked the car and opened the trunk. "Think it'll fit in here?"

Burke strolled over to size up the space. The false bottom that concealed their stash of illegal weapons and questionably acquired cash reduced the available storage, but it was still plentiful. Apparently, people in the 1950's had expected to be able to travel with everything but the kitchen sink. Their duffels and a little bag of snacks from a convenience store were in there, but they'd fit in the back seat without a problem.

A muffled thump came from inside the trailer, the sound of a very large, very unhappy animal waking up.

Richard reached for the handle.

Burke's heart leaped into her throat. "Grandpa, don't!"

But it was too late.

The pig burst through the doors with a screech not unlike that made by a banshee in the moments before an untimely death. In three seconds flat, it had taken in its surroundings and pointed its snout in the direction of a distant patch of scraggly-looking trees.

Burke searched the trunk for something—a net, a hook, a dang lasso would do—but then her eyes fell upon the bag of snacks. She thrust her hand into the sack and snatched out the first thing she latched onto, which happened to be a half-full package of Oreo cookies. Ignoring the ache creeping through her muscles, she threw the treat so it landed in the pig's path.

The animal almost passed it up before putting the brakes on and shifting its half-ton of bulk to sniff the cookie. In three quick crunches, the little chocolate and cream sandwich disappeared. Burke threw another, not quite as far this time.

Both men stood frozen as she lured the Saehrimnir ever closer. At last, she lay a cookie on the back seat of the car and backed away.

Crunch, crunch. Gone.

Burke scrambled to the other side of the car, yanked open the rear door, and dropped a cookie in the middle of the seat.

The freakishly human eyes stared at her. Burke could have sworn the pig knew it was being tricked and was trying to decide whether or not the cookie was worth it.

Apparently, it was.

One surprisingly small hoof was lifted to the floorboard, and then another onto the seat, and in a flash of frantic motion, all three hunters and the gods' livestock were tucked into the Caddy. The white wall tires tossed a cloud of dust into the air and the Peanut Festival became another story in their past.

CHAPTER THREE

Albert

ALBERT PETERS KNEW IN HIS HEART OF HEARTS THAT HE WAS special. His mother had told him so. When he attended second grade and the fourth grader with facial hair and his gang of ogres attacked him on the playground, his mother bandaged his wounds and told him not to mind those guys. They had brawn, but Albert had brains. Someday, he would rule the world and they would be his paltry little servants.

When he lost the Science and Math Olympiad in Jr. High to a team of girls from a nearby private school, his mother had explained that no one was more clever than her little Alby. Those girls came from rich families who probably bribed the judges.

When not a single one of the thirteen young ladies Albert invited to prom said yes, his mother promised him that women would be begging to be with him when he was a rich and famous computer scientist.

Some days, memories of his dear saint of a mother crept up on him like an intruder, bludgeoning him until he wept and begged them to stop. Life had been hard since she'd passed. He had to find time to work and cook his own meals and wash his own laundry. All the hardship of life was more than a man could bear alone. Men, as a rule, were not designed to handle domestic tasks and so could manage them in only the most basic terms of survival. Even worse than going to the grocery store for himself was the cold, cruel fact that his mother had never seen him live up to his potential. When she died, he was only a grunt at a superstore, driving around fixing computers for old ladies.

But things were looking up. Maybe Mom was helping from above, because a couple years back, not long after she died, he'd come across an advertisement for IT help. Coleum Corporation was a hot new up-and-comer. Everybody knew about them. There wasn't a soul in the tech world who hadn't heard the name, but no one seemed to know exactly what they did. Some guessed they were going to blow Apple out of the game with a new communications device unlike anything seen before. Others compared them to the hottest app developers—they'd take over the software world.

Albert went to his interview and a fat, sweating man who smelled vaguely of bad eggs and wore a suit from the 1970s called him into an office and asked him to take a new computer out of a box and connect it to the local network. Albert was given one hour and left alone. Child's play. When the guy came back, the task had been done for thirty minutes and Albert was on his phone, flirting with a busty fairy in an RPG.

The boss grunted, sounding like a dog choking on a bone, and gave Albert the job. "We're flying to Mars. You're staying here to make sure the computers work."

Albert laughed.

The man stared at him with bloodshot eyes. The left side of his face drooped as if the skin weren't firmly attached.

"You're serious?" Albert pushed his spectacles up to the top of his nose.

"Do I look like I have a sense of humor?" the man asked.

The news hit the wires that same week and the world exploded. Everywhere you went, people were talking about Coleum Corporation—where there was space for all. Albert mentioned his job and people took notice. They asked questions. They found him interesting. At last, the world began to see the truth of his greatness.

Of course, jobs always sounded more glamourous than they really were. A great deal of his day involved stringing cable between offices and wiping viruses from the computers of executives who'd "accidentally" stumbled into ethically questionable and often illegal websites. No one needed to know all that.

Almost overnight, the world had learned the name and face of John Jones—the public face of Coleum Corp—and Albert had been inside Jones's office. That single degree of separation made him interesting, and being noticed was intoxicating.

The thing about intoxication, though, is that an addict grows accustomed to his addiction and more fuel is needed to fuel the fire.

Albert Peters knew he was special, and he knew that being a regular old IT guy wasn't enough anymore—not even an IT guy for a company as prestigious as Coleum Corportation. He wanted more.

He adjusted his paisley print tie in the mirror and told himself, "Don't worry, buddy. You'll be on top of the world. Your break will come. You're so close now. Just keep your head down and your eyes open and, any day now, opportunity will knock at your door."

CHAPTER FOUR

Richard

Covered in grease and terrified, clearly the pig did not enjoy being saved. Burke crooned to it like a baby, but the pig, apparently, saw the cookies as the only good in a bad situation. Unfortunately, what goes in a pig must come out, and when Stanley pulled to a stop to release the animal near the banks of the West Fork Choctawhatchee River, they all burst forth from the vehicle, desperate to escape the stench.

Burke, still angry about being denied her day at the fair, seated herself upon a rock next to the shallow, murky water and announced that she would stay right there until Stanley had the mess cleaned up. Covered in dry mud, fairground dust, pig drool, whatever lubricant had been used to grease the pig, and a good many Oreo cookie crumbs, she sat with her back ramrod straight. She folded her hands in her lap and brushed the end of one broken thumbnail against the pad of the other thumb. Her long black braids hung over her shoulders in wet clumps that just reached the place on her arm where she'd attained a six-inch-long bruise wrestling the pork chop of the gods.

Richard longed for Stanley to challenge her at that moment but, alas, among the good many descriptors he could use for the old Brit, "stupid" had no home.

"Well, old chap, you and I will take the Caddy to clean her up and—"

Richard broke forth in a wheezy laugh that brought tears to his eyes and tottered toward the riverbank. "We will expect you upon your return," he said, easing himself down onto the rock next to his pungent granddaughter.

A muscle twitched in Stanley's jaw but he made no protest. With a nod, he turned away and left them. The powerful purr of the Cadillac hummed to life and faded into the distance.

Richard's eyes met Burke's and they both burst into laughter.

He'd laughed more in the last six months than he had in the past six years combined. Heck, maybe in the past sixty. Something about running headlong toward death took away the weighty seriousness of staying alive that he'd labored under for most of his adult life.

"We should walk into Mom's house just like this," Burke said.

He wiped his eyes and rubbed his aching knees. "We'll tell her the whole truth and nothing but the truth."

"And she'll listen and say, 'How absurd. There is no such thing as Norse Gods. Any fool knows there is One God and Jesus is Lord. Now go wash up, Burke Dakota. No respectable man wants a woman who smells like swine. I swear, it's no wonder you couldn't keep the one you had.'"

"Speaking of that, you heard anything from Dim Ditty Dimwit lately?" he asked.

She stretched out her legs, letting the toes of her boots fall to the sides.

Richard wondered when she had given up her fancy, high-priced girlie shoes for boots with reinforced toes. The change signified by the difference in wardrobe struck him as indicative as something far deeper than clothing. They'd seen the face of true evil in the past half year. They'd waged war and come out still standing, more or less.

"He called me a while back, when we were in Texas. The divorce from the underwear model is final. He's thinking about joining an Ashram in Colorado."

"He called just to tell you that?"

"I think he wanted me to understand he's no longer begging me to come back. He's seeking enlightenment now."

Richard blew a raspberry.

Burke laughed. "Exactly."

Across the river, a doe and her fawn emerged from thick green foliage with watchful caution. The mother deer led her offspring to the water's edge and they both lapped up their fill while Burke and Richard watched, silent and unmoving. If they'd had a mind for it, they could enjoy venison for months.

Richard wondered how often humans, like those deer, went about the business of life completely unaware of the still presence of a watchful predator. Only the luck of good timing kept them off some creature's dinner menu. If people really knew, they'd be too scared to function.

The animals returned to the lush green cover of the forest.

"We've put this visit with your mother off for too long," he said.

She chewed on her lip.

"She's been worried sick, you know."

"Yeah, I know."

Richard shifted. He had more than enough padding around his middle and none at all on his backside. Rocks did not serve as adequate seating for a man whose ninetieth birthday loomed just the other side of the horizon. "She's got a good heart. Wants the best for us both. Always has."

"Undeniably," Burke agreed.

"So, you're ready for this visit, then?"

"Nope."

"Me either."

"She'll have some loser lined up for me to meet—an accountant or an architect looking to impregnate me quickly before time runs out."

"There will be brochures for a new nursing home. One more recreational than Everest. She'll say, 'They have a pool, Dad. Didn't the doctor say swimming is good therapy for your hip?'"

"How is your hip, anyway?"

He chuffed. "Well, I ain't usin' a walker no more and I ain't fell over yet."

Comfortable silence settled between them once again. Their shadows stretched long across the river's tumbling current as the sun slipped down the western slope of the sky. Nature's choir, punctuated by the bass of a bullfrog and the high, chirping soprano of a little yellow goldfinch, sent up a song of birth, death, and the sheer joy of living the moments in-between. If he'd had the luxury of a well-padded chair with a footrest, he'd be sound asleep by now.

"Grandpa?"

"Hmm?"

"Don't let her talk you into living in a nursing home again, okay? Not even a really nice one with a pool." She slipped one strong brown hand over his pale, arthritic fingers.

Richard squeezed her hand, keeping his eyes resolutely fixed on some distant point on the other side of the river lest she see the waterworks welling in his eyes. Weren't no reason to be sitting in a forest, crying like a little girl. "You got it, kid," he said.

Stanley made it back just before the sun dropped below the horizon. Both he and the car had a freshly scrubbed shine and smelled faintly of citrus and chlorine bleach. "I figured we'd had enough fun for one day and rented three rooms at the Wyndham. Tomorrow we can head north."

Burke rose and stretched long limbs toward the sky. "Is it run by goblins? Staffed by vampires? Are the housekeepers all witches? Do demons live in the sewer lines under the building?"

"Demons would never deign to live in a sewer. They're quite proud," he replied.

Her gaze remained steady.

"Only humans, so far as I noticed," Stanley told her through his grin.

She held out a hand and Richard allowed himself to be helped to his feet. He waited until the blood flow returned to his legs before releasing her hand.

"You know," Stanley said as they hiked back to the road, "just because there are no monsters at the hotel doesn't mean it's perfectly safe. I've seen a good many humans who were much more frightening than any monster."

Burke grinned. "Oh, I know. By this time tomorrow, you'll be eating turkey with one of them."

THE TRIP NORTH WAS REMARKABLE ONLY FOR ITS NORMALCY. While the Caddy gobbled up the miles, Richard reflected that one year ago, as the holidays approached, he'd been certain the future held nothing for him but a painful decline toward a slow, lonely death. He'd still been relatively young when his wife, Barbara, passed away. At the time, he'd believed she'd been stolen from him by a rare, crippling illness. After he buried his one true love, he continued rising every morning, making the bed, eating his morning bran flakes, and going to work at Wellington Plastics. After all, what else could a man do? No matter that only a shriveled raisin remained of his soul, the sun rose and set. And then one day the company gave him a gold watch and sent him home for good. He watched afternoon talk shows and slept as much as he could for lack of an alternative, until the day he fell and broke his hip and landed in Everest Senior Living, lovely home for old geezers who couldn't care for themselves. There, he met Stanley Kapcheck.

Stanley Kapcheck had strutted those bright and cheery corridors of death like a gamecock on the prowl. He ate pudding and never got fat like everyone else. He still wore shoes with laces and had all his own teeth. His very existence irritated Richard right up until the moment he saved Richard from a strigoi—a vampire-like creature that feasted on the memories of humans until only a mindless, drooling husk remained. Sitting in a diner in the middle of the night, Stanley opened Richard's eyes to a world of supernatural wonder and gave him a place in the order of things, a purpose for his remaining years.

Richard became a hunter.

He'd never meant for Burke to get sucked in, but there she was, in it now, as deep as dung in a cow pasture. The trio had settled into a new kind of routine where the only constant was change. Thirty-nine states in six months. They'd challenged things bigger than themselves, faster, stronger—invisible things, things that could fly, The Devil Herself, and, truth be told, he couldn't remember ever feeling happier, more content, more utterly alive.

Death at the hands of an angry djinn or a hungry rougarou was infinitely preferable to dying in a nursing home. He'd settled his mind to live every single day. He'd go down swinging in the end. No more mere survival, thank you very much, and he wouldn't let his daughter convince him otherwise. He couldn't.

He was afraid of how hard she would try.

He was afraid of her tears and her confusion.

How to explain this new life? Impossible. Far better to avoid her, which he'd done. Until now. Because Stanley had convinced them to go back.

Friggin' Stan Kapcheck.

I-69 to I-94, an exit ramp, three stop lights, and a stretch of twisting little side streets dotted with potholes and speed bumps, and there they were. In silence, they clambered out of the car and stood in the driveway. The season's first snowflakes drifted down, fat and slow and lazy as if an enormous down pillow had been ripped open far above. A biting wind drew harsh criticism from Richard's joints, and he marveled that they'd eaten food on a stick under the sun just a few days earlier.

Burke offered him a reassuring smile. Stanley rocked on the toes of his shiny shoes. Richard squared his shoulders and took a fortifying breath. A man had to do what a man had to do.

Like a soldier storming the beach at Normandy, he marched straight to the front door, lifted his fist, and prepared to knock next to the wreath made of tiny pumpkins and autumn leaves, but his plan turned sideways when the door popped open.

His daughter squeaked in surprise. "Dad!"

"Oh." Richard's hand fell back to his side. "We're here."

She pressed a hand to her heart. "You startled me. Well, come in! Come in! Goodness, is it snowing?" She pulled him into a short, fierce embrace. "You can put your shoes on the mat."

As if he hadn't been there a hundred times over the years and been fussed at for every footprint and water ring.

"Oh, Burke, you braided your hair. I love it. You're a vision. I simply can't understand why you don't have a man." She pulled Burke into a tight hug and then pressed a hand against the row of braids.

"Hi, Mom. I'm glad you like the hair," Burke said in a weird, flat voice. "This is our friend, Stanley Kapcheck."

"The man who lured my family away from their lives." She held out a hand in Stanley's direction. "Madeline Hallman."

Stanley pressed her hand between his. "Madam, the pleasure is mine. I can't tell you all the things I've heard about you."

Richard toed off his shoe and got ready to knock Stanley to the ground if he started repeating all the things he'd heard about Maddie.

"Strong, confident, faithful, concerned for your family's welfare and social connections," Stanley said. "But for all that, no one mentioned how lovely you are. Though, of course, I should have known Burke's mother would be a true heartbreaker."

Her mouth opened and closed again. Her head cocked to one side. She blinked three times in quick succession and gave her head a little shake as if clearing away a lingering haze. "You can leave your shoes on the mat," she said.

Stanley bowed as if granted a privilege by the queen.

"I didn't... I don't have... Are you all thirsty? Hungry? You made good time. I didn't expect you so soon. Dinner is all but done already, but I was on my way out to the market. I forgot to get decaf when I was there earlier, and I know Dad can't have—"

"Don't make a special trip for me," Richard said. "I'll take it fully leaded just like I always have."

"Dad, you know the doctor said—

"The doctor said I oughta curl up and die. Man didn't know his butt from a hole in the ground."

Maddie sighed. "Dad, you'll be up all night."

"Not like I got school in the morning, is it?"

"Well, I'm certainly not going to argue with you about it."

"Good." Was he shouting? He didn't mean to be.

"I don't know why you're being so contrary."

"I ain't contrary. I just don't drink cow piss for coffee."

"Fine." She closed her eyes and took a slow breath. When

she opened them again, she asked in a cheerful, high-pitched voice, "Shall we go in and sit?"

Burke's father had been an avid collector of anything avian. As a result, American Audubon prints adorned the walls. A large clock with a different songbird representing each hour hung between two picture windows that framed a view of the back yard with its wide deck and now-dormant vegetable garden. Life-like bird sculptures dotted the mantlepiece as though hopping and pecking in a grassy yard where family photos grew in place of trees. The central portrait showed Burke and her ex-husband on their wedding day.

As far as Richard could remember, each object in the room occupied the same exact space it had on the day his son-in-law died. His daughter, having been raised in a shrine meant to preserve the memory of her dead mother, now lived in the shadow of her husband's death.

Richard shoved the feeling of hot guilt down deep and cleared his throat. "You still got the birds, I see."

Maddie perched on the edge of one high-backed chair and primly crossed her ankles. She'd learned manners from reading eighty-four-thousand girlie magazines, and now the rules of etiquette and self-carriage were tattooed onto her soul. "Well, yes. Of course. There's a new one, there on the mantel. The red-winged blackbird. The ladies at church gave me that after I organized the summer lemonade fundraiser."

The little blackbird stared at him with soulless black eyes. He suppressed a shudder and found a place to stand where the sun coming through the window warmed the stiff muscles of his back. If he sat down again too soon after the long car ride, he would risk every joint south of the boarder locking up solid. Better to let the blood flow for a few minutes.

Stanley relaxed into the twin of Maddie's chair and leaned back, each arm resting on an arm of the chair, legs crossed, like a king holding court. "I had an opportunity to travel to

Australia once. Do you know that birds there don't sing? They screech, call out, holler, and mimic, but none of them whistle a tune."

"Did you travel a lot for your work?" Maddie asked.

"Yes. A fair amount."

"My own family, on the rare occasion they manage time to call, doesn't share many details." She clicked her fingernails against the little wooden strip on the end of the chair's arm.

Burke, curled like a cat in a corner of the sofa, rubbed her forehead with her fingertips.

"Exactly what kind of work did you do before you retired?" Maddie asked.

Stanley rubbed his chin with the knuckles of his right hand. "I was a private investigator of sorts."

"How exciting." She caught her long strand of pearls between two fingers and twisted it.

"The silver screen has given that impression, but I assure you, I spent more hours with my nose in a book than chasing bad guys in exotic locations."

"Did you ever catch anyone I'd have heard of?"

"I once staked an offspring of Vlad the Impaler in a pub in Romania," Stanley replied.

Burke's hand dropped lower, pressed against her closed eyelids.

"Oh, a stake out," Maddie exclaimed.

"More of a stake in," Stanley said.

She giggled.

Richard rolled his eyes. "I gotta use the sandbox." He traipsed through the kitchen and down the hall to the half bath. More birds. Birds on the wallpaper border. Birds embroidered on the towels. Little soaps shaped like birds, so old they'd taken on a cracked, dusty appearance. An enormous cardinal in an ornate golden frame stared at him while he peed. "Don't judge the stream, old boy. The water pressure ain't what it used to be, but at least the hose ain't leakin'."

He used the soap that smelled like oranges, dispensed from the beak of a glass robin, and headed toward the kitchen to snoop. Passing through the dining room, he noticed the table had already been set for dinner. The sight pulled at his heart. Lacy blue scrolling decorated the edges of the dishes. They'd been hand-painted, all matching, yet no two exactly the same.

Barbara's dishes.

After so many years, how could it be possible for her to jump out and surprise him like that? After all this time, her death remained a scar on his heart, healed but still prone to occasional, painful flare-ups. Finding and killing the creature who'd killed her didn't make her loss hurt any less. If anything, revenge left a hollowness in his chest, a feeling that he hadn't done enough. He wanted to kill the skinwalker again and again. Then again, people in hell wanted ice water, and look how that worked out for them.

"Dad?"

He turned to find Maddie watching him from the doorway. A little line marred the space between her brows. "You okay?"

He gestured to the table. "I saw your mom's dishes." The words sounded stupid uttered aloud. What was a dish? No more than a piece of glass from some factory in Mexico.

Maddie drew near and ran one finger over the blue lines. "I hope you don't mind that I used them. They're my favorite. Much prettier than the plain modern things they sell now."

He shrugged. "Just dishes."

She smiled up at him. "Not really just a dish."

"No. I suppose not," he agreed.

She took a deep breath. "So, your friend Stanley seems an interesting fellow."

"Don't he, though?"

"I'm glad you're here. I've missed you, Dad."

He raised his eyebrows. "Really?"

She rolled her eyes, just like Burke. "Of course. You're my father and you disappeared in the middle of the night and haven't come home for six months. I've missed you, and I've worried about you, and I've wondered what I did to make you want to stay away from me."

"I didn't go to be far away from you." That was the God's honest truth. Maybe he didn't want to be preached at day and night, but going off with Stanley had nothing to do with getting away from Madeline.

"Someday, maybe you'll take the time to explain to me exactly why you did go. Everest was a good place, Dad. I didn't dump you in some nasty nursing home or something. I spent a lot of effort to find something nice for you."

"I know, kid." It had been a lovely facility. Not a single thing in the world wrong with it other than the staff members who literally feasted on the souls of the elderly. No one had thought to mention that part in the brochure.

She tapped a nail against the back of a chair. *Click. Click. Click.* Like a deathwatch beetle. The shiver from earlier escaped and scuttled up his spine.

"Well," she said with a sigh, "I just need to check the turkey. Burke and Stanley went to wash up. Dinner should be ready on time. I don't want you to eat too late. It can't be good for your digestion and you need to get your rest. I worry about you gallivanting around the countryside. You should be somewhere safe and pleasant."

"Safe and pleasant aren't all they're cracked up to be," Richard said. "A man needs a little adventure to stay alive."

"Rosalie Adey and Edith Porter had an adventure when they took a senior's bus tour to see the leaves on the coast of Lake Michigan last month. It was all booked through the place where they're living. I got a brochure from them. I'll show you later, after dinner. You're going to love it."

He wanted to inform her, in no uncertain terms, that he would not be moving into the old folks home with the widows, but she'd already given his arm a little squeeze and drifted off into the kitchen. Right before she disappeared around the corner, she called over her shoulder, "They even have a big heated pool, Dad."

Lord, but she made him feel old.

CHAPTER FIVE

Albert

ALBERT RODE HIS BIKE TO WORK WHENEVER HE COULD. November had brought below-freezing temperatures, but he could still bundle up and make it work. In another month or so, snow and ice would hold the world captive and he'd be forced to drive his car like all the other sheeple.

Where would he be in another month? By then, the launch would be old news and the world would wait for news of the first settlers setting foot on Mars.

The settlers would be big news. History makers. The folks children would read about in history books a thousand years into the future.

But what would Albert be?

Just the guy who was left behind.

He pedaled harder and gritted his teeth against the cold that bit into the skin of his face.

They need people like me. They don't understand how much I can do for them. I need to tell them. This is the time. Carpe diem, Albert. Now or never. Go big or go home.

A plan formed. When he arrived at the office, he'd lock up his bike, stop in the lobby restroom to tidy himself up, march into Jones's office, and announce that he deserved a spot on that ship.

Resolve warmed his frozen bones and carried him along with the effortlessness of a bird in flight. He reached the office parking lot, wrapped the lock around the front wheel of his bike and rammed his way through the big glass doors like an invading marauder. Adrenaline fogged his mind and, before he knew it, he was in front of Jones's receptionist.

"I need to see him," Albert managed.

Her red-painted lips formed a perfect, joyless smile. "I'd be happy to take a note and see if he is able to schedule an appointment."

Albert's limbs buzzed and tingled. Maybe he'd pass out. *Please, God, don't let me vomit.* "No. Now. It's important."

"I'm sure it is. Mr. Jones's schedule is full of meetings regarding important matters. It's necessary for us to sort the important from the crucial."

"I'm Albert Peters," he shouted, slamming his palms down on her desk. Why was he shouting? He didn't know and he couldn't stop. "It's important. I'm important. He needs me!"

Behind him, a door opened with a click and a gentle voice asked if everything was okay.

Albert spun and met the gaze of John Jones. Tears sprang to his eyes and he blinked fast to make them go away, certain he'd die of shame if he cried in front of this man. Words deserted him. He scrambled and clawed for any semblance of an intelligent sentence.

"I'm Albert Peters. You need me."

A fly passed between Jones and the overhead light fixture, sending a little black shadow across the space between the two men.

Jones held out a hand and Albert took it.

The remaining shreds of control left him and a tear spilled over his eyelid.

"Everyone has their place in the food chain, Albert. Pond scum is no less important than a lion roaming the savannah. You are valued."

Albert nodded and, without another word, left the office on legs that carried him along as if they operated separately from his will. He rode the elevator to the second floor and sat down in his cubicle.

John Jones values me. I am special. I knew it!

He tugged a tissue from the box on his desk and blew his nose. He'd been thinking about the upcoming changes at work all wrong. The launch wasn't the end. It was the beginning.

His eye fell on the calendar.

He had a date coming up. His first real date in...well... It didn't do to dwell on how much time had passed. It was a blind date, but a date, nonetheless.

This was the one. No doubt about it. He felt it in his gut. He was a man of great value and this woman would recognize his worth and nothing would be the same for him ever again. John Jones said so.

Or...well...he said something like that.

CHAPTER SIX

Richard

MADDIE INSISTED THEY STAY AT THE HOUSE. SAID SHE HAD plenty of room. Pleaded the case that they were only giving her a few short days before they set off again to who-knows-where, only to return for another visit who-knows-when. They'd conceded to her demands in order to shut up Stanley, who lectured them about the wisdom of choosing your battles.

She did not have enough space.

Apparently, she operated under the sorely mistaken assumption that Richard and Stanley would be comfortable sharing a single room containing a queen-sized bed. When they first saw the arrangement, Stanley slapped Richard on the back and said, "No worries, old boy. I promise not to steal the covers or peek under your skirt."

Richard dropped his duffle in a fussy, spindly-legged chair and declared, "You're two pickles short of a barrel if you think I'm sharing a bed with you. I'd sooner sleep in the car."

Maddie padded into the room with a pile of towels. "You try

sleeping in the car in this weather, I swear I will call the cops and have them drag you back in here and cuff you to the bed."

Stanley unzipped his garment bag and hung the contents in the closet, giving each a little shake to avoid any potential wrinkles. "What do you say, Dick? Will you share the bed with me if handcuffs are involved?" The corners of his eyes crinkled in amusement.

"Mr. Kapcheck, I would think a proper British gentleman such as yourself would be above such bawdy humor." Maddie deposited the towels on top of a vanity in the corner.

"Madam, don't believe the old myth about the French being the world's greatest lovers. We Brits may be laced up tight on the outside, but behind closed doors we remain the race that descended from men and women who worshipped the gods of pleasure under the silver light of the full moon as it glimmered upon their beds of leaves within the primeval forest."

A deep crimson blush bloomed upward from Maddie's prim, high collar all the way to the grayish roots of her dyed-auburn hair. She pressed one hand against her ample bosom, opened her mouth to reply, blinked three times in slow succession, closed her mouth, and scurried from the room.

Richard had to give credit where credit was due. He'd never seen anyone silence his daughter more effectively.

Stanley chuckled at the observation when Richard told him and clicked the television on to hear the news while they dressed for dinner.

Now, Stanley stood before the full-length mirror adjusting the absurd, elaborate knot on his orange silk tie, while the newsman talked about some famous billionaire getting ready to launch a passenger ship to Mars. "Coleum Corporation spokesperson John Jones once again used today's press conference to reiterate their mission's focus on peace, prosperity, and a future where there's space for all."

"World moves too danged fast." Richard tucked his wrinkled blue Polo shirt into his Chinos. "I remember when folks got excited about being able to cross the Atlantic in one jump."

Stanley retrieved his waistcoat from a hanger and buttoned it up over his flat stomach. "You're not telling me anything I don't know. I remember when Mr. Peabody in the next village purchased a Model T. My mother went to mass and lit a candle for him, convinced anyone with a desire to travel faster than a horse could run must surely be possessed by the devil. We're old men, Dick, doomed to succumb to the vigorous forward momentum of the young."

Richard scowled at his reflection. With his shirt tucked in, there could be no mistake. The one thing he'd succumbed to was the furniture disease—his chest had fallen into his drawers. He tugged the shirt out of his waistband. "Speak for yourself, ya old goat. Least I came out of the baby chute this side of the twentieth century."

Stanly met his eyes in the mirror and raised his brows. "Yet now we're a fifth of the way through the twenty-first, and we may just live long enough to see a human colony on another planet. Who'd ever have imagined?"

Richard remembered being a boy, hiding under his covers with a flashlight after being told to go straight to sleep, the slick pages of a new comic book from the Tombstone Pharmacy beneath his fingers. The bright colors and wild, improbable images crawled into his imagination and painted an image of adventure more real than anything he'd ever experienced with his five senses. In those pages, good was good and evil was evil and the guy who did the right thing got the girl every time. "All them science fiction writers in the 1950's went mad imagining about it. It never did end in peace and prosperity and a future with space for all."

A knock sounded at the door. Richard crossed the room to open it. There was a time when he'd have just shouted for the person to come in, but that particular habit had nearly resulted in disaster one night in a seedy hotel on Ventura Boulevard, and he was a man smart enough to learn from his mistakes. He opened the door a crack.

"Just me," Burke said. She wore a floor-length patchwork dress that swirled around her legs like water when she entered the bedroom, and draped from her straight shoulders in a way that brought to mind ancient monarchs on gilded thrones who ruled with god-like authority. Peeking over her grandfather's shoulder, she smiled at Stanley. "You look absolutely dashing."

Stanley bowed his head in her direction. "A pale moon to your dazzling sun."

Richard rolled his eyes. "I'm gonna barf."

"Oh, Grandpa, stop. Aren't you going to dress for dinner?"

He gestured to his body. "Am I naked?"

She ignored his question. "Has she pressed for info yet?"

"Nothing outside of what you heard," Richard said. "She told me about a great facility with a heated pool, though."

Burke faked a gagging noise that made him smile.

Stanley turned off the television, silencing a darkly handsome man with a scar over his left eye speaking from behind a podium about a new day dawning in which no member of the human race is unvalued or without purpose. "I suspect the two of you have worked this whole visit up to something sinister in your minds. Madeline has been nothing but gracious thus far."

The two of them stared at him.

Stanley raised his hands in surrender.

The doorbell rang and Burke sank onto the bed as though hearing a death knell. "There it is."

"What's the matter with you?" Richard asked.

"I'll bet you the next turn in the shotgun seat, that's some horrid date she set up for me."

Stanley left the room, his argyle-stockinged feet silent against the thick padding of the carpet. A moment later he returned, hands stuffed in the pockets of his pleated trousers. He shrugged. "He might have a fantastic personality."

Burke groaned and dropped her head into her hands. "It's not too late to go back and find those carnies. A good hunt would be—"

"Oh no!" Stanley exclaimed. "You mustn't ever hunt them. They're—"

"Don't," Burke said, holding up a bejeweled hand that sparkled in the orange sunlight streaming through the window. "Did I tell you I don't want to know? I wasn't kidding. I really don't. I love carnivals. You will not ruin carnivals for me."

Stanley shrugged again.

Richard caught sight in the mirror of the wiry white wisps floating around his head. He patted them. They sprang back up, heedless of his wishes. "Come on then," he said, giving up on his appearance entirely. That ship, if it had ever sailed, left the harbor a long, long time ago. From an early age, it had been clear he would never cruise through life on his good looks. "Let's get this over with."

Three months earlier, he'd decapitated a rugaru with a chainsaw. How bad could Thanksgiving dinner with family be?

CHAPTER SEVEN

Burke

MADDIE SAT IN THE LIVING ROOM SIPPING TEA WITH NOT one, but two men. The younger, a thin, beak-nosed man with wire-rim eyeglasses, had a face that appeared to be three quarters forehead. The other, who was maybe sixty-something, brought to mind Mr. Rogers, right down to his reddish-orange cardigan. They both rose to their feet when Richard, Stanley, and Burke entered. The skinny guy rubbed his palms against the legs of his baggy brown slacks.

"This is my father, Richard, my daughter, Burke, and their friend, Stanley Kapcheck," Maddie said, gesturing to each of them in turn. "Everyone, this is Albert Peters and Luke Castleberry."

"Richard, Burke, it's a pleasure to see you again, and very nice to meet you, as well, Mr. Kapcheck. I'm one of Madeline's neighbors."

Luke lived three doors down from Maddie and had been friends with the family since Burke made his acquaintance while selling lemonade back in the days when people didn't worry much about their kids being snatched off the streets by perverts. He shook hands all around and made all the appropriate niceties when Stanley insisted on being called by his first name.

The other guy bobbed his head at them like an agitated cockatoo. He flashed a smile, revealing a row of teeth so straight and white they gleamed when the light hit them, just like the old Saturday morning cartoon characters. His watery gray eyes settled on Burke. "I have to say, you're just as lovely as your mother said. I really like your braids. They're very exotic."

A muscle jumped in Burke's jaw. Maybe it wasn't too late to go hunting at the carnival, after all. Stabbing something sounded pretty good at that moment. "Mom, you didn't mention anyone was coming for dinner."

"No? Well, I'm sure I meant to. Sit, everyone, please."

Stanley crossed to the couch and dropped down between the two visitors, a little closer than was strictly necessary to Albert, who gave him the side-eye. He slung an arm behind the little nerd's shoulders and crossed his legs. The corners of his mouth twitched upward.

Maddie perched on one stiff, hi-backed chair. Richard plopped in the other, causing the thin chair legs to squeak in protest.

Burke settled on the raised brick hearth in the corner, as far from the group as possible without actually leaving the room. From there, she could make a break for it if she needed to, and they'd be hard-pressed to catch her.

"Are you one of Madeline's neighbors, as well?" Stanley asked the twerp.

"We're just brand-new acquaintances," Maddie answered for him. "It's quite a funny story, actually."

Albert snorted.

Richard startled, looking alarmed.

"I suppose you could say it was funny," Albert agreed. "If being run over amuses you."

Burke drew back. "My mother ran over you?"

Maddie waved a dismissive hand. "No. I most certainly did not run over him. I just bumped into him."

Albert snorted again. "It was my fault, really. When I'm cycling, my mind travels off to another dimension. I zipped behind her when she was backing up."

"You know how those parking spaces downtown are," Maddie said, picking up the narrative. "Well, you just can't see a thing. The only way to get out is to put the car in reverse and hope for the best."

"I'm just thankful she hit the brakes fast when she heard the thump," Albert said.

"And thank God there was no oncoming traffic," Maddie said.

"I would have been deader than Christ on Saturday," Albert said.

Richard's gaze darted back and forth between them during this verbal tennis match, but finally settled on Maddie, who folded her hands in her lap and said, "Obviously, there was no choice but to extend some hospitality. It was the least I could do after nearly killing the man."

Luke wrung his hands like a nervous old woman. "Madeline, if you're ever worried about driving downtown and need a ride, I would hope you'd never hesitate to ask."

"Aren't you sweet to offer, Luke. I'm fine, though. All's well that ends well."

Stanley's smirk had grown into a grin.

Burke rubbed her forehead with the tips of her fingers. Were her headaches more frequent lately? Maybe it was an aneurysm. That would be a quick and easy way to go.

The Audubon Society grandfather clock announced the

hour in the high-pitched, somewhat annoying chirp of the spotted woodpecker.

Albert scooted an inch away from Stanley and pointed his unsettling smile in Burke's direction. "Your mother mentioned you're a software designer."

Burke dropped her hand into her lap. "I was. I'm retired now."

"Far too young to be wiling away the days with afternoon television," he said.

Television? Seriously? Something popped inside her brain. It must not have been the aneurysm, because she was alive enough to be annoyed. "Last week I saved a twenty-six-year-old mother of three by chasing down a banshee on foot and stabbing it through the heart with a wooden stake."

Albert's pale eyes grew wide behind his wire-rimmed spectacles.

Luke spoke up with a hint of amusement in his voice, "I flirted with death myself, last week—ate bacon five out of seven days and never once gave a thought to cholesterol. I've heard women find it attractive when a man knows how to live dangerously." His eyes flicked to Maddie, whose full attention remained on Stanley.

Maddie fiddled with her pearls. "You're quite fit, Mr. Kapcheck. You must be very careful about what you eat."

"You're sweet to say so, my dear. I must confess, though, based upon the aroma, any consideration of moderation I may normally exercise will be set aside for this evening's feast. If your cooking tastes half as good as it smells, I shall gain five pounds before I leave here."

A timer rang in the kitchen and Maddie leapt to her feet. "That'll be the turkey." She paused long enough to point a finger at Burke. "And no more weird humor from you, Missy."

Luke jumped up, as well. "I can help you."

"Not necessary," Maddie called over her shoulder. "Stay and visit."

He sank back down, his smile somewhat faded.

Stanley slapped his hand on Albert's shoulder, causing the geek to jump half out of his seat. He'd inched himself so tightly against the arm of the sofa, he and Stanley were now sharing a single cushion.

"So, tell us about yourself," Stanley said.

Albert wiped his palms against his pants. "Well, uhm..." He tried to scoot, found himself tightly wedged and settled for putting one forearm on the arm of the sofa.

Burke wondered if the man would pull himself up and over and run from the room to escape from Stanley.

"I bike a great deal," Albert finally managed. "I have a car, of course, a hybrid, because I'm quite conscious of the environment, but still, there's no cleaner form of transportation than good old, people-powered bikes."

"Maybe we should get people-powered cars like they drive in that cartoon with the cavemen," Richard suggested.

Albert snorted three times in quick succession, his shoulders shaking in laughter. "Maybe so," he agreed as though it were a perfectly reasonable idea.

This was the man Burke's mother wanted her to hook up with? She'd sooner join a convent.

Maddie called them in to be seated at the table and directed each of them to their place—Richard at the head with Burke on his right and Albert on his left so the two younger people would be directly across from one another, and Maddie at the foot, between Stanley and Luke. "We should each say what we're thankful for," she said. "I'll start. I'm thankful to have my family home again, at last, even if only for a few days before they once again take off to God-knows-where to do God-knows-what, leaving me here all alone. At least they're here for today and I am thankful." She raised her glass toward them and sipped. "Now you, Burke, dear."

Burke drained her wine and carefully put the long-stemmed glass back down on the table. "I'm thankful that it's been several days since anything tried to devour my soul. I'm hoping to make it two weeks in a row, but it's not looking good."

Maddie huffed. "If you're not—"

"Silly girl," Stanley interrupted. "If you're referring to the nachzehrer in Tulsa, he would never try to ingest a human soul. It's hearts and livers they're primarily interested in." He sipped his wine during the resulting silence.

Burke watched the blood drain from her grandfather's face. He probably worried Maddie and the men would actually believe them. Fat chance. Half the time, even Burke didn't believe that their ridiculous lives were real.

Luke spread his napkin across his lap. "Well, I certainly hope that whatever is roaming this neighborhood isn't anything like that," he said, tipping his chin to peer at them with mock seriousness.

Stanley leaned in. "You have a monster roaming the streets?"

"Mrs. Dister would have you think so."

Maddie scoffed, "Mrs. Dister is so flighty she jumps at her own shadow."

"I love a good monster story," Stanley said. "What does she say?"

"Well, apparently, something ate nearly every vegetable in her garden. When she got fed up with going out to pick her ripe harvest only to find it missing, she asked her grandson to hook up some kind of fancy security camera. The camera picked up the image of something like a small hunched up man with broad shoulders, naked as a newborn babe, sitting right there in the middle of the zucchini vines, munching away. When a car drove by it, scrambled off on all fours."

"It was probably some drunk teenager," Maddie said. She

focused her attention on Stanley and told him, "When I was raising Burke, I kept a tight rein on her to be sure she was studying and making good choices. Parents today leave it to their electronic gadgets to raise their kids. Poor things don't stand a chance."

"Perhaps it was," Stanley agreed.

Maddie patted her hair and fluttered her lashes in his direction.

Good Lord. Burke had never seen her mother pay attention to any man other than her father. To see her like this with Stanly, of all people, was unsettling, to say the least.

"Well," Maddie said. "Enough of all that. The food's going to get cold if we sit around telling every bit of nonsense the neighborhood's been gossiping about before we eat."

Luke's shoulders slumped an inch or two.

"Stanley, what are you thankful for?" Maddie asked.

Stanley gestured toward the feast laid out before them. "I am thankful for the opportunity to enjoy a good, old-fashioned, home-cooked holiday feast with loved ones. I dare say it has been far too many years since I've had such an opportunity." He sipped his wine again. "How about you, Dick? There must be some gratitude somewhere in that wrinkly old heart. Spit it out, chap. What are you thankful for?"

Richard appeared to be fighting the urge to peg Stan's face with one of Maddie's over-cooked dinner rolls. He took a deep breath and said, "Reckon I'm thankful to be able to sit up and take nourishment."

Albert chimed in, his nasally voice grating across Burke's ears like a rusty old washboard, "Me, too! I'm thankful Maddie didn't kill me." A long series of shoulder-shaking snorts followed the proclamation. "Really, though, it's quite nice to spend the evening with two beautiful ladies." He waggled his eyebrows at Stanley. "Two pretty girls are better than one, am I right?"

Stanley inclined his head. "You may be right, but I find that ladies respond most positively when you admire them for their unique beauty as individuals." He winked at Maddie.

Maddie blushed and looked down at her plate.

Is it too soon to refill my wine glass? Burke wondered.

"A woman's real beauty comes when the experience of her years ripens into something full and rich," Luke said, color rushing into his pale cheeks.

Maddie took a deep breath and said, "That's enough of all that, now." She led them in a short prayer of thanks before telling them, "This food is going to go cold. Go on and fill your plates." She lifted the bowl of sweet potatoes, passed it to her left, and the next several minutes were dedicated to passing dishes, filling plates, and exclaiming about how wonderful everything looked. Richard mashed up the soft, lumpy potatoes between his gums and declared them not too bad.

Once all the serving dishes had been returned to the center of the table and the first wave of compliments ebbed away, Stanley asked Albert, "You told us about your hobbies, but what do you do for work?"

"Oh, it's very exciting," Maddie exclaimed. "Albert works for that company that's getting ready to fly a spaceship to Mars. Can you even imagine? Living on a whole other plant—why, it's just like a movie."

Burke had been so wrapped up in her own wild ride lately that she hadn't given much thought to the subject on everyone else's mind. She didn't find the idea of flying a spaceship to Mars so unbelievable, though. Earth wasn't in the very best shape. Having a Plan B seemed like a reasonable call.

Albert swallowed a mouthful of turkey and washed it down with water, doing his cockatoo imitation the whole time. "Coleum Corp," he said at last, as if they hadn't all heard about it on every news show for the past six months. "I'm a technical advisor. I've even worked on Umbra's personal server." He leaned toward Burke. "I think that's one reason your mom figured we'd get on well. We're both computer nerds."

Burke made a face that might have passed for some kind of agreement and stuffed an enormous scoop of sweet potato into her mouth.

Stanley leaned forward. "Umbra, you say?"

"Yup," Albert confirmed. "Umbra's the one who makes the whole operation go. 'Course, you don't hear much about that. They put John Jones out there, mostly. Umbra stays holed up in the labs in Italy, working like a darn dog to make big dreams into reality."

"Yes, it's Jones I see on the television," Stanley said.

"Jones isn't the brains, but he's pretty and he talks good. I figure that's why they always put him out front. Don't get me wrong. He's high up the ladder, but Umbra is the god on the top of the pyramid. Wouldn't mind walking in those shoes for a few days, eh?"

Maddie wagged a finger in his direction. "There's only one God, dear. Don't ever forget that. Dad, could you pass the corn casserole, please?"

Richard lifted the glass dish and handed it to his daughter. Burke wondered what would happen if she brought up the Norse gods and their hunting pigs.

"Madeline, I don't mean to be contrary. Perhaps you are right that there is only one true God, but I must add you to the pantheon. A goddess of the kitchen. This turkey is the most moist and flavorful I have ever experienced," Luke said.

Maddie waved his words away with her fork. "What do you think, Stanley? Was it worth waiting all that time for my humble home cooking?"

Stanley dabbed at the corners of his mouth like a prissy little dandy. "A delight to every sense, my dear."

A person didn't need eyeglasses to see Madeline's head swell under the praise.

"So, have you been to those offices in Italy?" Stanley asked Albert.

Maddie deflated a bit.

Albert shook his head and answered around a mouthful of potatoes, "Once. We're mostly in contact by phone." He swallowed and grinned at Burke, displaying a piece of parsley stuck in his perfect teeth. "You'd love it there."

"I've been," Burke replied without looking up from her food.

"Burke, dear, sit up straight," Maddie admonished her. "A woman of your age needs to care for her bones. Hunching like an old crone is going to add years you can ill afford to your image."

Burke jabbed the poor, defenseless piece of turkey on her plate. It felt good to stab something.

"I would love to see Italy," Luke offered. "I'm determined to travel more, now that I'm retired. In fact, I've been considering a trip to Iceland. Do you know there are hot water springs all over the place there? It's not really particularly icy, at all, due to the geothermic activity."

"What are hot water springs good for?" Richard asked.

Luke seemed surprised by the question. "Well, they're quite lovely for a soak, and romantic, as well, I hear." His eyes darted to Maddie and back to his plate.

Richard scowled at him.

Stanley's focus remained fixed on Albert. "They're launching from Michigan, though, right? Just a few hours drive from here?" Stanley asked. "Surely, the boss will be here for that."

Albert's head bobbed. "Yup, yup. Sure. Everyone'll be here for that."

"Why did they choose Michigan?" Stanley asked. "I'd have thought a warmer climate, like those chosen by NASA and some of the other tech companies."

Maddie leaned toward Albert. "Burke won a trip to NASA

back in her schoolgirl days, for a computer program she wrote. She had a lot of potential back then."

Nope. Not too soon to refill, Burke thought. She reached for the wine bottle in the center of the table and refilled her glass.

Albert raised his eyebrows. "Yeah? I was at space camp once, but I had to go home early. I got sick. I was allergic to the natural fibers in the shirts. I'm strictly a polyester guy these days."

"I bet," Burke mumbled.

He went on, clearly undaunted by her lack of eye contact. "Michigan's actually a pretty natural choice. It's sort of perfect, what with all the empty factory space up along the I-94 corridor and the labor force with lots of assembly line know-how and not many jobs. Plus, there's some historical—"

"Your office is off I-94?" Stanley asked.

Albert stuffed the better part of a dinner roll in his mouth and nodded.

"I've been up there once or twice," Stanley said. "I notice there's sometimes a lingering scent of sulfur. That ever bother you?"

Richard's fork clattered against his dish. Burke didn't blame him. Stanley's questions had taken an unsettling turn. Only the nastiest monsters left a sulfur stench in their wake.

"Dad?" Maddie looked at him with an over-solicitous expression Burke knew would irritate him.

"I'm fine," he assured her.

Burke sat up straight, her eyes fixed on Stanley.

Albert's head weaved left and right. It was almost as if his joints were made of springs instead of flesh and bone. He didn't appear as tightly screwed together as he should have been. "No. Can't say I've ever noticed a sulfur smell."

Burke's heart resumed its normal rhythm. She didn't know what had prompted Stanley to ask about sulfur, but she knew for sure she had less than zero interest in being carjacked in Detroit by anything that went bump in the night.

"Only thing that ever bothered me is the flickering lights," Albert said. "Don't know if it's the power drain from the assembly lines or what, but the lights never burn steady. Gives me a headache, you know?"

The crazy heart rhythm returned. Stanley had managed to sniff out a monster right there at Maddie's holiday dinner table. Two monsters, if you counted whatever had batty old Mrs. Distel's panties in a bunch.

Burke met her grandfather's eye and gave a subtle shrug. By the stunned expression on his face, he didn't have any more information about the situation than she did.

"Anyway," the little worm went on, "it'll all be worth it soon as we launch. Nothing much left to do on my end but check over the odds and ends and go to the big celebration."

"A city on Mars! Amazing," Luke said.

"That sounds exciting," Maddie exclaimed.

"It will be," Albert agreed. "Everyone who's anyone will be at the party. Umbra's got a whole Dreamliner booked to bring the staff from Italy." He cocked his head in thought. "You know, Burke, you ought to come with me. My plus one is still available."

"That's hard to believe," Burke said.

"Well, a man in my position doesn't have a lot of time to socialize."

"I'm sure Burke understands. When she worked in IT, she couldn't even find time to make a baby," Maddie said.

Burke's grasp on the sharp-tined fork tightened.

Stanley piped up, "You should go."

Burke's mouth fell open. *The man has lost his mind completely. He's going to drive me to deadly assault with flatware.*

Stanley's smiling eyes watched her over the rim of his wine glass as he took a dainty little sip before continuing, "Really,

Burke. How many people get the opportunity to brush shoulders with a *creature* like this Umbra? It's a *rare chance* to see what others may never have the occasion to witness."

"I know I'd go. Wow! To hobnob with the people making history. That's something special, don't you think?" Luke said.

"It's unanimous, then," Maddie said, though Richard hadn't voted and Burke was quite certain she had not agreed.

Her gaze narrowed on Stanley.

Stanley nodded encouragement.

She sighed and rolled her eyes. "Fine."

Richard scowled at his food and said nothing.

Ha! See if I stick up for him when the subject of nursing homes comes up.

Maddie pointed at Richard with her fork. "Don't eat too much if you're planning on having pie, Dad. You know how all these rich foods tie up your digestive system. A man of your age needs to be careful with his body."

Richard's eyes darted to the wine bottle but Burke had already polished it off.

CHAPTER EIGHT

Richard

AROUND MIDNIGHT, BURKE SLIPPED INTO THE LITTLE bedroom and shut the door carefully behind her. "She's finally asleep," she announced. "I double checked to make sure."

Richard adjusted the pillow that cushioned his spine against the wall. Stanley had beaten him to the bed, which left him no reasonable choice but to stretch out with a blanket on the floor. He had doubts about whether or not he'd actually be able to get up off the floor again when the time came, but if he'd learned anything in the past six months, it was to deal with one problem at a time. An aching back was a fair price to pay to escape spending a night in bed with a donkey's hind end.

Burke cocked her head. "Why are you on the floor?"

"You're two pickles short of a barrel if you think I'm sleeping with him." He jerked a thumb in Stanley's direction.

"You're not even going to be able to get up in the morning," she said.

"I ain't a cripple. I can get up off the floor just fine, thank you." The note of confidence in his voice pleased him. "Now, are we gonna jaw all night about my preferred sleeping arrangements or are we gonna get down to business?"

Burke rolled her eyes and perched in the rickety little chair. The thin legs creaked but held her muscular form without collapsing. A full day's worth of annoyance breathed a frosty mist over, "Spill it, Stanley. And it better be good. Why am I whoring myself out to that slimy little creep?"

Stanley's eyes crinkled at the corners. "Aw, you're too hard on him. He's a bright guy, just a little socially awkward."

Burke held his gaze without wavering.

Stanley held up the battered journal he'd been studying to pass the time until Maddie fell asleep. "I looked it up to make sure I wasn't mis-remembering. Umbra is thought to be the name of one of the top leaders of an organization known as The Children of Cain. They operate out of a remote part of southern Italy. Any hunter who's been around for more than a minute has bumped into them in some way, shape, or form. Busar battled them more than once."

"They met up with Busar and lived to tell about it?" Burke asked. Neither she nor Richard had met Stanley's old mentor, Busar, but to hear Stanley talk, the man had been a cross between Chuck Norris and James Bond. He'd learned hunting at his father's knee and creatures across the world quaked at the sight of the powerful Ugandan. A few years back, Busar met his match—a story Stanley had never quite mustered up the will to share.

"A man can no more destroy The Children of Cain than he can destroy the concept of God within the minds of the human race. They are part of our collective consciousness and so deeply entwined in our society that to pull them out would unravel the entire tapestry. But it's more than that. They are mist. Just an idea, a thought so ancient, the first of them wrestled the Nephilim before the time of Noah's flood."

The number of things about Stanley that Richard found

annoying were too numerous to count, but his habit of dropping tidbits like 'Noah's ark was a real thing' into casual conversation ranked in the top five. Well, maybe the top ten.

Stanley opened the book to a page dotted with familiar symbols—the all-seeing eye atop a pyramid, a five-pointed star in a circle, the Masonic compass, and a dozen others. Symbols associated with power, the Illuminati, the not-all-that-secret secret elite who supposedly rule the world. "The Children of Cain are the fathers of every one of these and more. They outdate the Knights Templar by tens of thousands of years. When the cornerstone to the first pyramid was laid, you can bet the master architect knew of them, an ancient authority, even then."

Imagining the squirrely little cyclist as one of the Great Powerful Elite stretched credibility as far as anything Richard could think of in the last half year. Burke voiced exactly that.

"I don't think he's one of them," Stanley said. "I think he works for them, as many unwitting men and women do."

"At the company that's getting ready to build a colony on Mars," she said.

"Precisely." Stanley beamed at her, the star pupil.

"Ain't no monsters in space, are there?" Richard asked, once again playing scenes from black and white movies in his memory.

"I'm sure I don't know," Stanley said. "But there will be in just about a week if we don't do anything to stop it." He turned to Burke. "You need to see if Umbra is who I think he is and, if he is, we need to find a way to stop them from launching."

A bizarre half-grunt, half-laugh exploded out of Burke and she threw her hands up. "Oh, is that all I need to do? No problem. I probably won't even need to stay any longer than the cocktail hour."

Stanley crossed his legs under him, sitting on the bed like a little boy, and leaned forward with his elbows on his knees.

"Can you imagine, Burke, an uninhabited planet—a whole world ripe for the picking—settled by monsters with their very own hand-selected crop of humans?"

Silence grew in the room like a cancer while they all digested that thought.

Once more, Richard thought about that cookbook, *To Serve Man*. The Sci-Fi guys had proven again and again to be prophets, foretelling the dangers of the future. How long before society began taking them seriously? All those politicians in Washington squabbling over the funding for a highway over here and a new national park over there when one of their daddy's contemporaries had flat out warned them they'd end up in the literal stew pot if they didn't watch their step. Did they pay attention? No. They rolled their eyes and stuck to the safer, less controversial, subjects like gun control and immigration.

Stanley's oft-repeated words drew Richard back to the conversation at hand.

"Hunters are led to the hunts that are theirs to accept. Perhaps we are here for just such a time as this. You're not alone, Burke. Your grandfather and I are going to do whatever we can as well, but *this* hunt"—he lifted his hands in a gesture of helplessness—"this hunt was laid before you."

Burke rubbed her forehead with her fingertips.

Stanley went on, "You'll need to walk on eggshells. There isn't a monster on earth who doesn't, in some way, ultimately owe allegiance to the Children of Cain. Anything could be at that party."

Richard realized his mouth had dropped open at some point and he clamped it shut again, lest the fish-out-of-water routine become habit. He made a mental note to work on his poker face. The pressure of the blood pumping furiously through his veins ignited little spots of darkness and light that popped at the edges of his vision. Friggin' Stan Kapcheck. "You can't seriously be suggesting the kid go in there alone?"

Stanley remained unperturbed. "She's been invited to attend a very high-profile dinner in a public forum. I imagine every major news network and half a dozen style channels will be filming. She'll be in no danger at the event. Well, no more danger than she can handle."

"My life wasn't so bad," Burke said. "I had a lovely routine, exercised every day, read a lot of good books."

"You were dying of old age in your forties, my dear. You are not a woman destined for a life of quiet reading and reflection," Stanley said. "You're only regretting it because you're focused on the dirt and long car rides instead of the lasting importance of the work to which you've been called."

Richard considered the ease with which she'd stalked through the forest in combat boots with an automatic weapon in her hands. Stanley was a donkey's hind end, but he wasn't often wrong. "Is that what crapped in your corn flakes? You been grumpy because you're regretting this life?"

Burke slumped against the back of the chair. The chair yelped a little protesting squeak. "I thought, in hunting, I'd found some great purpose. I thought I was finally making a difference," she said. "But there's always another monster. Always. There's no end to it, and there never will be, and now you're telling me that the monster wranglers are actually the most powerful beings on earth."

Stanley stretched his legs out before him once more and leaned against the headboard. He smoothed the blanket that covered him and folded his hands over his stomach. "A man was walking on the beach one day at low tide. At his feet, stretching hundreds and hundreds of yards, were countless starfish, stranded by the receding waters. With the patience of Job, the man picked them up, one-by-one, and tossed them back into the sea.

"His neighbor came along and scoffed at him. 'Why bother?' he asked. 'You can't possibly save them all. Not even half of them. There's no way you can make a real difference when such a vast number of them are stranded here.'

"The man bent and picked up one fish and returned it to the water. 'I made a difference for that one,' he said."

Richard rolled his eyes. Now the man had resorted to telling parables as if he were the Lord Jesus Christ himself. Tomorrow he'd probably try walking on water.

Burke stood and headed toward the door. "Tone it down, Stanley," she said before leaving. "Your messiah complex is showing."

A wheezy laugh catapulted straight up and out from Richard's chest as his granddaughter departed the room following her fantastic exit line. He lay down on his cold, uncomfortable pallet and drifted off to sleep with a grin on his lips. No troubles or worries like those expressed by Burke plagued his mind. He understood the score in no uncertain terms. In his time at Everest Senior Living... Heck, in all the lonely years before that, he'd never once fallen asleep smiling.

MORNING DAWNED BRIGHT AND COOL. RICHARD FLOPPED onto his back like an octopus washed up on the beach and stared at the ceiling, contemplating the best way to lift himself from the floor. His left hip throbbed in a dull bass-note rhythm. His right arm tingled and buzzed as circulation restored itself. Both feet had grown so cold during the night he'd woken up in pain before they passed into the stage where he couldn't feel them anymore. Presumably, they still resided in their usual place at the ends of his legs, but he couldn't see past the swell of his gut to verify the fact.

Shifting his head left, he could see the bed was unoccupied and neatly made. He drummed the fingers of his right hand on the floor, trying to speed the process of waking his muscles.

The door creaked open. "Oh, Dad," Maddie groaned. "Why on earth are you sleeping on the floor?" She bustled over to him and squatted down. "Maybe if I hold both hands and pull you forward—"

"I don't need no help," he declared. "Maybe I just ain't ready to get up, yet. I ain't no cripple. Why's everyone always treating me like one?" As soon as the words left his mouth, he wished he could suck them back in. His entire life, he'd been plagued by lips that moved faster than his brain.

Her whole body sagged like a half-deflated balloon. "Fine." She rose to her full height and peered down at him. "Stanley said he was going to the library. Burke and I are going to the mall. We'll be home in time for lunch. If you're still laying there when we get home, I am checking you into a facility, if I have to get a court order to do it. A man your age ought to know better." She spun around and huffed out of the room. The slamming door cut off her muttering.

A few minutes later, the garage door rattled, sending a vibration through the floorboards beneath him, and he heard the hum of Maddie's sedan fade into the distance.

Whatever tiny seedling of guilt had sprouted a moment earlier, withered and died. A man his age? Who was she to lecture him about what was and was not appropriate? Did she harp on Stanley about his socks with the stupid little neon pizzas on them, or about the way he trotted along the slick sidewalks with his hands in his pockets as if he'd bounce like a twenty-year-old if he fell? No! She flirted with him. *Bah*!

Spurred on by righteous indignation, he flung the covers off.

His right arm had returned to full functionality. Both feet felt cold again. He could do this thing. Rocking a little to build momentum, he rolled onto his belly. From there, he managed to get his knees under him, crawl to the edge of the bed and leverage himself up. No way the whole operation took more than five minutes. "Hmph," he muttered into the silence. "In time for lunch, indeed. I ain't no cripple," he declared again, just to remind himself.

After giving his body a chance to figure out he'd shifted from horizontal to vertical, he fetched his clothes from the suitcase along with a little flat tin full of balm given as a gift from a Healer in New Mexico. He wasn't crippled, that was for sure, but he wasn't too vain to acknowledge that his hundredth birthday was closer than his fiftieth was to the current date, and he did have a handful of titanium screws drilled into his bones, after all. He vowed once more to be the first to the soft, warm bed that night. Let Stan Kapcheck enjoy a night on the floor since he was so almighty spry.

After showering, he made himself a lovely, heaping plate of leftover stuffing smothered in steaming-hot gravy with a slice of pecan pie on the side for breakfast, and settled onto the sofa to eat in front of the television. Four remotes lay spread out before him. By the time he'd poked enough buttons to figure out how to turn the thing on and change the channel, his food had cooled to lukewarm. He flipped through hundreds of stations—talk shows, soap operas, a live-feed of one man on the floor of the Senate talking to no one about nothing in particular. How had he spent years of his life entertained by this?

You weren't entertained. You were just passing the time until you died.

Oh yeah. Well, no more of that!

Only a scattering of crumbs remained on his plate. He licked his thumb and used it to clean them up and pop them into his mouth. "Don't scold me," he told Barbara's ghost, whom he could feel preparing to admonish him. "Manners only count if there's someone around to see them."

Poking the power button that had brought the screen to life accomplished as much as pissing on a forest fire. Patience exhausted by the ridiculous electronics, he walked over to the television, reached behind it, and unplugged the contraption. Ha! Who needed buttons?

Earlier, he'd noticed a stack of books next to his duffle and assumed either Burke or Stanley had left them for him, hoping he'd have a chance to do something useful with his morning. Leather covers invariably meant difficult curly-cue text, and these thick tomes failed to be the exception to the rule. He squinted at the pages as he flipped through *Powerful Occult Leaders of The World, Nineteenth Century Edition*. Not exactly hot off the presses, but the book did indeed speak of a mysterious individual by the name of Umbra who operated out of an estate on the Italian coast and moved among the supernatural community with a power far greater than that dreamt of by the average man or monster. Maybe this Umbra was father or grandfather of the current Umbra. Could well be the same guy. Stanley had burst into the unsuspecting world during the final years of the nineteenth century. No reason someone else couldn't have bent a few rules along the way.

UMBRA LIVES A RECLUSIVE EXISTENCE, SEEN DIRECTLY BY ONLY A handful of most trusted associates. All known information points to his being fully human and mortal with the strength and advantages one would expect from the highest order of witch, shaman, or healer and more.

RICHARD IMAGINED CALLING STANLEY A WITCH AND chuckled. Little witch. Haha. Have to get him some black and green striped pantyhose and fancy red shoes.

Darn peacock would probably enjoy it.

Maybe someone would drop a house on him.

The thought stirred a murky mixture of emotions in

Richard. It seemed prudent, at that moment, to leave them unexamined and focus on the issue at hand.

THE UMBRA ESTATE, SHIELDED BY POWERFUL SORCERY, IS ALL BUT impossible to locate. Rumored to be a great gothic structure surrounded by labyrinths and moats, it has been the subject of centuries of wild speculation. Umbra himself seems to move in and out of the protected space without hindrance as the intrepid detective will have no difficulty finding that enigmatic name listed among the most powerful influences on the most powerful nations in the world, from the Great British Empire to China.

A close inspection of financial records will show that Umbra, or some corporation attributed to him, has made donations in the millions of dollars to political campaigns, war efforts, and business ventures. Those backed by him have never failed to thrive as long as the partnership continued.

Occasionally, there is a rift and the tide of world politics will shift. No greater example of this exists than the famous instance when King George III bragged to the world in the summer of 1780 that his empire was nigh on to undefeatable due to his having an "Italian sorcerer on a leash." Throughout the months that followed, a powerful sense of fighting pride previously unseen in the history of modern man swept through the back country of the so-called "new world" and the raggedy little street-urchin of a nation, The United States, with few allies, drove back her enemies and placed herself solidly upon the world stage.

Not surprisingly, whispers of an alliance between General Washington and a certain Italian diplomat with bottomless pockets abounded as he ascended to the presidency. In fact, some of those closest to him spoke of him having nearly God-like powers.

. . .

"Well, I'll be a suck-egg mule," Richard mumbled to the empty living room just as the rattling of the rising garage door reached his ears.

He slammed the book shut, sending a little puff of dust into Maddie's flawlessly sterile, filtered air.

Burke stalked into and through the house carrying an armful of bags. Moments later, a bedroom door banged shut with more force than was strictly necessary.

Stanley appeared a minute later. His keen eye landed immediately on the book. "Reading about the days of your childhood?" he asked.

"More like the history of your middle age, ya old coot," Richard retorted. "Where'd ya ditch my kid?"

Stanley settled into one of the padded chairs in the living room and crossed his legs. "The ladies pulled in right ahead of me. Madeline is making a pot of tea. She really is a gracious hostess."

Richard grunted. "Said she was crazy. Never said I didn't teach her manners. Did you know Umbra helped George Washington win the Revolution?"

"Did you know David Bowie was driven mad by his refusal to play tricks with Umbra?" Stanley asked in return.

"Who's David Bowie? Related to Jim?"

Stanley roared with laughter.

"What's so funny?" Maddie asked as she entered the room carrying a little silver tray bearing four cups and a teapot arranged around a dent in the center. Barbara's tray. A wedding present that Richard so clearly remembered opening, he could still remember the sound of the paper tearing.

They'd sat on the couch side by side, her in a tiny nightie that left him practically drooling and utterly at her mercy, him in nothing but a pair of striped pajama pants. On the floor to his left, picture frames and glass bowls, Tupperware containers, flatware, embroidered napkins, and kitchen gadgets of various sizes and usefulness formed a haphazard mountain. The remaining wrapped gifts, no longer a tower but still a formidable pile, covered the coffee table in front of them. How had he survived his years of bachelorhood without all this stuff? Did people really require a matched set of ten pots and pans, or three different size colanders?

"Your turn to pick," she told him.

"Do the big one, then," he said, mostly to clear off space on the table.

"Oh, yes! I've been saving that one. It came from my rich Aunt Sylvie."

"You have a rich aunt?"

"Doesn't everyone?"

He thought about that. It was true, there was rumored to be a wealthy relative on his mother's side of the family, but he suspected she was more legend than fact. Certainly, no wedding gifts had come from that quarter.

Barbara knelt in front of him and leaned forward to rip the paper off the box. Desire smacked into him like a tidal wave of lava, so powerful it made him dizzy. It took him a moment to tear his eyes away from the teeny, tiny ruffled bloomers covering her round little backside and focus on the fact that she'd said something.

"What's that?" he asked.

"For real!" she exclaimed. "Just look!" And, laughing, with her dark hair still tangled from their loving, and wearing that silly little scrap of fabric, she lifted a silver tea set from the box and set it out before them. Then, lifting the tray in her strong, capable hands, she asked in an absurd accent that he assumed was intended to sound British, "Like a spot o' tea, Gov'nr?"

Reason left. A man could only take so much. Grabbing her by her round hips, he dragged her down onto the sofa. She let the tray and its contents fall in a clatter of metal and met his passion with her own fiery desire.

Later, they laughed over the dent in the tray and speculated if it had happened when she dropped it or when they rolled off the couch and landed on it.

Just a few short years later, she was gone. Stolen away from him and their child by a monster who, in turn, had been slain by their granddaughter.

Richard blinked back the memory and forced himself to focus on the moment. In this house, the past jumped out at him from behind every corner as surely as the monsters they hunted did in a shadowy forest. He'd rather face the monsters.

Burke needed to go on this date and wrap up whatever this business with Umbra and his minions was so they could pack up the Cadillac, hit the open road, and fix their eyes on the adventure ahead rather than the pain of the past.

He rubbed his eyes and accepted a cup from Maddie. "Ain't nothin' funny. Stanley's just acting like an idiot."

"Dad!" She passed a cup to Stanley. "I noticed last night, you prefer a dollop of cream, so I got some of the good stuff from Whole Foods while we were in town."

"Madeline, the beauty of your thoughtfulness exceeds that of your countenance and that is, indeed, an astonishment," Stanley said.

Richard resisted the urge to blow a raspberry at the puffed-up horse's patootie and silently congratulated himself on growing as a person.

CHAPTER NINE

Albert

ALBERT STOOD IN FRONT OF A VENDING MACHINE, TRYING TO figure out if peanut butter crackers or potato chips had a greater overall negative impact on the environment. It was important to make wise choices. Maybe not as important as it was before a whole new planet became available for settlement, but still—one must do what one could.

It was hard to concentrate. He had moved on from obsessing about his status at Coleum to obsessing about Burke Martin. When the old lady who'd nearly killed him invited him over for an early Thanksgiving dinner, he'd been ready to refuse. Then she mentioned her daughter would be there—her "quite lovely" and "all-too-single" daughter.

He'd been intrigued. The daughter had to be on the sunset side of life, judging by the old lady's age. In his experience, women of a certain age weren't terribly choosy about their sexual partners and, if he was being entirely honest with himself, he was long overdue for a sexual partner.

Apparently, the girl was also in IT. At least, she wouldn't be completely clueless when he talked about the things that interested him.

Butterflies, or something a little less pretty and hope-inspiring, fluttered in his stomach when he thought about the date. Or, more accurately, the night after the date.

An obnoxious, high-pitched male voice popped his thoughts like the tip of a butcher's knife slamming into a latex balloon. "Hey, Al, need help figuring out how to work the keyboard? You have to push the letter that matches the one in front of your choice. It's hard, we know."

He bumped the button for the chocolate and marshmallow candy bar. Damn! Chocolate would be the death of the great apes and now he was a contributor. Not that he wouldn't eat it. Wasting food would not do a single positive thing for the apes or anybody else. He snatched the candy from the machine's tray and turned to face his tormentor. "Hi, Tim. How's it hanging, buddy?"

Tim's ever-present sidekick, Bob, stood next to him snickering. "Why do you ask, Al? You think about other guys' junk a lot?"

If he could be sure the rocket would get lost in space, dooming everyone onboard to a gruesome death, he'd secretly suggest a spot for these goons. "I noticed your avatar took some bad hits in the game last night."

"Noticed your avatar is the weakest, most pathetic one in the whole of Middle Techtopia."

"His powers have yet to be fully realized."

"Like your adolescence," Tim said and jabbed an elbow at his friend.

Albert squeezed the candy bar so hard it squished beneath the pressure. The two losers blocked his exit from the vending room. "Excuse me, guys. I gotta get back to work now."

"Why? Does the janitor need help rebooting his computer?" Tim asked.

"I heard you solved the mystery of the laptop on the fourth floor that needed to be plugged in," Bob added. "Surprised you had the brain power to figure that out."

Tim laughed. "He probably spent an extra twenty minutes crawling around under the desks trying to get a peek up someone's skirt."

Albert's face burned. The fact of the matter was, he may have stolen a glance or two, but who could hold that against him? He'd been under a table where eight of the youngest, firmest girls of the secretarial pool were working. "You know, you should have more respect for me. I was talking with Jones himself this morning and he told me he valued my work here at Coleum. You don't want to get on the wrong side of someone who could end up being your boss one day."

The men howled.

"He probably mistook you for the guy who's been doing a stellar job of keeping the executive toilets clean," Bob said.

Tim held his gut and doubled over in glee.

Albert shoved his way past them and out of the room. Someday, they'd pay. The two of them and every other low-life idiot who didn't understand the greatness that simmered at his core.

CHAPTER TEN

Richard

BURKE EMERGED FOR LUNCH AND ATE HER TURKEY SANDWICH wearing a black and silver sweat suit and a scowl.

Maddie dished an unsolicited spoonful of olives onto Burke's plate. "Really, Burke, I'd think you'd be more excited. A first date. You never know what could come from that. A whole world of possibilities lay before you."

Burke made a face. "I'm sure he'll offer me the moon."

Maddie raised her brows. "He may be one of the few men in the world able to deliver on that promise." She dabbed at her lips with a rose-colored linen napkin. "You know, the three of you, you've been on some kind of adventure. I get it. I do." She tucked the napkin over her legs and held up her hands as though someone were arguing. "We all need a little change now and then."

Oh, boy. Here it comes. Richard rolled his eyes at his cranberry sauce.

"But you've had your fun. You need to come home now. Dad, there's no way you're getting the proper doctor's care you should have while you're gallivanting around the country sleeping in sleezy motels. And Burke, it's not too late for you to start a family. They've got all these fancy fertility doctors and such. Why, that woman from that show on Wednesday nights just had a baby and she must be at least five years older than you. Right now, you're still young enough to think you'll never really be old, but let me tell you, one day you're going to realize you're at the end of the line and there's no one there with you because we'll all be long gone by then."

Stanley leaned forward as if to say something. The movement drew her eye. "And Stanley, dear, a man of your age, you ought to be pampered, comfortable. You said yourself that real meals with loved ones are too few and far between. Why not come with Dad and me to check out this new facility? I just know he's going to love it there. They have all sorts of activities and they even offer turn-down service in the evening. Maybe the two of you could be roomies!"

Stanley grinned.

Richard resisted the urge to throw an olive at him.

"Madeline, dear, I have never known another kind soul so interested in the welfare of others," Stanley said.

Maddie blushed and waved his words away. "Isn't that what the Good Lord told us to do?"

"Indeed, it is," Stanley agreed.

"Well, it's settled then. You'll come with Dad and me when we go to our appointment."

"What appointment?" Richard asked.

"Why, the appointment to fill out paperwork, of course. There's an opening right now. It might not be there if you hesitate. We need to jump on it. I'll call them and set it all up. Burke, you can stay here with me until we find you a place." She gave a funny little side-eyed smile. "Or until you settle in with a certain Mr. Right."

"I settled in with Mr. Right, remember? He left me for an

underwear model," Burke said.

"I'm sure you'll do better this time." Maddie clicked her fingernails against the edge of her dish.

The sound tapped against Richard's brain. He wondered what kind of weapons the girl had strapped to her person and thought it might be a good idea to run interference before Burke did something that would land her on the six o'clock news—and not in a good way. "Could be the kid likes being single," he suggested. "Maybe not every woman needs a man and a baby to turn her into a whole person."

Burke and Stanley both gaped at him as if he'd said something astounding.

"What're you staring at me for? I been listening," he said.

Maddie puffed up with a long-suffering sigh. "No one *likes* being alone, Dad. Don't you remember how lonely you were after you retired? Ambling around that house by yourself? Wasn't it so much better at Everest? I mean, you met Stanley there. Everybody needs a friend, right?"

His final night at Everest, a bat-winged, fanged creature with a glossy ponytail and pink surgical scrubs had tried to suck his memories away, leaving him a dry husk of flesh. It was the only halfway enjoyable evening he'd spent at the place.

"Oh! Look at the time!" Maddie suddenly burst out. "Burke, we need to be at the salon in twenty minutes. Ida Wolf agreed to squeeze you in. We don't want to keep her waiting."

"What's wrong with my hair?"

"Nothing's wrong with it, dear. I like the braids. They're lovely. You want something a little fancier for this party, though, don't you? There are going to be Italians there."

Burke stared across the table at her mother as if trying to decipher a foreign language. It really was impossible to argue with logic like Maddie's.

THE GIRLS LEFT AGAIN, WITH MADDIE FUSSING AS SHE backed out the door, "Don't you touch those dishes, Stanley Kapcheck, or I'll kick you out in the cold tonight. If you're my guest you're going to let me take care of you and you'll be doing no cleaning up in my kitchen."

"Oh, now, Madeline," he replied. "You know I can't just sit around with my feet up while you work your fingers to the bone taking such good care of us. I'll wash dishes and I'll be pleased to do it, and when you come back tonight, I'll happily help you dirty them again." He followed her all the way to the car, tucked her in behind the steering wheel, and closed the door for her, even waved from the drive like a little housewife seeing her honey off to a hard day at the office.

"Something's wrong with you," Richard told him when he returned to the house.

"No doubt, a good many things," Stanley agreed. "Come on, old boy. You can help dry."

Richard would have been perfectly content to take a nice long nap, now that his belly was full to bursting after his second big meal of the day, but pride dragged him along in Stanley's wake. Darned if he'd let the old goat be the hero of the day while he lazed around like the old man his daughter saw him as.

Stanley filled the sink with hot, sudsy water and set to scrubbing, and Richard dutifully took each dish, wiped it dry, and set it among its mates in the cabinets. He sent up a silent thanks that these plain white plates bore no resemblance to the fancier dishes they'd used last night. How many times had he dried dishes for Barbara while they talked about their day, the weather, the neighbors, the meaning of life, or the future they'd both assumed they would share together?

"What'd you find at the library?" he asked. "Anything about Coleum and the Italians?"

"I wasn't looking for them," Stanley told him.

Richard scowled. "Well, what in tarnation were you looking for then?"

"I was looking for accounts of a naked, vegetable-eating monster prowling the suburbs."

Richard flung the dish towel over one shoulder and leaned against the counter. "Find anything?"

"I did," Stanley said, setting a pot upside down in the rubber dish rack. "In fact, there have been no less than six separate reports of similar incidents. Gardens torn apart, garbage cans riffled, a short, naked man streaking through neighborhoods after dark. All six were in the police reports of the papers, but because three different precincts come together not far from here, it doesn't appear that anyone has put it all together as related. Since it's not anything more than a misdemeanor, I doubt anyone's really tried."

"Six, eh? Any bodies?"

"Nope. Not that I could find. In fact, not a single out of the ordinary death in a twenty-mile radius for months. Last one I could find was in the summer. Wife took an axe and gave her husband forty whacks after finding him in bed with the babysitter."

"Bloody, but not out of the ordinary. Nothing but good old human nature at work there," Richard said.

"Indeed." Stanley placed the last glass in the rack, took the towel from Richard, and dried his hands.

"So, what do you make of it?"

"No idea, old boy, but I thought a stake-out might be in order."

"A stake-out?"

"Do you have a better idea of how to figure out what's on the streets of this neighborhood, or some other way to pass the time while Burke is out with Albert tonight?"

Richard had to admit he did not. "I looked through the books you left in the bedroom while you were gone."

"What books?" Stanley took a bottle of water from the refrigerator and cracked the seal.

"I just told you what books. The ones you left in the bedroom. You going senile in your old age?"

Stanley's eyes crinkled at the corners. "If I was, I don't suppose I'd know it. I'm sure I don't know what books you're referring to, though."

Richard harrumphed. "Well, maybe it was Burke. Anyway, I read a bit about Umbra and I was thinking... Seems strange someone so reclusive would, all of a sudden, show up in front of the paparazzi at some high-falootin' shindig in the city. I mean, this Umbra fella is a ghost in the shadows. Ain't no one seem to know anything at all besides a name that makes everybody's guts go watery."

Stanley took a dainty sip of water. "I had the same thought. It leads me to wonder about John Jones."

"We got time between now and nightfall to do some digging," Richard pointed out. Ferreting out dirt on Jones promised a more interesting afternoon than staring at the nonsense flashing across the television. He remained determined to keep that part of his life in the past.

They set up a little office with laptop computers and a fresh pot of coffee on the dining room table. When Richard opened the browser, the song sparrow on Maddie's clock chirped out the hour. By the time the wood thrush started singing, his back hurt and his eyes burned. He closed the laptop with more force than was probably advisable.

Stanley stretched, his spine snapping like someone walking on bubble wrap. "You look frustrated."

"Well, for one thing, there's too dang many John Jones's in the world. It's like trying to do a search for every book in the library that has the word *and* in it. They're all on Twitter, too, twatting about politics and award shows."

Stanley smirked. "Tweeting."

"What?"

Stanley twisted back and forth and shook his arms. "They're tweeting, not twatting. There's a significant difference."

"What's the difference?" Richard asked.

"Google it. Anyway, common names are always fantastic choices for aliases."

"I thought of that, but he seems to check out. I musta read two dozen articles about his good old days at the University of Illinois and all the money he made with that photo app startup."

Stanley closed his computer. "Yes, it's a clear trail all the way back to his early days. Right back to when he got into trouble in high school."

"I read about that, too," Richard said. "His dad died, and he cracked up a bit. Ran into trouble with the law. Ended up in some sorta halfway house with a kid who knew about computers."

"Did you see anything about how his father died?" Stanley asked.

Richard couldn't remember any specifics, other than having the impression the loss had been sudden and unexpected.

"How about where Mom's been all this time?"

"Nothing," Richard told him.

"Ever come across the other kid's name?"

Richard checked the notes he'd scribbled down, squinting at his own shaky chicken scratching. "Anthony."

Stanley rubbed his chin with the backs of his fingers. "Sounds Italian, don't you think?"

The dots connected in Richard's mind, but no clear picture formed. "Kid was in juvie in the Chicago suburbs. Half the boys there are probably Tony or Vinnie." He twisted, trying to work the knot out from under his right shoulder blade. "I got one thing here that's pokin' me like a piece of dry hay in my undershorts."

"That does sound unpleasant," Stanley said.

Richard chose to ignore that and stick to business. "It ain't nothing I can think to do anything with. Just strikes me weird. In an interview with some business rag, they asked him about a trip to the rainforest. They were trying to make it out like maybe he went there on some big mission to save the savages or, maybe he was trying to convince them to give up the secret location of some vast resource or something, but he denied it all. Told them"—he consulted his notes again, to make sure he got it right—"'I barely spoke to another soul from the time I left the airport. I just sat under the trees and communed with the shadows. When I came home, I was a whole new man.'"

Stanley didn't appear to be impressed. "So?"

Richard shrugged. Now that he'd said it, he was hard-pressed to say why it stuck out at him. "I don't know, really. It's just the timing. Wasn't a month after he got home when he had the big press conference and told everybody he was gonna fly to Mars and take the cream of the crop with him. Something about that—"

The front door slammed hard enough to shake the house and they caught a flashing glimpse of Burke, long hair hanging in thick waves around her shoulders. Maddie came in a moment later, looking five years older than she had when she left. "I swear she refuses to see reason!" she exclaimed without preamble. "Sometimes, I look at that child and wonder how we could share any DNA whatsoever." She sighed and patted her own tidy hair. The silver roots visible the day before had disappeared after the trip to the salon. "It's like she doesn't even care that she'll be hobnobbing with the world's elite. She'd rather be tromping through a swamp in those god-awful, hard-toe boots of hers. How can we be related?"

Richard had no good answer, but he empathized deeply with the sentiment.

CHAPTER ELEVEN

Burke

Burke hadn't been on a date in two years and that suited her just fine. She'd tried the relationship thing in her younger days and found herself chasing self-esteem on a treadmill while her smarmy, good-looking husband banged a Swedish underwear model. Her divorce had cost years of her earnings, but she came to realize it was the best money she'd ever spent.

Nowadays, she lived as a forty-something divorcee, spending her days traveling around in an antique Cadillac with her grandfather and their... Stanley.

Before that, she'd been a forty something divorcee who spent her days working out in a gym and reading.

The jury remained undecided in regard to which version of mid-life was preferable, but either indisputably trumped the soul-sucking abyss that was marriage to a narcissist.

The point is, for Burke, dating held less appeal than stalking a foul-smelling, four-armed swamp monster through the alligator infested wetlands of the Florida Everglades. As far as she could deduce, her agreement to go out with Albert from IT meant one of two things. Either she had a butt-ton of respect for Stanley Kapcheck and his wild hunches or being back in her mother's house had officially robbed her of the last tattered remains of her sanity.

When the little dweeb greeted her by petting her hair as if she were a sheep at the county fair, she almost turned around and called off their date. Then Stanley appeared out of nowhere and tucked her into her coat. Her mother pressed the silly little purse they'd picked out to go with her dress into her hand, and before she knew what happened, she was watching the reflection of her scowling grandfather standing on the front step in his stocking feet recede in the side mirror of Albert's tiny humming insect of a vehicle.

A voice in her mind screamed for Albert to stop. Sudden certainty that she would never again ride in the Cadillac flooded her imagination with such force that her fingers twitched in the direction of the door handle. She could tuck and roll at the stop sign and walk away with no more than bruises.

How would I explain that to my mother? No one hates dating that much.

It's not a date. It's a hunt.

Oddly, that was the thought that calmed her enough to remain in the car.

Yup. Crazy, for sure.

The gala celebrating Coleum Corporation's impending victory over the bonds that had tied humanity to Mother Earth since the first people emerged from the salty waters of her womb was being hosted on the rooftop of the tallest sky scraper on the I-94 corridor. A clever idea—hosting this particular shindig among the clouds.

Albert squeezed into a line of traffic inching forward along the circular drive in front of the building.

Burke continued to tune out his stories about how Super IT

Man saved the day by informing someone all they needed to do was unplug and re-plug their modem. He scrubbed a virus from a laptop. He replaced a mouse-chewed charger. He remained so entranced with his own genius that not much was required of her in the way of conversational participation. She grunted and nodded every so often and he prattled on and on for the entire forty minutes they spent in the car.

Free from the burden of thinking up things to say, she studied the other vehicles around them—a Honda Accord, a Mercedes S-class coupe, a snazzy little Jaguar convertible, a Ford Expedition. Apparently, folks on every rung of the corporate ladder had received an invitation to the big soiree. Valets in puffy red coats opened doors on economy and luxury vehicles alike and whisked the cars away in the general direction of an adjacent parking garage. How very equal opportunity. And odd.

Again, that hissing voice in the base of her brain ordered her to run.

From what?

No answer.

Stop being stupid.

Run.

From what?

No answer.

She focused on the slow breathing that would draw adrenaline-diluting oxygen into her body.

When they finally reached the building's front doors and she escaped the confines of the little hybrid, the fresh breeze blew away the last vestiges of inexplicable nerves.

"Take good care of my baby," Albert told the man who opened his door, then he snorted obnoxiously.

Burke rolled her eyes at the guy on her side of the car and imagined that the smile he gave in response carried a sympathetic undertone. As Albert's date, she'd been labeled an object worthy of pity by the hired help. Fantastic.

At the entrance, a man with skin several shades darker than her own freckled beige, and a build approximately the size of Albert's car, checked their invitation, scanned Albert's employee ID, and peeked inside the absurd little purse. He failed to notice that the lipstick-shaped thing was actually a single-shot pistol loaded with a silver bullet. A girl could never take too many precautions.

Dating might not be at the top of her things-to-do list, but that didn't mean she remained oblivious to the bouncer's undeniable hotness. She winked at him.

His gaze darted to Albert and back to her and his left eyebrow twitched upward. "Enjoy the party," he rumbled in an excellent Barry White baritone.

Yeah. Sure.

Burke trailed along behind her runty little escort, determined to keep in mind it was a hunt, not a date. Yes, a hunt. An adventure. Let the good times roll.

CHAPTER TWELVE

Richard

THE LITTLE DWEEB HAD SHOWN UP RIGHT ON TIME TO PICK up Burke. Points for promptness, but his suit looked like something out of the 1972 Sears Catalogue, and when Burke politely asked for "Just a moment, please. I'm afraid I've misplaced the lipstick I was hoping to take with me," he told her he'd never known a Black lady who spoke so nicely.

Richard had waited gleefully for her to kick the dipstick in the face, but she just ground her teeth and walked away. Such was her loyalty to her position as a hunter. Richard grinned in pride.

His smile faded when the dingus made eye contact with him. At least three dozen different comments raced from his mind toward his lips. The one that burst out was, "You've got a lot of room for growth, Buddy." He huffed. That was inadequate by a long shot, but Burke returned before he could say anything else.

"You come home safe, kid." There. Those words said exactly what he meant.

She offered him a tiny smile and a promise that she would, and then she followed the egghead out into the night. He stood on the stoop and watched them drive away.

"Dad, come inside." Maddie's voice rang out from inside the house. "I'm making popcorn. There's a *Jeopardy* marathon on channel thirty-six."

Richard went inside and shut the door. The click sounded too loud. His guts crawled. He hated the idea of sending the kid into a hunt by herself. He hated the idea of her being with that snot-nosed little dork. He hated being cooped up in a house where he was made to feel like an old man.

Stanley emerged from the kitchen with a full tea service on a tray. "Come watch television with us, Dick. Sometimes a man has no choice but to wait."

He wanted to tell Stanley to stick it where the sun don't shine, but he'd been working on keeping his cool—becoming a better man and all that.

In the living room, Maddie beamed at him. "It's been a long time since I had anyone to compete with when I watch this show."

Wow! Madeline believed he was a real threat when it came to this trivia stuff? He'd assumed she viewed him as a doddering old fool, but maybe she had some respect for his intelligence, after all.

Maddie went on, "Now that you've introduced me to Stanley, it'll be a true battle of the wits."

Richard plopped onto the couch. Friggin Stan Kapcheck.

Richard dutifully stared at the television, munching on bland, butterless popcorn and sipping nasty tea that smelled like roses, but after half a dozen episodes, he thought he'd scream if he heard one fact about world geography or nineteenth century French poets. His mind kept returning to Mrs. Dister's story. From the bedroom window, he'd be able to see just about the entire neighborhood. Maybe he'd be able to catch a glimpse of something and figure out what was going on.

"I'm going to bed," he declared.

Stanley stretched extravagantly and nodded. "Yes, it is about that time. I think I'll turn in, as well."

The two men retired to the bedroom to see what they could see in the Neighborhood Where Nothing Exciting Ever Happens.

CHAPTER THIRTEEN

Burke

COLEUM CORPORATION'S LOBBY BOASTED A SOARING CEILING adorned with Art Deco-inspired features and a black and white marble floor that caused the clicks and clacks of dozens of high heels and shiny leather dress shoes to bounce around like the clatter of beans in a maraca. The racket set Burke's teeth on edge and left her yearning for the days when she spent most of her time alone in a room with Dan Brown's latest mystery novel.

The men and women surrounding her smiled brightly at one another, greeting each other and making small talk. No one acknowledged Albert from IT, not even the long-haired, bearded guy in the powder blue tuxedo with the ruffled shirt. A little pinprick of pity struck her heart and she warned herself to be careful lest she start feeling truly sorry for him. Then where would the night end up? With sympathy kissing?

I think not. All the crazy voices in her head agreed on that much, at least.

In groups of a dozen or so, guests piled into golden-doored

elevators like so many cattle being driven down the chute toward the transport truck. Elaborate light fixtures around the upper edges of the big metal box cast long shadows that crawled up the walls of the small enclosed space.

The hairs on Burke's neck stood up. Her reptile brain hissed again. While others watched the numbers above the doors, she studied the blurry reflections of faces avoiding each other's gaze in the mirrored doors. A great many monsters looked human to the naked eye but appeared as their true, undisguised selves in a reflection. So far as she could tell, all the people sharing the cramped space were actually people—or, at least, they were the kind of monsters who could easily pass for people. Someone reeked of way too much Channel Number Five. No one stank of sulfur.

They reached the top floor, the doors slid apart, and all the probably-humans stepped out onto the plush carpet. The herd flowed around the corner and down a long hallway lined with glass doors and windows that showed nothing more exciting than oodles of conference rooms and meeting spaces with impressive views of the city stretching in both directions. The murmuring voices blended into one soft susurration, infinitely quieter than the racket in the lobby, but somehow more unsettling to the part of Burke that still thought the tuck and roll at the stop sign at the end of her mother's street would have been the wise choice.

Why am I so nervous? What's out of place, here? What does my gut know that my brain refuses to see?

She asked herself the questions she'd learned to ask over the past half a year of intensive on-the-job hunter training. These were the questions that had kept Stanley alive for the past century and a half. If she trusted his instincts so much, it seemed only wise to put some small amount of faith in her own.

At the end of the hall, they climbed a short, steep staircase guarded at the top by two more beefcakes in fancy black suits, and stepped out into a wonderland.

On the street level, the night had carried the promise of winter's bitter domination of the coming months, but up here among the clouds, the folks at Coleum Corporation proved they were undaunted by the terrestrial limitations that so often held the rest of humankind back. Sub-freezing temperatures and a light snowfall were no reason to move a party indoors. Rather, enormous heaters and stunning glass-and-stone fireplaces blasted out heat that raised pleasant goosebumps along Burke's arms. A vast white canopy with rainbow colored silk banners draped from center to edges protected the space from falling precipitation while leaving the sides open to the breathtaking scene of glittering lights laid out across the surface of the planet far below them.

Albert rocked on his toes and tapped his hands against his skinny legs. "Pretty fancy, eh? I bet half the world wishes they were here tonight, but you couldn't even buy your way in. Have you heard how many celebrities pitched a fit about that?"

In fact, she had heard about it at great length from her mother. Madeline hadn't shut up about it the whole time they were shopping and getting ready. Clearly, she was trying to live out some kind of fantasy vicariously through Burke.

Story of my life.

Burke wandered along in Albert's wake, distracted, for the moment, by pondering whether her mother would be thrilled and energized if she knew exactly how Burke spent her days. *I could tell her about the wendigo in Colorado that I burned with an actual military-issue flamethrower, and the mummy in Virginia that I drowned in a vat of ammonia.*

In her imagination, Maddie scolded, "Burke Dakota, that's disgusting. No proper lady spends her days wrestling with monsters. My goodness, it's no wonder you're getting muscly like a man. What kind of husband will you find if every man you meet is scared of you? Men prefer a woman who's soft and feminine."

Nope, nopety, nope, no. There would be no big revelation to Mom regarding the hunter life. They'd all be doing Maddie a favor by leaving her in blissful ignorance.

Burke wove her way through the candy cane forest of bright silk and sparkling jewels under a sky of twinkling white Christmas lights that cast their soft but insistent light on the crowd, banishing the shadowy darkness to exile in the world outside this magical square of luxury. Laughter trilled heavenward like birdsong. Musicians dressed in silver played soft, futuristic-sounding songs on unfamiliar instruments.

Albert found his name on a card set atop a table in a corner farthest from everything and held it up for Burke to see. "This might seem far from the action, but it's actually great because we don't have to worry about people constantly bumping into our chairs."

What Burke wanted to say was, *Whatever you need to tell yourself so you can sleep at night, buddy*, but she held her tongue and eeked out some sound she hoped would pass for agreement. Two sullen-looking single men and a woman in a dress that Burke guessed had been brand new around the time she'd danced to Whitney Houston's latest hit at the high school prom, sat in silence. The men gawked at them. The woman stared out at the party with eyes as blank as if her mind were already on a rocket ship to Mars.

"Hey freaks and geeks! We're here. You can start the party now!" Albert fell into a fit of snorts and shoulder shaking.

Their wide eyes looked from him to her and back again. When he'd sufficiently recovered himself, he gestured to her grandly. "This is my date, Ms. Burke Martin."

Their gazes settled on her again.

"It's a pleasure to meet you," Burke lied politely. Her mother would be so proud.

They stared so long she began to wonder if they were mute. Finally, one of them asked, "*You* came here with *Albert?*"

"I did, yes." A painful but undeniable truth, thanks to her mom and Stanley Kapcheck.

"Don't seem so surprised, Tim. It's not like I've never brought a lady to a company party before," Albert said, pulling out his chair and dropping into it.

"You brought the sixty-year-old crazy cat lady from across the hall of your apartment building to the Christmas party last year," Tim replied.

Albert grinned at Burke. "She's a real cougar, that one. Don't be jealous, though. It was never a real thing. I confess, I had a bit of a dry stretch, but things are downright exciting these days. Am I right? The fates have smiled on me."

She assured him she'd find a way to overcome her raging envy and took her seat in a folding chair covered in bright white canvas.

From nowhere, servers appeared and, thank God from Whom all blessings flow, she had a glass of wine in her hands within moments.

TIM, ALBERT, AND THE OTHER GUY WHOSE NAME NO ONE ever mentioned had fallen into a heated conversation about what Burke assumed to be some sort of online fantasy role-playing game. She knew it was all BS because they kept saying that a stalker could kill a mage without batting an eyelash and in her experience, killing a mage was like fighting a god. A mage could be bound, captured, or banished, but hardly ever killed. Whatever a stalker was, it would end up as toast in a real-life battle.

She took advantage of their distraction to scan the crowd. Lots of creepy rich guys, but not a single Caroline creeper.

Dozens of shifty eyes, but none that glowed yellow. Not a single guest, so far as she could see from her seat in this luxurious corner of Siberia, sported tell-tale drops of blood on their starched white shirt.

What am I supposed to be looking for anyway? Stanley had been infuriatingly vague on that point. There could be anything at the party. Or nothing at all. Every sort of human, or perhaps just the powerful elite who control the destiny of the entire planet. Gather information. Stop the launch. Don't let anyone notice you.

No problem.

Having effectively tuned out the men at the table, she leaned toward the silent woman next to her. "Do you work for Coleum?"

The woman fiddled with a bit of lace on her skirt. "I'm here. I'm really here."

"Yes, but why?" Burke asked.

The woman startled at the question and met Burke's gaze as though she was noticing her for the first time. "Half the world wishes they were here tonight, but you couldn't just buy your way in. This is quite a privilege."

Her bizarre echoing of Albert's statement pinged on Burke's *Something Is Weird* Radar. "Yes. A privilege." Burke reached for the water glass next to her wine. "So, you work for Coleum, then? Are you in IT, the same as Albert?"

The woman frowned and blinked. She seemed to think about the question for a long moment before replying, "I'm here."

"Are you sure?" Burke asked.

"Oh, yes. I'm here and it's a real privilege." Her attention, dubious as it was, drifted back toward the crowd.

While Burke pondered how best to press for more information while remaining utterly unnoticeable, the music stopped and the man who'd been playing something that resembled a metal lute requested that the group turn their attention toward the stage. In a rustle of expensive fabric and metal chair legs scraping against polished concrete, the masses settled, leaving only a ring of servers standing around the edges of the rooftop.

Burke watched with a hunter's eye.

Maybe five hundred men and women had gathered for the momentous occasion. Most smiled and whispered, fidgeted, cleared their throats, sipped cocktails and water, and did all the things anyone would expect from a crowd that size, but here and there, like so many mannequins in a crowded mall, someone sat in perfect stillness in a state of expectation, exactly like the woman next to Burke. She counted ten, maybe twelve of the zombie freaks visible from her vantage point.

Not real zombies, though, or the sterling silver flatware would have presented too much of a problem for them as it could cause their flesh to sizzle on contact. Plus, they weren't decomposing or trying to eat their tablemates. That was a dead giveaway.

Ha! Dead giveaway. She couldn't help but grin a little at her own unintentional pun.

With everyone settled in, someone new stepped up to the microphone, a tall, skinny guy with thin wisps of sandy brown hair. "It is my distinct honor and privilege to introduce to you a man who needs no introduction. Not the god of war, but one who will lead us to a land unfortunately named after the red deity, and usher those lucky enough to be chosen into a new era of peace heretofore unknown by those on this blue marble."

As one, the zombies leaned in. Next to Burke, Weird Lady's breath quickened, and she made a tiny noise disturbingly sexual in nature.

Apparently, Albert noticed it, too. He snorted, although to give credit where credit was due, he snorted quietly. "The ladies all swoon for Jones," he whispered in Burke's ear. His overly minty breath tickled her nose and threatened to make her sneeze.

At the door through which they'd exited the building onto the rooftop, one of the goons stepped aside and John Jones himself emerged from the dark space—six feet tall and gorgeous, with eyes so blue they sparkled under the twinkle lights. He strode toward the stage with shoulders back but head bowed, confident in his power, striving for humility, failing completely at being humble. The scar across his left brow shown far more visibly in real life than on television, but somehow the jagged line only served to increase his appeal. Without it, he'd have been nearly boyish, too smooth and sleek. With it, he became both mortal and dangerous. In a word, *interesting*.

The not-really-zombies leapt to their feet, clapping and cheering, fully animated, at last. The entire crowd followed. Burke could easily say she'd never seen any group of employees so overjoyed to see the boss. She peeked in Albert's direction and noticed the tears glistening in his eyes.

Jones possessed undeniable sex appeal, and he positively radiated charisma, but to bring a grown man to tears... What did this guy have that every other boss in the history of corporate America lacked?

At the podium, Jones made motions in the air as if patting his screaming fans on the head in a weak attempt to make them quiet down and settle back into their seats. The crowd screamed even more wildly.

Burke wondered if the people on the street could hear the ruckus. On the heels of that thought came the realization that, while she'd noticed several news vans and cameras down there amongst the common people, she'd not seen so much as a cell phone camera up here on the roof. She wondered what would happen if she pulled out her iPhone and started recording John Jones' speech. Probably not the best way to remain invisible.

Eventually, the crowd spent their ecstasy and settled back into their seats. John Jones beamed at them, a benevolent king looking over his subjects, a father gazing out upon his loving children.

Burke leaned close enough to Albert to smell the Irish Spring scent of his skin. "Where's Umbra?"

Albert held a finger to his lips without ever taking his eyes from Jones.

"Five days, eleven hours, eight minutes until launch," Jones said.

The crowd surged to their feet again, roaring, screaming, weeping. The woman next to Burke performed a fantastic imitation of a fourteen-year-old girl at a boy-band concert. Burke clapped politely while stitching together a hasty plan of action should the lady faint.

An absurd amount of time passed before the group hushed again. Everyone resumed their seats, sniffling and wiping their eyes. Burke carefully smoothed the WTF frown off her face and focused on John Jones, who encouraged them all to dream big, and reminded them that the launch was a win for the whole team. Each of them played an essential role. High praise was doled out to the engineers and designers, the agricultural scientists and the architects. A brief mention of the technical people who kept the wheels of progress turning caused Albert to visibly swell with pride.

The man displayed great skill at the artform of talking a lot without saying anything.

At long last, Jones paused, during which time he managed to appear as though he made eye contact with each and every person present. "After we do this thing, there will be no need for those who have lingered under oppression to cower and hide from their oppressors. There will be no squabbling over land and resources, which threatens to escalate into nonsensical wars that threaten the existence of us all. There will be, I promise you, space for all."

Burke braced for another eardrum-shattering standing ovation complete with screams and fanatic shouting, but the crowd maintained a hush that gave her the same sense of holy awe she'd experienced at well-preached Christmas Eve masses. The prophet had spoken. His disciples cowered in awe of their god.

But the god is nowhere to be found, Burke thought. *Where is Umbra?*

Jones raised his hands, palms up as though in offering. "In the meantime, let us celebrate our success, both past and future."

Servers appeared at the tables with tureens of steaming soup and enormous crystal bowls of salad, baskets of steaming bread and bottles of wine with which they topped off every glass.

CHAPTER FOURTEEN

Richard

WITH THE BEDROOM LIGHTS OFF AND THE DRAPES PULLED aside, the nocturnal happenings of Maddie's neighborhood played out before the watchful eyes of the two hunters like the world's most boring midnight movie. Mrs. Dister waddled by in a pink running suit with matching pink trainers and a pink baseball cap. Her short grey ponytail poked out of the hole in the back. The ponytail appeared almost identical to the tail of the little gray mutt on the other end of the leash she clutched in her chubby fist. Her head twitched constantly left and right, leaving no doubt that she kept a keen eye out for the veggie-thieving monster. A handful of smallish SUV's, four-door sedans, and one ancient station wagon rolled by in slow succession over the course of an hour or so, each one carefully obeying the twenty-five-mile-an-hour speed limit and the general rules of safe driving.

Luke Castleberry dragged his rubbish bin to the curb, peeking several times in the direction of Maddie's house. Maybe Mrs. Dister's mystery creature would jump out of the bushes and eat old Luke. After all, he had about as much personality as a head of cabbage.

Richard chuckled at the thought.

"What's on your mind, my friend?" Stanley asked from his seat on Richard's left. They'd arranged the two ugly, uncomfortable chairs in front of the window with a little table between them as a convenient place to rest their loaded pistols and hot cups of coffee.

"Watching paint dry'd be more exciting than keeping an eye on this street."

Stanley shifted. The soft rustle of expensive cotton blend, magnified by Richard's hearing aid, stirred an itch deep inside his skull. He fiddled with the hearing aid's dial in an attempt to adjust the volume. Stupid thing was smaller than a tick turd.

"Is Mr. Castleberry an old rival of yours?"

The hearing aid buzzed again. "You're irritating my head," Richard told him.

"He seems like a very upstanding gentleman," Stanley said.

"Luke Castleberry has as much personality as wet concrete." He continued messing with the volume dial. Too low and it buzzed. Too high and a weird bass pulse thumped in counterpoint to his heartbeat, as if one of the neighbors several houses away played rock music with a baseline just loud enough for the sound waves to jab at his brain. The sensation left him shifting in the rickety chair, unable to settle in with any degree of comfort.

"Could it be you don't appreciate the affection he clearly feels for your daughter?"

Richard pulled the offending device from his ear and tossed it on the table where it slid and settled to a stop against one of the pistols. *Ah, blessed quiet.* "Need a battery," he told Stanley. "I can't hear you." He glanced at the clock and took note that it had been almost five hours since Burke left in Albert's prissy hybrid.

CHAPTER FIFTEEN

Burke

Burke leaned over and told Albert she had to powder her nose. He nodded vaguely as though not quite sure what to make of that information, and she left him sitting there to figure it out. Rather than make her way through the middle of the crowd, she skirted the edges to get a good glimpse of the group as a whole.

The not-really-zombies ate, just like everyone else. They sipped their wine and seemed to all be using the correct forks—pure silver forks. None of them appeared to be drooling, so far as she could tell, but neither did any of them speak or make conversation, with one exception.

A young man, strikingly handsome, with ebony skin and deep dimples, muscles apparent even under the layers of his tuxedo, and eyes the exact golden brown of polished oak, who'd earlier acted just like the others, was now nodding along and engaged in conversation at the side of a rather plain-looking woman . She patted his arm affectionately and basked in the glow of his attention, but the moment she looked away, his countenance faded back to a flat forward stare.

This wasn't anything Burke had seen before. Monsters could suck away memories or even souls, leaving a drooling, mindless husk, but these Stepford people were something entirely new to her experience. Clearly, they weren't blood-thirsty monsters, but something smelled witchy, to say the least.

She continued around the perimeter of the space until she reached the doorway that led back into the building. The goons let her pass without comment, and she descended from the heavens back into the tower. She'd already noted nothing more exciting than a series of meeting rooms and closets between the elevators and the rooftop entrance. No major revelations came to her as she retraced her path through that space. No bodies with vampire bitten necks or unexplained pools of blood appeared in plain view inside any of the conference room windows. Not one of the little golden plaques on the wall appeared to be hoodoo symbols.

Two men passed her, both of them doing that absurd up-and-down thing with their eyes that men do as if they're checking out livestock. After that, she found herself alone in the hall. She jumped on the opportunity to accidentally on purpose walk right past the bathroom and around the corner. More meeting rooms. Apparently, the executives at Coleum Corporation used the top floor to impress visiting guests with the lofty view of the top layer of smog hanging over the city on a sunny day. But at the end of the hall, two big glass doors led to a waiting room dominated by a fancy wooden desk.

Jiggling the door confirmed that it was locked. She peeked over her shoulder and prepared to jiggle a little more strategically—with a hairpin in hand—when she noticed a tiny camera mounted above the track lights aimed in that direction. Five seconds later, a new goon, this one in tactical gear rather than a tuxedo, appeared around the corner.

"Help you?" he asked.

Burke found it easy to smile her flirtiest smile. The guy was as adorable as a puppy on steroids.

Do you have to be gorgeous to work for Coleum security?

Burke twisted one of her curls around her finger. "Sorry. I know I'm probably not supposed to be in this part of the hall, but curiosity was killing me. I had to take a peek around and when I saw that desk through the doors... My goodness." She pressed a hand to her heart, an attempt to draw his gaze to her cleavage. "Is that a genuine Louis the fourteenth? It's just stunning."

His focus never left her eyes for a second, but a little line formed between his brows. "That's a limited-access area."

She pouted. "Couldn't you just flip the lights on for one quick minute to let a girl take a peek?"

A muscle twitched along his powerful jawline. "I'm sorry, ma'am. Our instructions are to maintain all secure areas for the duration of the event, no matter what."

She took a step in his direction—a move that placed her decidedly within his sphere of personal space. "But...a *real* Louis the fourteenth," she crooned. "Please?"

He swallowed hard. "I'm sorry, ma'am."

"Can you at least tell me who gets to sit there? Maybe I'll be lucky enough to meet them at the party and work it out to come back during business hours."

His massive shoulders relaxed as he realized Burke had no intention of pushing the issue. "Of course. Mr. Jones' receptionist sits there. This is his private office suite."

Burke batted her lashes. "I should have guessed. Only the best for the big guy, eh? Who's going to get this space once he flies away to Mars?"

One corner of the puppy dog's wide, luscious mouth twitched upward. "Only thing I know is it won't be me."

"You don't seem like the type to be content in an office anyway," she said.

He shrugged. "Wouldn't like the work, but wouldn't mind the pay." He glanced up at the little camera and his smile faded. "Not that I'm not grateful for this job. Coleum takes fantastic care of their employees. All of us."

"I'm sure they do," Burke said. She sighed. "Well, if you're sure I can't talk you into letting me in, I suppose I should head back up before I miss dessert."

He stepped aside to let her pass. As she did, she stopped and looked back over her shoulder. "Can I ask you a weird question?"

He cocked an eyebrow.

Adorable.

"You haven't seen any antique coins around here, have you?"

"Antique coins?"

"I just thought...maybe..." She gestured toward the locked office. "If that's old, maybe there'd be other stuff, too. But no? No coins? Fat leather books full of dead languages? Hand-carved bowls with strange symbols on them?"

He stood there, bewildered.

"I know it's bizarre. I'm just a sucker for old stuff, but never mind." She winked at him. "Maybe I'll get lost again after dessert."

"I wouldn't recommend that, ma'am."

Huh. So much for my mighty powers of flirtation.

CHAPTER SIXTEEN

Richard

THE UGLY RANCH-STYLE HOUSE ACROSS THE STREET WENT dark when the porch light clicked off and the blue glow in their front window flickered and went out. The humans of the world were drifting off to sleep feeling safe and secure, oblivious of the monstrous things that shared their planet, looking for a heart to eat or a soul to suck dry. He'd be lying if he said there wasn't some satisfaction in being one of the people in the know after a lifetime of living like a mushroom—kept in the dark and fed a bunch of crap. Of course, being in the know meant he spent a good amount of time fighting, running, falling, and sometimes screaming like a little girl, but, hey, a man learns to take the good with the bad.

"She's a vibrant woman, not a child, you know. I honestly don't see what all the fuss was about. She seems just as kind and lovely as a flower on a warm summer day."

That sound wasn't like the bass rhythm of music, exactly. It was more familiar.

The hairs on his neck stood at sittention.

"Would you shut your danged pie hole for a minute?" Richard snapped. "You hear something?" He fumbled to find the stupid hearing aid in the dark and managed to knock it onto the floor. Aware that he was muttering under his breath and unmotivated to stop, he got down on all fours and started feeling around under the table. His joints popped like sappy pine in a campfire. From his position on the floor, the sound came to him again, as if carried through the wooden frame of the house itself, a low, deep, guttural *whomp, whomp, whomp* that prompted his lizard brain to send a little burst of adrenaline into his heart.

Stanley rose with fluid grace, his pistol gripped in both hands, and closed the distance between himself and the window. "Adieu fear bit sit breeding?" he whispered.

Richard stretched forward, searching with his fingertips. "What?" He strained to focus on the noise and identify its source, but the excitement sent his guts churning and now those noises covered up anything else he might have been able to hear.

Stanley's gaze remained fixed on the scene outside. "It's how slike breeding sue me."

"You having a stroke or something?" Richard asked just as a car turned the corner, its ridiculously bright headlamps cutting across the window, highlighting Stanley's pasty complexion. "Come away from the window, Stanley. Something ain't right," he said.

Breathing. Not rock music. It was the low, grunting breaths of something leaning against the house, just under the edge of the window in front of them.

"Come away from the window!" he shouted.

An inhuman shriek pierced the night.

Fangs.

A hideous, wide mouth stretched wider, less than three feet away.

Black eyes fixed on Stanley.

Richard reared up.

Crack!

The back of his head slammed solidly into the underside of the table hard enough to lift it from the floor. "Son of a—" He rolled onto his side, clutching his head. The lights in the room blared to life, illuminating his gun and his hearing aid, both lying on the carpet right in front of his watering eyes.

"Oh, my goodness, Dad!" Maddie's voice came from the direction of the bedroom door. She must have been the one to flip the light switch.

Stanley knelt at his side and leaned over him, much too close over him. His left hand flicked the pistol under the bed. "You okay, Dick?"

Richard shoved at him with the hand not clamped to his head. "Get off me, ya dang fruitcake!"

Stanley obliged, sitting back on his heels. The wrinkles at the corners of his eyes scrunched up in that annoying way that made you know he was laughing at you, even if his lips weren't moving.

Maddie scurried into view and stood with her hand pressed to her heart. "What in the world happened?"

"I'm so sorry we gave you a fright, dear," Stanley said. "Your father and I found ourselves restless and decided to sit up for a while and watch the world go by. His hearing aid fell on the floor and he got down to retrieve it and...well...I'm afraid we caused a commotion and woke you."

Her hand remained on her chest, but her shoulders relaxed. "Goodness," she said again. "Here, Dad. Let us help you up." She extended a hand.

Richard chose to ignore it. "I don't need no help." Grunting and panting as much as a greased pig after a chase, he managed to get himself up to his feet again. Gingerly, he explored his scalp with his fingertips. It throbbed in protest, but his hand came away free of blood. When he looked at Maddie again, her hands were balled in fists at her sides.

Her eyes narrowed to slits. "I swear, you're the most stubborn mule of a human being on the face of the Earth."

He drew back, more surprised than insulted. He couldn't remember her ever actually insulting him outright.

CHAPTER SEVENTEEN

Burke

By the time she hiked back up the steps and circled around to the table, the dinner dishes had been cleared away and replaced with dainty little plates displaying an assortment of tiny cakes and pastries. "This looks lovely," she remarked as she took her seat.

Albert mumbled something unintelligible around a mouthful of food.

"We're so privileged to be here. Half the world would kill for tickets, but you couldn't buy your way in, no matter what," the woman next to her said.

Burke arranged her napkin over her lap. "I got that. Thanks."

The woman's gaze drifted off to nowhere in particular and she continued to eat.

Burke nibbled at the treats laid out before her, watched the crowd for clues about the weirdos, and ignored Albert who rambled on at great length about the crucial part the IT team played in the day-to-day operations of Coleum. There was no way they'd be able to figure out the payroll, let alone fly to Mars, if it weren't for him and his team.

John Jones caught her eye when he stood up from his place at the table closest to the stage and began mingling through the crowd. A tiny woman with a perfect hourglass figure and glossy brown hair that brushed her waist trailed along behind him looking submissive and saying next to nothing. His smile stretched as wide as the Great Mississippi River and looked every bit as slick and cool. There wasn't a doubt in Burke's mind, if there had been any babies around, he'd have been kissing them and taking photos.

She leaned over and interrupted Albert in the middle of a story about a supposed rocket scientist who couldn't figure out how to re-boot his own modem. "Can you introduce me to him?" she asked.

Albert followed her gaze. His face turned a shade pinker than usual. "Mr. Jones?"

"Yeah. I really want to meet him."

Albert snorted. "Well, yeah. You and half the world."

Burke held up a hand. "All of whom would give their left arm—"

"It's quite a privilege to be here," the woman on her left reminded her.

Burke slumped back into her chair. "So I've heard. I just thought, since you're such an important part of the team, you might be able to...you know...do a tiny favor for your special lady. But if you're not high enough up the ladder, I completely understand."

"It's not like that," Albert objected.

The guys next to him exchanged a knowing glance and giggled like middle school girls.

Sensing progress, Burke pressed on, "No, really. Not everyone can be Mr. Big. Companies need little men, too. In fact, the average Joes are crucial to any operation."

Albert's face glowed brighter than the boiled lobster tails they'd eaten for dinner. "I am *not* an average Joe. I programmed the whole—"

Burke gave his forearm a reassuring squeeze. "It's all right, Albert. Really. I understand."

He shook his head. "But you don't," he whined. His gaze darted back and forth between Jones and Burke. His scrawny chest rose and fell in quick, sharp rhythm. "Okay. Come on."

"What do you mean?" Burke asked.

"Dude. I wouldn't—" one of the nerds started to say but Albert cut him off.

"No, man. My girl—my special lady—wants to meet Jones, she's going to meet Jones. He owes me."

The zombie-woman-who-wasn't-really-a-zombie gasped out loud at that.

Albert glanced around as if to see if anyone else had overheard, then bolted out of his chair with such force it teetered on two legs for a moment before thumping back down.

Burke jumped up next to him before he lost his nerve and let him lead her through the crowd to Jones and the gorgeous girl, who were schmoozing with a group of men she recognized from the evening news—state politicians, one of whom was rumored to have his eye on the next presidential election. Albert set a pace akin to that of an Olympic runner in the one-hundred-meter event, scattering wait staff like so many bowling pins. At the last second, he drew to a dead stop five feet behind Jones and stood there as if paralyzed.

Jones' voice flowed from his lips like jazz from a master's saxophone. "Well, Senator, as you know, space is international territory. We've been over this repeatedly. Claiming it for any one nation is against international law. I will swear to you, though, we will not forget who our friends are, and when it comes time to mine for titanium or magnesium, or whatever else we may be able to find up there, I will have your name at the top of my list." He stopped talking and his shoulders stiffened. Though his smile never wavered, when he turned and peered down his flawless nose at Albert, for just one moment, a shiver of terror as intense as any she'd experienced while facing down The Devil Herself raced through her body. A split second later, warmth and joy flowed out of him as naturally as if he were the midday sunshine in June. "May I help you?"

Albert made a sound like a slowly deflating balloon.

The woman behind Jones snickered.

Burke reached out a hand, which Jones accepted without hesitation. His skin was soft and dry, his grip sure and confident. "Please forgive our intrusion. Albert was kind enough to invite me to join him tonight and I just couldn't help but push my luck by begging him to introduce me to you."

He didn't release her hand, but somehow the pressure of his grasp filled her with a sense of calm reassurance—a sense that if she trusted him to take care of her, everything would be okay. He directed his smile at Albert. "What department do you work in, son?"

Son? No way they had more than five years age difference between them.

"Information technology, sir," Albert whispered, staring at the floor.

"And are you a technical specialist, as well?" he asked Burke.

"I was. I was a programmer before I retired. I'm taking care of my grandfather now."

"How noble of you. Our older generation is too often neglected. We fail to give them the honor they deserve. What's your name, dear?"

"I'm Burke. Burke Martin."

He dropped her hand as if she'd burned him. "Not the Burke Martin who turned Compufest into the most profitable app corporation of all time?"

"I didn't do it alone," she told him, trying to hide her surprise that he'd heard of her.

"Albert, however did you come to know this charming creature?" he asked.

Albert managed to peek up at his boss. "Her mother ran over me with her car, sir."

John Jones roared with laughter. The senator and his tablemates smiled in their direction. No way had they been able to overhear what had been said, but obviously, if Jones was laughing, they should be amused, as well. When he finally pulled himself together, he slapped Albert on the back hard enough to cause him to stumble forward. "Well done, son. Well done. Listen... It is Albert, right?"

Albert nodded, apparently stunned mute. "There's something I want to talk to you about. Stop by my office in the morning, will you?"

Burke had often heard of people "turning green," but before that moment, she'd never thought of it as a literal phenomenon. Albert's skin took on a weirdly chartreuse tint and she wondered if he was going to throw up on his boss's beautiful Farragamo derby shoes.

"Ms. Martin, it's been truly a pleasure and an honor. I'm glad you came here tonight." Jones shook her hand again, and again she found herself leaning into the comforting warmth of his aura. "I'm confident fate will cause our paths to cross again very soon."

He put an arm around the waist of the little slip of a woman that Burke had all but forgotten was standing there and the two of them wandered off into the crowd, no doubt to schmooze with those who lived life far higher up the ladder than the IT guy and his unemployed date.

The band switched to dance music from the era when girls pretended to be happy and proud that every boy in town was running off to fight the forces of evil on the other side of the world.

Albert mumbled something and took off, and she suspected he was headed to the bathroom to pull himself together. She wandered toward the open bar, trying to make friends with overly helpful servers. Consummate professionals, each and every one, to the point where they skirted her questions about Umbra with the slick skill of veteran politicians. Everyone agreed that it was very exciting sharing space with the Great One. No doubt, it was a great privilege to be at the party, even as a lowly servant. Half the world would give their last dollar to be there. Not one of them would actually point him out to her.

She made note of the not-really-zombie people and watched them carefully. A pattern emerged. When spoken to by certain people, they animated, even beyond what you'd expect from someone in that context. They doted and adored and positively fawned over their companions, but when their companions looked away, they took on the personality of storefront mannequins.

By the time Albert found her, her feet were screaming inside her shoes like two dogs howling in their crates. The frustration of knowing something was going on with the stranger people but having no way to figure out what it was reached a boiling point. Being told Umbra was right there under her nose but being unable to figure out which of the partygoers might secretly be ruling the world served as hot-burning fuel for the fire.

She teetered back to her own chair on her aching feet and slumped back. "Why am I even here?"

The woman next to her raised her eyebrows. "Oh, it's a great privilege."

"I'm pretty rich, you know," Burke told her. "I could afford to go buy a pretty house and putter in the garden every day for the rest of my life."

"Why would you want to do that?" The woman squeezed her folded hands together so tightly her knuckles turned white. "No matter how much money you have, you'd never be able to buy an experience like this one."

"Yeah, you know what would make it really great? Meeting Umbra in person."

The woman blushed as if Burke teased her. "Don't be silly."

"Why is it silly?"

"Well...no one... I mean...maybe someone but... I don't think..." The woman twitched twice and then relaxed. "Look! John Jones is coming this way. Maybe he'll stop at our table and say hello. How exciting!"

Burke harrumphed. "Yeah. Super radical, dude." But she'd be lying if she said some part of her didn't sort of hope he'd come talk to her once more before they left. The part of her that had longed since birth to fit in and be accepted by society nearly swooned at the very thought.

CHAPTER EIGHTEEN

Richard

FROM THE BED WHERE HE'D BEEN TUCKED IN AND GIVEN Ibuprofen and an icepack for his head, Richard saw Burke in the hallway.

"What happened?"

Stanley and Maddie turned as she paused in the doorway.

Maddie made extravagant gestures with her arms as she explained, "Your grandfather and his friend, against every bit of common sense known to humanity, decided to spend the night drinking coffee and spying on the neighbors, which turned into him bashing his head on the furniture and scaring the wits out of everyone. This, from the man who insists he is perfectly sound enough of body and mind to take care of himself, so far be it from me to offer him any kind of a helping hand. No! Not me! He can do it himself. So fine, just fine. Fine! It's fine! Just *fine*!" She took a slow, shuddering breath while they gaped in wide-eyed silence. "So," she said in a high, honey-sweet tone. "How was your date?"

Burke blinked three times before answering. "He told me he

wanted to kiss me. I said I'd rather not. He tried to kiss me anyway. We had a brief but intense conversation about consent and then I got out of the car. I don't think his nose is broken, but I can't give any guarantees."

Maddie rubbed her forehead with the tips of her fingers. "I just..." She took another of those shaky breaths before announcing, "I'm going to bed," and without another glance in Richard's direction, she left the room. A moment later, her own door shut with a bit more of a bang than seemed necessary.

IT TOOK A FEW MINUTES TO GET RE-ORGANIZED. BURKE disappeared to her own room to change into pajamas. Stanley pulled the drapes shut and pushed the furniture back into place.

"What in tarnation was that thing?" Richard asked.

Stanley admitted he'd never seen anything like it.

Richard thought of the pale skin, black eyes, and sharp fangs. "Well, don't you think we ought to go after it once Maddie's settled in? We can't just leave it running around the neighborhood. It could be dangerous."

"Only to vegetable gardens, it seems. If I had to hazard a guess, I'd say we'll find Madeline's kale patch has been murdered. Whatever that creature is, it appears to be an herbivore. It made no move to attack through the window. It ran from Albert's headlights. No one's been hurt around here, not so much as a missing chihuahua."

Richard snorted. "An herbivore with fangs? Ain't that contrary to some basic fourth-grade science?"

Stanley sat down in the nearest chair, crossed his legs, and smoothed nonexistent wrinkles from his slacks. "Everything evolves with some sort of defense mechanism. Even a bunny rabbit can give a nasty bite when frightened."

The memory of the shriek wrought a little shiver. "That

wasn't any kind of bunny rabbit."

At last, Burke returned, shed of the fancy dress, cleansed of the thick make-up, and sipping a cup of herbal tea that smelled faintly reminiscent of the stuff the nurses used to rub on his hip at Everest Senior Living. Where did Maddie find that crap, and what possessed her to spend good money on it?

"I'll tell you my story, but I don't know exactly what it all means," she said before launching into the story of her evening with the four-eyed geek.

When she'd finished, Burke set her empty teacup on top of the dresser. "That's all there is. No wild reflections when I checked my lipstick in my compact mirror. No ancient warding discretely carved into the doorframes. No second bar serving up calf's blood. Real silver on the tables. Weirdness all over the place, to be sure, but nothing like anything I can put a name to."

"Well, that's about as useful as tits on a bull," Richard said.

"Yeah, well, what great mystery did you solve tonight?" Burke challenged.

Stanley ignored the bickering. "It's not witchcraft." He rubbed his chin the way he often did when trying to remember something he'd learned before either Burke or her grandfather had even been alive, let alone hunting. "But it's close, related somehow. Not demons, either, but it feels almost the same."

"Explain?" Burke asked.

He held out an empty hand. "Like you said, no hex bags. No fat leather books. No bowls with symbols or funny-smelling herbs. No strange drinks at the party. Nothing witchy in any way, shape, or form. The craft, well-practiced, can be powerful beyond imagining, but it invariably leaves traces."

"But it does sound witchy," Richard argued.

Stanley nodded. "Indeed, in many ways it does, my friend."

"Maybe this Umbra is like Lord Voldemort from the Harry Potter books. He can fly without a broom and cast spells without a wand because he's gone farther down the dark path than any other witch," Burke said.

Leave it to the book nerd to compare real life to a kid's story. If we live in a world where witches and wizards really do run magical schools, you could bet your bippy that everyone would know about it. You couldn't hide something like that.

A different internal voice objected.

Isn't Umbra the head of a major international magical conglomerate that basically rules the world in secret?

Richard's mind thrummed like a hive of irritated bees inside his skull. Ibuprofen had its limits.

Stanley folded his hands in his lap. "Anything is possible."

"You going to give a straight answer of some kind or just sit here yanking our chains all night?" Richard asked.

"I don't know the answer, Dick. It's not witches or demons. Not in any sense I've encountered. Like Burke, I sense the otherness in every part of what's going on, but I have no answers except to confess that I am very concerned about this situation."

Richard didn't like the sound of that one bit. They'd faced some truly creepy stuff and it was a chilly day in Hell when Stan Kapcheck actually started to worry.

"Burke, I'm not sure sending you there was the right thing to do. I may have made a terrible mistake. I want you to stay close, all right? Stick around the house. Don't go outside alone. Don't go anywhere at all with Albert again."

Amusement did a little tap dance across her face. "Oh, don't worry. I don't think the IT guy and I will be running off on any romantic trysts in the near future. I have to ask, though, do you really think any of this has anything to do with him directly? I mean...Albert? Really? What's he going to do to me? Ambush me with his pretend Dungeons and Dragons army?"

Stanley grinned at her. "If he did, you'd be hard pressed to fight them on your own."

Burke rolled her eyes.

"All right then, since we don't know squat and we ain't gonna figure it out tonight, are we going to bed?" Richard asked. "I'm beat. Seems like we oughta be able to think about this over breakfast better than now."

Stanley rubbed his chin.

"Bed sounds fantastic," Burke said. She kissed them both and left the room.

Richard lay down and pulled the blanket over his chest, too tired to take the time to properly gloat about getting first dibs on the bed, but alert enough to note that Stan still hadn't moved. "You pullin' an all-nighter for some reason?"

"Hmm?" Stanley mumbled.

"What crawled into your craw?" Richard asked.

Stanley met his gaze. "Demons."

"Pardon?"

"I just can't stop thinking that demons can work magic without a wand and fly without a broomstick."

"Do witches really fly on broomsticks?" Richard asked.

"I was just sticking with the earlier comparison," Stanley explained.

"Ah. Well." Richard thought about it. "There's no sulfur smell. Burke and Albert both said that."

Stanley nodded. "Yes. They did, and I've never heard of a demon that didn't stink of the pit."

"But," Richard prompted.

Stanley sighed. "I don't know, my friend. I just don't know." At last, he settled into the makeshift bed on the floor.

"That makes you frustrated as a woodpecker in a concrete forest, don't it?" Richard asked.

"Leaves me feeling crazier than a long-tailed cat in a room full of rocking chairs," Stanley replied.

Feeling mocked, Richard harrumphed and turned toward the wall. He felt Stanley laughing at him in the silence.

CHAPTER NINETEEN

Albert

ALBERT SHOWED UP AT WORK FIFTEEN MINUTES EARLY. ANY earlier and he would have appeared over-anxious. Fifteen minutes said I'm prompt and efficient, but not a drooling little lapdog. His stomach churned and a thin sheen of sweat refused to leave his palms.

His appearance in Jones' office generated a response entirely different than he'd received last time. The secretary turned her creepy red smile on him. Her pale skin appeared almost translucent under the bright lights. He could see the blue veins beneath the surface. Something about that was oddly titillating. "Go on in, Mr. Peters. Mr. Jones is expecting you." Her pink tongue darted across her bottom lip.

Albert struggled to focus. "Thank you." With a trembling hand, he opened the door and then entered the inner sanctum.

John Jones was practicing his putt on a thin strip of artificial grass. "Come on in, my boy," he said without looking up.

Stars swam in front of Albert's eyes. A bead of sweat dripped down from his temple. The night before, he'd been bolstered by more than a few glasses of wine and the desire to impress a beautiful woman. In the harsh light of morning, he could barely stand in the presence of the Great Man Himself.

"Do you know why you're here, Albert?"

Did he? "You asked me to come, sir."

Jones leaned on his golf club and looked Albert in the eye. "Calm down, son."

A peace that passed understanding poured over him like a warm waterfall. He sighed.

"That's better." Jones propped his club against a nearby shelf and ambled to his desk chair. "Sit."

Albert stumbled to the guest chairs in front of the desk and fell into one of them.

Jones sat in his leather executive chair and crossed his legs. "Your work is uninspiring, Albert."

Despair. A lump formed in his throat.

"But last night, you soared to new heights."

Redemption! He'd throw himself at the man's feet if the desk wasn't in the way.

"At first, I didn't know how an entry level loser like you managed to talk a woman of Burke Martin's caliber into...well... into giving you the time of day. But then I gave it some thought. Burke is into some...let's call them unique hobbies, shall we? Obviously, you have no idea about all that. She's a clever girl. So very, very clever. So, perhaps, she used you to get to me. Then again, maybe the fates brought her to me. Either way, I see this as the opportunity of a lifetime."

His hypnotic gaze never left Albert's. "I'm going to reward you, Albert, for bringing this horrifically divine creature into my inner sphere." He leaned forward with his elbows on the desk. "I want her mind, but oh so much more. I want those who love her to know that I own her and there is nothing they can do about it. Coleum exists to slap men such as them in the face. They can fight their little battles here on earth, but once we launch that ship, we'll be untouchable."

Albert shifted in his chair, uncertain if he was expected to say something.

Jones lowered his voice, "I'm going to tell you a secret, Al. Only the most privileged in this building know this."

Sweat dripped into Albert's eye. He swiped it away with his shirt sleeve.

"By myself, I couldn't have done a fraction of this. I had a magical experience. Umbra contacted me, chose me, through the most unusual means you can imagine. When that happened, a power unlike anything you can imagine gripped me. It changed me. It turned me into a god, Albert. Do you believe that?"

It didn't even strain the bonds of reality, as far as Albert was concerned. He nodded, afraid that if he opened his mouth, he'd whimper like a baby.

"I'm going to make you a god, too. You can have anything you want, all you have to do is bring Burke Martin to me."

"Take us on the ship," Albert blurted.

Jones smiled. "My pleasure."

Albert's heart hammered hard in his chest. Tears burned his eyes. "I'll do whatever you want."

Jones' smile grew. "I know." He pressed a button on his desk and shades rolled down over the windows, casting the room into shadow-filled semi-darkness.

A flash of movement caught Albert's eye, something cold touched the back of his neck, and then a peacefulness ten thousand times stronger than he'd felt coming from Jones filled him from the inside-out. Certainty rose up in him. *Power*, he thought. *This is what it feels like to have real power.*

Without really meaning to, he told Jones, "I'm your servant."

"Go get me what I want," Jones said. "Enjoy yourself along the way."

Albert didn't mind doing what he was told, but in a far corner of his mind he had just enough of himself left to feel a smidge of concern when his body stood up and left the room without him making the decision to do that.

CHAPTER TWENTY

Richard

A RARE DAY FULL OF GLORIOUS SUNSHINE HAD SHATTERED the usual stretch of cold, soggy, November weather. The colors of the leaves remaining on the trees were as vivid as the paint in any surrealist landscape and the glory of the autumn world took Richard's breath away. He relished the chance to be outdoors in the fresh air on just such a day. Checking the fluids on the Cadillac was no chore, but a privilege. DaVinci could only wish to have created anything so beautiful as a '59 Caddy. Richard slipped the dipstick back into place with careful reverence so as to let the machine feel and understand the awe and respect in his heart.

Burke watched from the canvas swing that hung from a low branch of a nearby sugar maple. She let her feet slide through the dry leaves, causing them to rustle in a pleasant way that brought to mind all the best things about autumn in the Midwest.

"I don't get it," she said. "Stanley was the one who all but forced us to come here and now he wants to high-tail it out of town."

The light streamed through the leaves above her, creating shadows that slipped across her smooth skin.

Richard wiped his hands on a grubby blue towel and popped the cap on a gallon of washer fluid. "He's worried about you."

"Haven't I shown some level of competence? Besides, there's still something afoot at Coleum, right? Dinner didn't accomplish much, but it did prove that. Plus, there's the mystery of the thing creeping around this neighborhood at night."

Washer fluid splashed over the opening in the reservoir. He adjusted and growled, frustrated that the weight of a one-gallon jug of fluid caused such a trembling in his hands. Old age was as annoying as a mosquito in the dark. Just when you forgot about it, it came buzzing in your ear again.

"We've never run from anything before," Burke pressed. "Why should we run from this?"

Richard finished up and snapped the cap back into place. "The fact that Stanley Kapcheck says it's time to run ought to be enough to make you just about as cautious as a burglar walking on a tin roof in cowhide boots."

She caught a leaf between her slim fingers and started shredding it into yellow and orange confetti. She smiled a tiny, knowing grin. "Grandpa, if I didn't know better, I'd say you respect Stanley's opinions."

He let the hood slam shut with a satisfying thwack of solid metal latches. "Stanley Kapcheck is a fine hunter. I respect him in that. In everything else, he's a wrinkled up, over-stuffed—"

The front door of the house swung open and Stanley emerged in tight jeans, a leather jacket, and black sunglasses. James Dean, dried up like an old raisin. *Idiot.*

"Good morning!" Stanley called. "A glorious day to head out on a new adventure, don't you think?"

"I'm not quite finished with the current adventure," Burke

said. Shadows from the tree played tricks over her face, making it impossible to read her expression, but there could be no mistaking her tone of voice.

"I'm afraid you are," Stanley said. "At times, prudence calls us to cut the line."

"I'm not fully clear as to why you think this is one of those times," Burke said.

Richard finished packing away the bottles and tools and wiped his hands again. "I've got to agree with the kid. We've heard a bunch of this and that but we ain't done a darn thing but jump at shadows."

"That's exactly it, my friend. I don't know what we're facing, and my instincts tell me we are woefully unprepared."

The whirring of an electric motor interrupted the conversation. A little hybrid pulled up to the curb and shut off. Albert stepped out, his ugly loafer squishing into a puddle of muck that had formed in the leaf-strewn road. His grin showed every one of those awful, sharky teeth. "Good morning! It's a lovely day!" The morning sun shone at a sharp angle, stretching their tall, slim shadows across the front yard.

"I think your mother wanted you in the house, Burke. You should hurry," Stanley said.

Burke stood and turned toward the house, but as she crossed through the dappled light, her steps changed to the slow, forced movements of a person trying to walk through deep water.

She halted and stood stock-still.

Albert stepped onto the sidewalk. "Hello again, Burke."

She turned around again and blinked at him, long slow blinks like an overtired child.

"I had a marvelous time last night." He snorted once through his swollen nose. "For the most part."

She eyed him over her shoulder and pressed a hand against

her heart. "Really? I was so worried that you'd be angry with me. I can't believe I was so mean to you at the end."

Albert's grin grew even wider and more terrifying. He brushed her words away with a gesture. "It's forgotten. I was wondering, will you go out with me again tonight? I want to show you something."

Burke bounced on her toes like an over-excited schoolgirl. "I love surprises!"

Stanley stepped in front of her. "Did you forget? We're leaving town today. You need to get ready to go."

She scowled at him. "I want to go out with Albert."

"We're leaving, Burke. You need to come with us."

"We'll go later. I want to go with Albert tonight. I want to see the surprise."

Albert beamed at her. "I'll pick you up early. How about four?"

Her expression brightened to pure joy. "I can't wait."

He seemed on the verge of saying more, but then turned and squelched back over to the geekmobile and drove away.

The two men turned toward Burke, who remained in the same spot, arms limp at her sides.

"Burke? Are you all right, dear?" Stanley asked.

"I'm very privileged. Half the girls in the world would kill to go out with a guy like Albert."

"Last night you were ready to shoot him in the foot and string him up for bear bait," Richard said.

She rolled her eyes. "I was just tired and cranky. Seeing him again, I guess I realized I was wrong. I'm very lucky he's giving me another chance." She pulled her phone from her pocket and glanced at the screen. "I'm going to hop in the shower and get ready. I want to look extra nice."

They watched her disappear into Maddie's house.

"This is bad," Richard said. "Something is very wrong here."

"It's certainly a complication," Stanley agreed.

Frustration and concerned boiled up in Richard's gut. He wadded the blue towel into a tight ball and hurled it at the car. "Dagnabit, man! What just happened?"

Stanley rubbed the bottom of his chin with the back of his hand. "I don't know, Dick. I wish to God I did, but I don't."

Anger, hot as a red poker, flared in Richard. "You don't know what the naked monster in the garden is. You don't know for sure who this Umbra is. You don't know what this mission to Mars is all about. You don't know why the people at that party were acting like a bunch of goll-derned warm-blooded zombies and now you don't know what's going on with Burke. Tell me what you do know, oh great and mighty hunter!"

Stanley put his hands in his jacket pockets and continued to stare at the door through which Burke had disappeared. "I know we're in over our heads, old boy, and we're going to need some help."

Richard deflated. "If only you knew where to find it," he said.

Stanley nodded. "If only," he agreed. "That would be a plus, for sure." He sighed. "But take heart, my friend. If I've learned anything over these long years, it's that help tends to come to those who are on the right path. The universe provides."

"Well what are we going to do?"

"I'm going to make some calls, but I think our best course of action is to wait and see what Burke has to tell us when she gets home tonight."

"That's your big plan? You want to sit around on your wrinkled up, bony old butt and wait to see what happens?"

"What are you going to do?" Stanley asked, finally meeting his gaze.

"Well, dagnabit, I'll tell you what I'm not going to do. I'm not just going to sit around here waiting for my beard to grow." He stomped across the yard toward the leaf-covered street, remembered he was unarmed, went back past Stanley, into the house, and fished his revolver from his duffle. Tucking the weapon into the back of his pants, he offered up a quick prayer that he didn't blow off a butt cheek, and headed back out past Stanley again, leaving him standing there in the yard waiting all alone. Best way to wait, in Richard's opinion, if that's all a man had the gumption to do.

The cool air whispered hints of winter and snowstorms, but the sun shone warm on his face and the brisk breeze carried the sweet scent of decaying leaves and woodsmoke. Autumn magic worked its way into his blood and soothed his angry spirit. Motion. Action. Doing something. That was just the ticket. Shoving worry deep into a dark corner of his heart, he focused on the moment.

When he'd lived in the southwest, autumn invariably left him homesick for Michigan. Sure, the winters could crush your soul and the summers would leave you prostrate with heat stroke, but the beautiful glory of autumn, Mother Nature's last wild burst of life before she gave up the ghost, made all the rest worthwhile. It occurred to him as he padded along, dry leaves crunching pleasantly under his sneakers, that if he saw his own life drawn out like a calendar, there was a good chance he was in his very own November. "Nothing wrong with that," he said out loud.

Mrs. Distel's porch was cleaner than the average modern housewife's kitchen. Despite being nestled in a neighborhood of old-growth maple and walnut trees, not a single leaf lay upon those white-washed boards. No spider dared spin its web upon the pristine surfaces. The glossy paint shone so very glossy in the afternoon sun that he could see a distorted, shadowy reflection of himself in the smooth columns that extended from the top of the half-wall to the roof above. A pretty cut-glass light fixture sparkled above the imitation-brass and ivory doorbell. He pressed his finger to the round button and a moment later one beady blue eye peeked out at him from between the slats of the window blinds. The sharp snick of locks being disengaged apparently meant he'd passed inspection.

Mrs. Dister opened the door only far enough to peek out at him—just far enough for him to observe that she wore a pink cotton muumuu with a pink cardigan over it and a little pink knit hat pulled down over her wispy silver hair. "May I help you?"

"Actually, I'm hoping I can help you," he said. "My daughter, Maddie Hallman, lives right over there." He gestured vaguely in the direction of Maddie's house.

Mrs. Distel smiled. "Yes, of course, I know Maddie. She drove me to church every Sunday when I was laid up with a broken leg two years ago. Fred Castleberry has the hots for her, you know."

Richard rubbed a hand over his mouth, willing the traitorous organ to stay shut and not get him in trouble. When he'd achieved confidence that he retained full control of himself, he forced a smile that he hoped didn't look like the crap-eating grin Stan Kapcheck wore half the time. "That's my girl. Everybody loves her."

"She wonders if you do," the woman said, arching a wiry grey brow at him.

"Excuse me?"

"She told me that one day when we were working in the garden. She said you always tried your hardest to do your duty by her and she hasn't the slightest doubt about your loyalty to her, but she has never been quite a hundred percent certain of your love."

If I leave right now, maybe the thing from the garden will come back and kill her in the night, he thought with some satisfaction and rubbed his mouth again.

The annoying voice of conscience on his opposite shoulder spoke the same words in an entirely different tone of voice, *If you leave right now, the thing from the garden may well come back and kill her in the night. What if it were to set its sights on Maddie after that?* He sighed and his lips betrayed his age by making the same flapping sound as an old stud put out to pasture, which only made him want to sigh again. If the monster killed her, the old woman's blood would be on his hands. He'd come to do a thing and do it, he would.

"So, anyway," he said. "My daughter tells me that you had quite a scare the other day and I was wondering if you'd tell me more about it."

"Why?" She pressed the door a fraction of an inch closer to closed.

"I'm a hunter." He couldn't help but stand a little taller at that. Of course, this crazy old bat had no idea the massively important connotations his statement held, but she didn't need to know. He knew. That was enough. Most of the time. "I'm not so bad at tracking things, figuring out what they are."

"I know what it is," she said.

This did not match up with the story he'd been told. "You do?"

She nodded and the door opened a bit wider. "Yes sir, I do. I might be an old dog, but I am pretty darn savvy when it comes to learning new tricks, and I got me a desktop PC. I went on the interweb and asked around in some chatter groups on the Facepage and no one knew anything for sure—just lots of guessing and speculation. But then I followed the surf and one thing led to another and when I connected the dots... BAM!"

He jumped at the exclamation. "Bam?"

"BAM!" she shouted again.

He waited expectantly.

She nodded at him with wide eyes.

"So..." he prompted.

She glanced around as if to make sure no one eavesdropped and then leaned out toward him. "El chupacabra."

"El chupacabra."

She nodded again.

He rubbed his mouth.

"You're not a believer," she said.

He held up his hands in surrender. "Oh, no. I believe."

"You look skeptical."

"No one is less skeptical than me," he assured her.

She lifted her saggy chin, as if to challenge him. "So, now tell me. You want to hunt el chupacabra?"

The merciless steel of his revolver pressed against the small of his back. "Very much," he told her honestly. "Mind if I take a look in your garden?"

She studied him long enough to make him feel as if she might be seeing right through his skin down to something he might not want the world to see, and then she shrugged and said, "Okay, then. Help yourself. Don't step in my kale. It'll go a few more weeks if you don't crap it up with too much plodding around back there in your big honkin' man feet."

She slammed the door in his face without so much as a by your leave, and for good measure, the blinds clicked shut a second after.

"Hmphf," he groused. "Oughta let it eat her," he mumbled out loud this time. He couldn't lie to himself, though. The thought of bagging el chupacabra intrigued him. Bonus points for doing it all on his own while Stanley sat around *waiting*. So, he tromped back down the freakishly clean steps and followed a path of identical fake stones around to the back yard.

The garden proved to be as tidy as the porch, a perfect rectangle of rich black dirt with a few neat bunches of kale and a handful of Brussels sprout stalks still growing at one end. Two apple trees and a small grape vine grew close to the back door. Two garden gnomes and a shiny blue glass orb adorned a flowerbed near the house. A blue jay shouted at him from its perch on a wooden feeder that hung from a black iron shepherd's hook.

"Mind your business, bossy," Richard told the bird.

It watched him with a suspicious black eye.

The dirt of the garden had been turned in long, straight rows. If forced to hazard a guess, he'd say Mrs. Distel used a gas-powered rototiller back here, and finished her work by drawing wavy lines along the paths with her rake. No way she'd turned rows that tidy by hand, but all around the kale the rows were marred by footprints. He crouched lower to get a better look. The clear outline of two bare feet, toes and all, were plain to see. A man didn't have to be Sherlock Holmes to deduce there had, indeed, been a barefoot human-like creature back here munching on the kale. Compared to his own sneaker-clad foot, the print in the mud was quite small—smaller than he'd expect from a college kid. More like a very petite woman or even a child.

He looked around for any other clues, not knowing what he hoped to find, exactly. Just when he was ready to give up and go back to Maddie's house, he spotted a bit of yellow under a nearby privacy hedge. Squatting down, he reached out and pulled a banana peel from under the fallen leaves. It was almost entirely brown, with only a few remaining spots of color. Richard dropped and looked carefully at the earth around the bushes. He found more footprints and an oval of squashed grass and leaves where the thief had clearly sat for some time. "Who the devil are you?" he asked, but only the rustling breeze answered him.

No closer to understanding and in no big hurry to return to Maddie's and hang around with Stanley, he took a slow walk around the block, eyes peeled for anything out of the ordinary. His mind whirled with worry about Burke, questions about Albert, visions of spaceships and Martian colonies, and ideas about what kind of creature looks like a human but runs around naked in the night. Not a single answer presented itself, but when he came upon Maddie's property by way of the back easement, he noticed a scattering of banana peels on the grass around her large wooden compost bin.

He crossed her yard and poked a banana peel with his toe. "Like your bananas, do you?" From there, he spotted another peel covered with empty shells under the hazelnut bush, and from the hazelnut bush, another in the hedge that grew around the foundation of the house. Here, too, bare footprints dotted the mud. Whatever the creature was, the night they saw it in front of Maddie's window wasn't a one-off event. The thing was camping out right under their noses.

All the rich holiday foods he'd enjoyed in the past two days churned in his guts. There were entirely too many questions in their lives right now and not nearly enough answers.

Maddie took the plate of heated-up stuffing and pie out from under Richard's nose and replaced it with a bowl of turkey and rice soup. She set a small glass of prune juice next to it and started to walk away.

"Hey!" he protested. "What gives?"

She called back from the kitchen, an annoying, disembodied voice of reason, "You're going to tie yourself in knots and end up sick if you keep eating like you have been. The feast is over. Time to take care of your tummy."

"Humph," Richard groused. "Ain't worried about my 'tummy' for seventy years, but apparently I'm in the second grade again."

"I can hear you," she called.

"Good!" he shouted back.

Burke picked up her spoon and started eating in weird robotic motions that sent shivers down his spine.

"Burke, do you remember what you told us about your table mate at last night's dinner?" Stanley asked.

Burke nodded without breaking the rhythm of scooping, swallowing, pausing, scooping...

Maddie set a bowl of soup at her own place and took her seat. "So, Burke and I were talking, and we agree that she's very lucky to have met Albert. Who would have thought a car accident could be so serendipitous? I was just telling her that I think she ought to—"

The doorbell rang before they learned what it was Burke ought to do, feel, obsess over, or believe according to her mother. Maddie dabbed at the corners of her mouth with a cloth napkin embroidered with a grinning pilgrim couple and dashed off toward the front of the house. Stanley met Richard's eye and then stood and followed her, one hand tucked in the pocket of his trousers where he, no doubt, hid some sort of weapon.

Richard watched Burke. She stared straight ahead and continued slurping soup. He wondered if they should hogtie the girl and get her out of town. True, she could take either one of them in a fair fight, probably both of them together, but there was a time when dirty tricks were the order of the day.

A soft murmur of voices rose up from the other room, drawing his attention in that direction. No one screamed or fired a gun, so presumably the visitor was a friendly. Stanley confirmed that by taking his hand out of his pocket and extending it toward whomever had entered. A moment later, Luke entered, hat in hand, and nodded in his direction.

"Good to see you again, Richard. I'm terribly sorry to have interrupted a meal. I simply wanted to bring Maddie a thank you gift for the lovely dinner the other day."

Maddie bustled by with her arms full of red roses. "This seems like more than a little thank you, Luke. My goodness. You probably could have bought groceries for a week with what these cost."

He twisted the cap he held. "It's not like I can't afford it.

Worked all those hours for all those years. Might as well spend it on the people I care about. Not like I can take it with me."

Stanley gestured toward the table. "Care to join us? Maddie made a fine pot of soup from the leftovers."

Richard scowled at him. Mighty presumptuous of Stanley to be inviting the neighbors over for soup that wasn't his to share. "Man didn't come over for lunch."

"No, he came with a grand gesture." Stanley clapped him on the back and gave him a wink and a smile. "Well played, old boy. Well played."

Color rose in Luke's cheeks like he was a pimply-faced sixteen-year-old picking his date up for the prom. "I just wanted to say thank you."

Burke finished her soup, lay her spoon down next to the bowl, and stared into space.

Worry lit a fire under Richard's butt. Sitting back and letting this date happen simply couldn't be their best option. Annoyance that Luke's presence meant he couldn't speak freely to Stanley only added fuel to the fire of his anxiety.

"I think we ought to stick to the plan. We ought to head out this afternoon. Soon. Now. Ten minutes ago," he blurted.

"Dad?" Maddie stood in the kitchen doorway, holding a large crystal vase in her arms, the flowers artfully arranged within it. "Why would you say that?"

Maybe he couldn't spill the whole can of beans, but he could keep one foot on the solid ground of truth. "I'm worried about Burke. Just look at her."

Burke beamed at him. "I'm the luckiest girl I know. Half the women in the world would give anything to go out with a guy like Albert."

Maddie cocked her head at Richard.

"It ain't natural!" he exclaimed.

"I think I know what's going on here," Stanley said. "Richard, may I speak to you in the other room?"

"Oh, there's no need to run off to the other room." Maddie thumped the roses down in the center of the table. "I get it. You've been a tight little trio, doing God only knows what for the past half a year and now Burke's got this date and it might break up your gang. Then what? Then you're stuck back here with boring old Madeline who insists on feeding you healthy food and driving you to important doctor appointments. Well, forgive me for wanting you to feel good and be healthy."

"I'd like to eat your soup," Luke said.

They all stared at him for a moment.

The redness in his cheeks turned a deeper shade of crimson.

"Richard, may I please speak with you?" Stanley asked.

Richard grumbled and groaned over every crack and creak his body made when he pushed himself out of his chair and stormed past Stanley toward the bedroom they shared. Stanley entered behind him and latched the door with care.

"I get it, Dick, I do. Your every instinct is to tie the girl up and drive her off to someplace safe."

The fact that Stan Kapcheck was apparently reading his mind only served to make him edgier. "It ain't right!" he exclaimed. "My guts are a mess. This ain't right. We're just sitting here. We're letting the monsters run the show. Something bad is happening, and it's happening to Burke, and we're just hanging around with our thumbs up our butts."

"Listen to reason, my friend," Stanley's voice remained as cool and calm as ever. "I don't know what this is. It's not a traditional binding spell cast by any kind of witch I've ever heard of. It's not demonic in any way that I know how to detect, certainly not that I know how to fight. If we try to take her away, at best she will break free of any bonds we create and do whatever she must, up to and including killing us, to get back to him." He pointed a finger at Richard. "You know she's capable of it, too. That girl is not a fighter to be trifled with. At worst, the spell will kill her."

The words poked a hole in Richard's balloon of self-righteous anger. "Kill her?"

Stanley shrugged. "I don't know. It's possible. She's clearly compelled to Albert. As to the degree of that compelling, I have no way of knowing. If she can't get to the object of her desire, if the spell is strong enough, then yes. The strain of that could be enough to kill her. I wanted to get her out of here before this could happen, but Umbra's people moved faster than I expected. Now we need to stay and find a way to break this spell."

Richard sank onto the edge of the bed. "So, we sit here and wait?"

"I'm afraid it's our very best option right now. I'll bug her coat, her bag, and her person. We'll track her every move. Maybe she'll return with useful information. If we can become a stumbling block to Umbra and his gang, I'd have not even the slightest objection.

"My guts are a mess," Richard said.

"The soup will help," Stanley said.

"I ain't talking about that!"

Stanley nodded. "I know, my friend. Mine, too. Mine, too."

CHAPTER TWENTY-ONE

Albert

THE LITTLE VOICE IN ALBERT'S MIND NO LONGER WORRIED. Fear had been crushed beneath the inexorable gravity of power. He had driven the six-lane highway at a comfortable one hundred and five miles per hour, weaving in and out of traffic without a smidge of concern. The other drivers moved out of his way. The road opened up before him. The universe opened up before him.

When he spoke to Burke, he felt the power slip from him, not a loss, but an extension, and then she was his. In an instant, she'd turned from the ungrateful bitch of the night before to a lovely marionette. The moment her eyes met his, he knew there wasn't a single thing in the whole world she wouldn't do for him.

And, oh, he did have so many ideas about what she could do for him.

His body ached deliciously at the thought.

Upon his return to Coleum, he turned into the parking garage and exited his vehicle, leaving the keys in the ignition.

No one would dare steal Albert Peters' car. If they did, there'd be hell to pay. Literally.

That gave him an idea.

He whistled as he jogged up the stairs to the second floor. Tim sat at his desk, looking at soft porn.

"Hey, Tim," Albert said.

Tim jumped, hit a button on his keyboard, and then let out a nervous laugh. "Al, what's up? Get lost on the way to your desk again?"

Originally, Albert's idea had been to walk into the shared office space, find Tim's cubicle, and smash his face into the desk until the white bits beneath showed. Now that he was there, it occurred to him that assault would be messy. His clothes might get spattered, and what kind of a man went on a date with brain matter on his tie? Really, it just wasn't good manners.

He put his hands on the arms of Tim's chair and leaned over him, casting the man's face into shadow. "After I walk away, count to sixty, stand up, go upstairs, and jump off the roof of this building."

Tears pooled in Tim's eyes. "I don't want to die."

Albert grinned. "Sure you do, pal."

Tim sniffed, wiped his eyes, and nodded. "Oh, yeah. I do."

"That's what I thought." He walked away, to the end of the room with the big windows that looked out over the city. The body fell past the window sooner than he would have expected. He was impressed with the way Tim burst open when he hit the pavement, and grateful that he'd kept his clothes clean.

The face on his watch told him he needed to get a move on. There were arrangements to be made before he picked up his girl for their big night together.

CHAPTER TWENTY-TWO

Richard

IT HURT A LITTLE TO ADMIT, BUT THE TURKEY AND RICE quieted his upset stomach and the prune juice cleared out the last of the offending greasy food. Maddie had sent him to bed as if he were eight years old and it was a school night and, more to avoid argument than anything, he changed into his PJs and figured he'd wait for Burke's return in the bedroom. His mind had been in such chaos over her disturbing transformation, he figured he'd while away the time pacing like a tiger in a cage. But now, free from gastric distress and pleasantly warmed by Maddie's froo-froo smelly flower tea, dressed in the soft cotton pajamas Burke bought at the over-priced department store, and stretched out upon the bed that smelled of lavender detergent, he thought maybe just a little nap was in order. He sprawled a bit, just because he could.

Sleep descended with the swift gentleness of an old favorite blanket spread open to fall upon him, so it was hard to say if he'd been out for ten minutes or two hours when a creaking floorboard jolted him out of a dream in which The Devil

Herself danced for him on a glassy black stage. Her long blonde hair fell in thick shining waves down her bare back. "Stanley's too easy. I prefer a man who presents a bit of a challenge," she purred while circling a tall silver pole.

He lay there with his heart thumping in his ears, wondering how quickly he could lay hands on the revolver in the side table drawer.

A shadow moved across the bed.

Richard threw his body left, hoping the sudden motion would delay his attacker's response. Unfortunately, he miscalculated his position in the bed and rolled right off the edge, except for his feet, which remained tangled in the fragrant sheets. He cracked his head on the edge of the side table and landed flat on his back, knocking the stuffing straight out of his lungs. Bright stars flashed in his vision. When they cleared, there stood Stanley, peering down at him with a frown.

"What in the world are you doing?" Stanley asked.

Richard kicked his feet like a capsized beetle trying to free himself from his bonds. "What are *you* doing, sneaking around in the dark like some kind of a creep?"

"It's two fifteen."

Richard's feet fell to the floor with a thump. "Is that the hour you always wake a man from a perfectly good sleep?"

Stanley extended a hand. Richard faced a choice. Accept the man's help or spend the next two minutes trying to hoist his old bones off the floor on his own. He reached up and took the hand, but made sure to grumble a bit so Stanley would know exactly how he felt about it. He expected to see the old familiar mockery in Stanley's face, so the worry that shown in his eyes brought Richard up short.

"It's two fifteen," Stanley said again. "Burke said she'd check in at midnight."

There'd been a terrible day in southern California when crossed signals left each of them convinced the other two had been in mortal danger from a vengeful baba yaga. In the end, it turned out the only real problem was the God-awful traffic in that part of the country. Around the dinner table, they'd agreed upon a standing rule: in addition to a rendezvous time whenever they were apart, there would be a two-hour clock. People ran late. Traffic jams, flat tires, dead cell phone batteries—any number of crazy things could cause a delay or a break in communication, but a two-hour window should be more than enough time to make contact and give assurances of safety.

Richard peeked at the green glowing numbers on the bedside clock.

2:17 a.m.

"I'll get dressed," he said.

Stanley nodded and left him to it.

Seven minutes later, the Cadillac rolled silently out of the sloped drive in neutral with the lights off. Stan let momentum carry the car backward past three houses before turning the key. The engine purred like the world's most powerful and well cared for cat. Headlamps sliced through the heavy shadows cast by the low-slung streetlamps dotting the subdivision, and they rocketed forward into the night guided by a red bubble floating over a map on Stanley's phone. The bubble winked out, returned, hovered, winked out again, came back. "I never saw it do that before," Richard said.

"Probably just a glitch. Do you know where that is?" Stanley asked.

Richard peered at the street names, squinting to make out the tiny black letters. "Not exactly. Not much in that part of town. Old assembly plant used to be out there, but they shut her down when Clinton moved all the jobs to Mexico. Ain't been nothing but rot and vines since." He fished his own small phone from his jacket pocket. Getting used to carrying the thing had been an adjustment. A few taps on the screen brought up Burke's number. The call rang and went to voicemail. He pressed the red button and let his hands fall back to his lap.

"I'm sure she's fine," Stanley said, but Richard noticed the speedometer climb a little higher.

WHEN MADDIE HAD BEEN A SCHOOLGIRL, THE FACTORY located just outside the western city limit up and moved to Mexico, taking half the jobs in the county with it. Richard remembered the churning fear of wondering if his own employer would follow suit, leaving him with a kid, a mortgage, and exactly $841 in the bank. Over time, the Earth took back the abandoned assembly plant. Holes opened in the ceiling and dandelions transformed the asphalt parking lot into dirt and stone. The passing decades had since brought more change.

A new facility stood in place of the old assembly plant, with solar panels on the roof and a gargantuan windmill in the parking lot. Three white metallic arms, each longer than the wing of a jetliner, spun in lazy rotation under the sliver of a crescent moon. As they crossed the blacktop wilderness, a nearly soundless *whoomp, whoomp, whoomp* reverberated somewhere deep inside Richard's core every time the arms completed a rotation.

The side of the building proclaimed "Coleum Corp. - Space for all."

Near one end of the building, a crowd of cars filled the spaces close to a door lit bright as day. Three workers in blue and white coveralls stood under a sodium lamp, snakes of smoke slithering skyward from the cigarettes clamped between their fingers.

Stanley maneuvered the Cadillac into a spot near the edge of the cluster of cars and tapped his fingers against the wheel. "Most decidedly not rot and vines."

"More full of life than an old cheese on a hot day," Richard agreed. "Also, not where I'd take a lady on a second date."

A few fluttering snowflakes zig-zagged through the air, high-lighted in the weird yellow light that cast a flickering shadow play across the blacktop. The movement stirred a vague, unsettled sense of motion sickness. Richard's gaze shifted left and right.

Stanly leaned forward over the wheel, squinting into the night. "Do you see anything strange?"

Richard readjusted his upper plate with his tongue. "Looks like any night shift I ever worked."

"No," Stanley said, his voice barely above a whisper. "Look again, Dick. Look with a hunter's eyes. Don't focus on what's right in front of you. Don't focus on anything at all. Just look."

This looking without actually looking was a trick Stanley and his cohort Nathanial had spent a full week trying to teach Burke and him. Burke picked it up right away, of course. Not a woman in the world had a right to be that darn smart. By the end of the week, he'd had the general idea, but his rheumy old eyes didn't like the queer, unfocused feeling of looking at nothing at all. With an exasperated sigh, he peered out past the bits of bug innards splattered on the windshield in the general direction of the well-lit entrance and let his gaze settle on an empty gray space next to the doors.

The shadows flickered, vying for his attention, but he ignored them and focused on exhaling to a slow count of ten.

A man slipped along the wall toward the roofline.

His eyes snapped upward to follow the creature's progress, but nothing was there. "What the Sam Hill?"

"Shadows," Stanley murmured. "No smell. No hex bags. Somehow, they bound her with shadows."

"I don't understand," Richard said, squinting into the dark.

"Neither do I, but I'm certain it's true."

Richard tried to look again. His eyes watered. He rubbed at

them, stared at the wall, took a deep breath. The inky black beings infested the property. They slid over the walls and curled around the lampposts. They hung from the backs and arms of the workers sucking on their cancer sticks and darted over the pavement. One of them slithered over the front of the car and peered at them with pure white eyes, no more than two spots of light in a man-shaped hole of darkness. It opened a gaping maw full of jagged black teeth and a hundred more pairs of white eyes turned in their direction.

"Go," Richard squeaked in a high-pitched, girly voice. "Go, go, go!"

Stanley's hand fumbled at the keys, grasped them, and the engine purred to life.

The creature crawled forward and reached a hand in their direction just as the headlights flared to life, bursting the creature like a balloon full of matte black confetti.

Stanley yanked on the gearshift and smashed his foot against the gas pedal. The white wall tires laid a film of rubber against the pavement with a piercing scream. At last, the tires gripped and the car lurched out of the space. He drew a tight circle that got them pointed toward the exit.

A broad-shouldered man with a black stocking cap on his head and a silver badge pinned to his chest punched a button that caused a yellow barrier to drop across the parking lot exit.

"Buckle up, Dick," Stanley said.

Richard wasted no time arguing. He managed to snap the buckle a split second before the Caddy's front bumper made contact, sending bits of wood flying into the night. The car bumped onto the road, scraping its belly on the pavement and throwing up a shower of sparks.

Stanley pulled the wheel hard, making a sharp left onto a two-lane city street as void of traffic at that late hour as any dark desert highway.

Richard peeked in the side mirror just as two sets of headlights bobbed around the corner behind them. "Company," he announced.

Stanley urged the car faster, not slowing as the light over the intersection in front of them flipped from amber to red. The headlights behind them drew close enough for Richard to make out a black SUV. "They're on your butt like white on rice!"

"I'm aware," Stanley replied, making an abrupt right-hand turn. The back tire caught the curb and the car bumped and shuddered, causing Richard's vertebrae to clack together like a row of castanets.

"Watch it, man! You want to kill us?"

"If I wanted us dead, I'd stop right here and let them—" The car hit a patch of ice on the overpass and slipped sideways, fishtailing wildly into the sparse stream of oncoming traffic. A rusty white delivery van clipped their front end and tossed them back into their own lane, which would have been fine if they were still pointed in the right direction. As it was, they sat at a dead stop with the front bumper facing one SUV while the second boxed them in. A thin stream of smelly white mist drifted upward from under the car's hood. The magnificent V8 engine sputtered and died.

Richard sat there, panting hard, taking inventory of his limbs. So far as he could tell, everything remained attached and fully operational. Too soon to say if his shorts were still clean. His family jewels crawled up into his belly to hide as the passenger door of the black truck swung open.

A pair of ugly brown loafers appeared below the door. Albert stood, illuminated in their headlights, his white teeth gleaming in the night. "Get out of the car, gentlemen," he called.

Stanley reached under the seat and snatched something that he slipped into his pocket so fast Richard didn't have time to make out what it was.

Richard looked down and was surprised to realize he'd had

the presence of mind to get the pistol out of the glove box during the short, wild chase. Feeling rather proud of himself, he pocketed the gun and tried to follow Stanley. Unfortunately, in the ruckus, his door had been smashed in, making it impossible to open it fully. He managed to push with his right foot until it cracked about a third of the way, but no way would he be able to squeeze through the tiny opening.

The driver's door on the SUV opened and a man emerged, the approximate size and shape of a wild buffalo—with about the same amount of hair, too. He came straight toward Richard, wrenched the door open with a screech of tortured metal, and informed him, "Mr. Peters said you need to get out of the car."

Richard levered himself upward and peered up into the man's face. The angle afforded him an excellent view of a vast amount of nose hair that fluttered like a party favor with every breath. His bowels churned around like a wooden water wheel had kicked into gear.

"Burke told me you'd come for her," Albert said, drawing Richard's attention away from the buffalo man. "She told me so many things. In fact, the past few hours have been the most informative of my whole life." He snorted. His shoulders shook. "The most lucrative, too. Who could have suspected getting run over by some batty old lady would turn out so well?"

Stanley stood with his hands open, held slightly out from his sides as if to show how harmless he was, just an old man at their mercy. He gestured with his chin toward the men climbing down from the delivery truck and the few cars that had already stopped to watch the drama and, presumably, offer their assistance. "Even the Children of Cain can't just get rid of us right here in front of God and everybody."

Albert snorted. "Ignorant old man, The Children of Cain could have you and every one of these people wiped out of existence so completely, not a memory of you would exist by this time tomorrow."

The water wheel churned faster in Richard's gut. The prune juice might have been a bad idea. He clenched his butt cheeks together and wrapped his right hand around the handle of the gun in his pocket.

Bang!

The bullet ricocheted off the pavement so close to his foot it sent up a spray of shattered blacktop that bit into his ankle. He hopped away, bumped into the car and, ironically, was saved from falling when the human buffalo grabbed his shirt front.

"They have guns! They're shooting at each other!" someone screamed behind him.

Albert ducked into the SUV and doused the lights, leaving the hunters' shadows stretched like long, man-shaped tentacles, velvety black against the charcoal gray of the pavement. Within the blackness, two spots of white appeared and blinked up at Richard.

Stanley's left foot shot out to the rear, shattering the lamp behind him.

Albert screamed from inside the vehicle, "I'll kill you, old man! I'll destroy you and everyone you ever loved! You have no idea who I am!"

Stanley's calm British accent floated atop the chaos, "You're no one, Albert. Just a slave to a man with real power. Tell him to give us the girl and do it quickly. And tell him we're coming for his little rocket ship."

Buffalo Bill jammed the cold, hard barrel of a gun into the soft spot under Richard's chin.

Someone made a pathetic whimpering noise.

Did I do that? Richard wondered.

Red and blue lights sliced through the darkness, turning the nightmare block party into a disco. Sirens wailed.

Richard had never been so happy to see the cops. He didn't even mind when they laid him across the hood of the car, took away his gun, and clamped his wrists in cuffs tight enough to squeeze the piss out of a flea. It was fairly annoying to realize, however, that Albert and his pet bovine had disappeared into the night. Tracking them from jail was going to be difficult.

Stanley sat next to him in the cruiser, peering into the darkness. "Bugger all," he mumbled, apparently having come to the same conclusion.

CHAPTER TWENTY-THREE

Albert

Burke trailed along behind Albert like a puppy—a curious little puppy who never stopped yapping.

How many people have access to the mainframe?

Can they really access it from Earth, even as far away as Mars?

What kind of signal are they using?

What programming language did they use?

What kind of core processor did it use?

How did they keep something that powerful cool enough to prevent meltdown?

Who the hell cares? Albert wondered as he pushed through the steel door in the Coleum Corporation basement that led to the underground rooms he'd only learned about that day. A maintenance worker hobbled past on thick grey tentacles.

Burke's eyes followed the creature. "There's nothing like that in Stanley's journal. What is it?"

Albert had been delighted to find that his mind had absorbed loads of information he'd never learned. He knew the average weight of a human being, and how much of that weight was meat. He knew the names and genetic strengths and weaknesses of every person on the ship's manifest. He knew that creature did not come from any place he could explain to Burke.

"Don't worry about it."

"Okay," Burke said.

She was very agreeable. It was a little annoying.

They rounded a corner and found the room he was looking for. Inside, three tall, slim girls with glowing green eyes were packing equipment into trucks. The tallest of the three gave Burke a thorough once-over. "She's the ride-along?"

"Yes. Jones wants her on the next flight north. When she gets there, you need to escort her to mission control. She'll be helping out with the last-minute programming details."

The girl sneered. "A human? Really?"

"She's a freaking genius," Albert snapped back. Apparently, the girl didn't care enough to argue about it. She rolled her eyes and went back to work. Albert turned his attention to Burke.

"Listen, this isn't how I wanted our first night to be, but we'll have lots more, right?"

"Lots more," Burke agreed.

"You're on our side now, right? So, you need to do whatever they ask of you when you get there. Help them out, okay?"

"Okay," she said.

Albert brushed a curl from her cheek. "I don't want to be away from you, but we both have work to do. Jones was not at all happy about the way things went with Stanley and your grandfather. He's working on a new plan and I need to go find out what it is. We can't have them coming after us, meddling in this launch. It's too important."

"They'll stop the launch," she told him.

She wasn't arguing. She was just stating a fact, as she saw it. The words caused the thing inside him to shriek in fury and he had to grit his teeth against the sudden burst of pain in his head. "They can't stop us. Believe that."

"I believe it," she said.

"Good." The thing settled down. Albert took a deep breath to re-center himself. "I'll get to you as fast as I can, all right? Be a good girl. Study hard. Learn lots up there. Make yourself useful to them and—" His own mind took control again and immediately replayed his favorite scenario. "Just as soon as I can get to you again, you can make yourself useful to me."

"Okay," Burke agreed.

"Kiss me," he said, and she did. She was a fantastic kisser. She didn't even object to his hands on her ass. Their time together was going to be even better than it was in his imagination. He just knew it.

But first, Jones.

He pulled away, savoring the longing. "I've got to go. Jones won't be happy if I keep him waiting."

"Okay."

It would be nice if she'd at least show a little emotion. It felt weird to tell her to show some feelings when the other girls were right there in earshot. No worries. It would take six months to fly to Mars—plenty of time to program her to be exactly who he wanted her to be.

CHAPTER TWENTY-FOUR

Richard

THE CITY JAIL WASN'T EXACTLY ALCATRAZ. HALF A DOZEN drunks snored loudly from the large cell at the end of the hall—the "drunk tank," so far as Richard could guess from eighty years of watching television. Across the concrete aisle, a woman dressed like a prostitute sat propped against the wall reading a magazine with a picture of a prettier-than-real-life celebrity couple on the front. Next to her, someone he couldn't see tossed and turned on their bunk. Richard couldn't blame him. The mattresses were thin as paper, smelled like pee, and he had the uncomfortable sensation something was crawling around within the pathetic stuffing. He couldn't see Stanley because they'd been housed side-by-side in cells separated by a block wall.

Arrested. Who'd have ever thought it?

Worst he'd ever been in trouble with the law had been a pile of speeding tickets he'd accrued trying to get to work on time on the days he had to see Maddie off to school before going in for his shift.

Now, he was officially a criminal, with black ink on his fingertips to prove it. He supposed that if this had happened at pretty much any other time of his life, he'd have been devastated. In high school, he'd have been kicked off the track team and whipped within half an inch of his life by his father—not a cruel man, but not one to abide shenanigans. As a young man, he'd have disappointed Barbara, who never missed a Sunday at church if she could help it. Poor woman wouldn't have been able to show her face at a garden club meeting ever again. Once Barbara was gone, there were all the responsibilities that came with being a single father. But now?

He grinned. It all struck him as kind of funny.

Darned if I don't laugh at the stupidest things, he thought, remembering being nearly hysterical with mirth after his first real hunt with Stanley.

Then he thought of Albert's words. "Burke told me you'd come for her." The laughter withered and dwindled away.

As if he sensed the weight of Richard's thoughts, Stanley said from the other side of the wall, "We'll get her back, my friend."

"Yeah," Richard mumbled, but his mind had already moved on to a different statement. The worm had said The Children of Cain could effectively erase him and Stanley and every person who'd witnessed their accident.

A vampire was one thing. Sure, they were strong and fast and vicious, but they were beings of flesh and blood, with weaknesses like anyone. Fighting such a creature presented a challenge, but it wasn't an impossibility. How did a man fight an organization designed on a foundation of smoke and mirrors? It was more futile than the nonsensical, never-ending "War on Terror" the politicians used as an excuse for every bone-headed decree they passed down from on-high.

Who was to say The Children of Cain didn't have agents right here in the jail? And for that matter, if the bad guys were working with some kind of shadow monsters, who was to say the creatures couldn't pop right up in his cell? If they'd been prepared to kill him on the street in front of God and everyone, why not here in the city jail?

One of the drunks retched and Richard jumped half out of his skin. He levered himself up off the nasty cot and crossed to the opposite wall. With his fingers wrapped around the steel bars of his cell, he felt like a character in a bad black and white movie. "Stanley?"

"Yes, my friend?"

"Can they get in here?"

"Quiet!" the guard at the end of the hall barked. Nearly seven feet tall and just about that wide, he loomed next to the doorway, glaring in their direction.

The prostitute shouted lewd suggestions and the drunks stirred and hooted with laughter.

Richard shuffled back to the bunk and sat down with his elbows on his knees. His thoughts ran to monsters and demons, family and love, responsibility and joy, pain and purpose until all of it turned into one big blurry tangle in his brain, no one part of it decipherable from another.

At some point, he must have drifted off to sleep, because he woke with a start to the sound of his cell door banging open in a clang of metal. "You're out, Bell," the guard said. A grin tipped the corner of his wide mouth. "But by the looks of the woman who paid your bail, you might be better off here with us."

Richard scowled at him and said nothing as he shuffled toward the exit. Screw pride and trying to lift his feet. He was tired and his bones hurt. If someone handed him his old walker, he'd take it and use it and be grateful. Stanley's footsteps sounded sure and steady behind him. He'd probably slept like a baby and woke up in a freshly pressed button-down. *Friggin' Stan Kapcheck.*

The guard hadn't exaggerated. Maddie stood at the front counter where she'd presumably just handed over a sizable check to the clerk to cover their bail. The anger rolling off her hovered like a black storm cloud in the lobby. Even the officers seemed to be making a wide berth around her and keeping their voices low.

Maddie drove back to the house in ominous silence. Three times, Stanley attempted to engage her, but never once did her eyes leave the road. The nail of her left pointer finger tapped a relentless beat that reminded Richard of a telegraph operator in an old black and white western. He loved those movies. Good guys were good. Bad guys were bad. The hero always got the girl. Life was simple and easy to understand. John Wayne never had to be rescued from the police station by his own daughter. Certainly, he didn't ride home in the back of the wagon, nervous about the scolding to come.

But she didn't scold. She did something much worse. She pulled into the garage and pushed the button to bring the door down, closing the bright, cold morning out, and then she turned to him with tears rolling down her cheeks and asked in a shaky voice, "Where is my daughter?"

Stanley piped up from the back seat. "Maddie, dear, what you must understand is that no matter—"

She raised a hand in Stan's direction, silencing him. "I would like my father to explain to me where my daughter is."

Richard's tongue was dry as a wooden god. He smacked his gums a few times to get them going and managed, "We don't know, exactly."

"You don't know."

The eerie calm of her voice raised the hairs along the back of his neck. "Well, we're pretty sure she's with Albert."

"Pretty sure."

"Nearly certain."

Her swollen red eyes narrowed. "And yet Albert is the one who called the police and had you arrested, was he not?"

"No. Not exactly. I think it was the guy in the delivery truck that called the police," Richard said, though he couldn't have sworn to that. It was all a little hazy. Seemed like the cop with the ugly blue suit said something about a night manager at Coleum and trespassing charges. No point in bringing all that up now.

Maddie fished a crumpled tissue from her purse and blew her nose. "Please go inside. Please just..." her voice caught and she swallowed hard. "Please just stay in one place and be safe and don't give me any more reason to worry." She shook her head. "I don't understand how everything got so strange. I don't understand why you can't just play Pinochle and go to physical therapy and stay in one place. I don't understand—" The dam broke and she sat there, sobbing into her Kleenex.

Richard cast a panicked look at Stanley.

Stanley mimicked patting her on the shoulder.

Richard reached over and pressed a hand between her shoulder blades. She flinched away. "Just go inside, Dad. And for the love of God, stay there."

ONCE THEY'D GONE INSIDE, STANLEY DISAPPEARED INTO THE bathroom. The shower ran for a few minutes leaving Richard time to fiddle with the lamps in the room, trying to figure the best way to make the least number of shadows. He finally took the shades off and stacked them in a corner. When Stanley emerged, he was still damp, with a towel around his waist.

"Put your dang pants on, man!" Richard said. "We have to find her."

"I'm not sure we should rush off just yet," Stanley replied.

"Well, yeah. You need to get dressed first. I ain't going to look for the kid with a naked man at my side."

"You could do with a shower, too," Stanley suggested.

"I don't wanna shower right now. We need to go find Burke!"

"You're exhausted and in pain, not thinking clearly or moving efficiently. You can't hunt like that. Not without being a liability to yourself and others." Stanley retrieved a stack of clothes from his suitcase and retreated to the bathroom, leaving the door open a crack. "There's Madeline to think of, as well. If you disappear again right now, she'll likely as not have you committed against your will. I can spring you from a place like that, but I'd rather not have to waste more time doing it." He emerged in a pair of plaid pajama pants and a tee shirt. "Take a shower, Dick. Rest. It feels like slowing down, but you'll be better off and faster for it in the long run."

Annoyance ate at him. Why was everyone telling him what to do? Worse, they were all too often right. Grumbling the whole time, he snatched up fresh clothes and stormed off to the bathroom. When he came out, Stanley was sound asleep in the bed. In a slow, somewhat painful process punctuated by a good many groans and the loud popping of his joints, he lay down on the floor where he slipped into a dreamscape full of monsters and Martians. The most frustrating moment of all came when he woke up in a world not so very different from his nightmare. The light had the golden hue of late afternoon. Apparently, they'd slept the whole day away. *Fantastic*. His granddaughter and the whole human race lay in danger and the two old men with enough knowledge to stop it were napping like fat lazy cats.

Well, knowledge implied they actually had some understanding of what they were supposed to be doing. That was a bit of a stretch.

"The GPS trackers are still going," Stanley said from his

perch on the warm, comfortable bed before Richard had a chance to speak. "The coat and purse are stationary, but she's all over the building. Whatever they're doing at that factory, Burke's been given full access. She must have covered every square inch by now."

Richard rubbed his sandpaper eyes. "We'll have to get past Maddie," he said.

"I think she's sleeping. Her night wasn't much better than ours. Dress quietly. We'll leave a note."

A note. Pathetic. She'd never be satisfied with a note. He was headed to the involuntary loony bin for certain.

Too bad he had no better plan to offer.

He dressed, admitting to himself that he really did feel infinitely better for being clean and rested. If he could put a decent meal in his belly, he'd be just about fit as a fiddle. Then again, if a bull had batteries, his horns would blow.

Stanley opened the bedroom door and stepped into the hall. Richard followed and they tiptoed toward the front door. They'd made it nearly halfway across the living room when a voice snapped, "You've got to be kidding, right?".

Maddie sat still as a statue in one of her fussy armchairs. "This is some kind of sick joke?" her voice trembled.

Way back when, Richard got caught putting a frog in Susan Morgan's desk. Susan had beautiful long red braids and eyes the color of emeralds. For the entirety of third grade, he had thought her the prettiest girl in the whole entire world. Why wouldn't a boy put a frog in her desk? Where else would you ever think to put it, for goodness sake?

But the plan had backfired when Mrs. Robbins heard the thing croak as he transferred it from his lunch box to Susan's desk. She had scolded him and issued a good many threats that started with a ruler and ended up with making a phone call to his father.

Mrs. Robbins was old, but she'd been a girl once. Why

didn't she understand the depths of his affection? Was it jealousy?

Girls. Did any greater mystery exist in the whole entire world?

Such were his musings as he walked to school the next morning in the moments before a frog hopped from the sidewalk, right onto the toe of his shoe. Not just any frog—the fattest, greenest, most moist-looking frog he'd ever seen in his whole entire life. A frog that held the very essence of frogginess.

The frog practically begged to be put in Susan Morgan's desk.

There could be no escaping destiny.

Richard scooped the magnificent animal up and cradled it gently against his chest with one hand while struggling to open his knapsack with the other. All thought of consequence vanished like mist in the morning sun. This was a mission from God. He could not fail.

The perfect moment presented itself when Susan chose to sharpen her pencil just as Mrs. Robbins excused herself to speak to a visiting parent in the hallway.

In a dance of sleek, covert actions, he opened the bag, scooped up the frog, leaned forward, lifted the lid of the desk, deposited the treasure, sealed it in, and sat down once more. The hard part was sitting, still and quiet, through the remainder of the time allotted for handwriting practice, waiting for the moment his glorious surprise would be revealed.

Victory. True love. A happy ending. Every good thing pulsed in his veins.

Mrs. Robbins called out for them to finish up.

Richard's heart beat faster.

Papers were passed to the front and collected.

He wiped his cold, clammy palms against his thighs, pressing hard to still the excited trembling of his hands.

The teacher announced that they should put their belongings in their desks and prepare to walk to the music room.

He leaned forward, clutching the sides of his desk.

Susan grasped the top of her own desk in her pretty pale fingers.

Surely his heart would burst right out of his chest from the strain!

She lifted the lid with her eyes turned toward the girl next to her, who'd just said something that could only be bland and unimportant in this spectacular moment.

The enormous, glistening frog played his role as though Richard had trained it lifelong for just this moment. It waited for the girl to face forward and look down. Even from behind, Richard knew the moment her eyes met the eyes of the frog. Her spine straightened. Her slim shoulders drew back.

If his grin grew any wider, his face would split.

Susan pushed her chair back and rose quickly to her feet, leaving the desk wide open.

The frog croaked, a magnificent, low-pitched, perfectly enunciated announcement that the water was *knee-deep* and then it launched itself straight at Susan's face.

The next few seconds passed in a bizarre flurry of action that seemed to happen in slow motion and yet, simultaneously, so fast, the Man of Steel himself would have been helpless to stop it.

Susan screamed. Her terror ripped through Richard's heart and the realization crashed down upon him that this did not rank among any of the top one hundred ways to get a young woman to fall in love with you. In her scramble to escape the monster she'd encountered, the girl's feet tangled in the shiny metal legs of her chair, which fell and clattered across the tiled floor. Susan herself went down hard, first hitting her bottom so hard Richard heard her teeth clack together, and then toppling over and cracking the back of her head against one of the desks behind her.

She lay on the floor, sobbing and calling for her mother. and Mrs. Robbins came racing to her aid.

The treacherous frog once more announced *knee-deep* and took three giant, moist, flopping hops across the classroom.

Mrs. Robbins, cradling Susan in her arms, watched it and then turned toward Richard with an expression far closer to bafflement than anger. "Really, Richard? Really?"

Anger would have been preferable. This astonishment over his immense thoughtlessness and repeated failure to comprehend the absurdity of putting a frog in a girl's desk struck at his heart in a way the number of spankings and other punishments he'd suffered over the years never had. Hot tears sprang to his eyes and, before the other boys could catch him crying, he turned and ran all the way to the river bank, scurried up a tree with the fleet-footed assurance of a squirrel, and hid there among the sticky, sap-dotted branches.

Maddie's voice, as she faced them in the dwindling light of the quiet room, brought every ounce of shame and humiliation back to him and heaped another sixty years of mediocre fatherhood on top for good measure. He couldn't think of any lie that could possibly explain their behavior to her, and he lacked the physical strength to run away and hide in a tree. That hadn't work out well last time, anyway. He'd still ended up on the receiving end of a wooden paddle. Left with no other recourse, he held out his hands in supplication and begged his only child, "Hear me out, Madeline. I'll tell you everything, if you just hear me out."

"Richard..." Stanley rested a warning hand on his shoulder.

"She deserves to know, Stanley," Richard said, shrugging off his hand. "It was one thing when it was just us, but she's in it now, deep as Mississippi mud, and she deserves to know."

"You can't tell her," Stanley said. "Some information must be sought."

Maddie kept her hands on the arms of the chair. Her nails bit into the soft upholstery. Her knuckles turned white. "Oh, you can believe I'm seeking information. I'd like very much to know what in the name of all that is holy is going on with my elderly father who barely left the house for the duration of my life and suddenly decides to up and run away from a nursing home in the middle of the night, bounce around the country for half a year, and then show up for Thanksgiving at my home and spend the duration of the visit sneaking around and getting arrested. Do tell, Dad. What the hell is going on here? I am sincerely seeking."

Her words opened up something inside Richard that he hadn't realized had been closed until that point. He sank down on the sofa and leaned forward, elbows on knees. "You're going to find some of this hard to believe."

She stared at him in silence, her jaw firmly set, looking so much like her mother when she was angry that it was almost possible to believe his wife had lived on past her thirties and forties and seen the age where her pretty dark hair started to shift into a glorious silver crown.

"It all started back at Everest, right? I settled in there and I was just waiting for my number to be called."

Her grip loosened. "Dad, it wasn't like that."

He brushed her words away. "It was and it is. Maybe that's not what you or anyone else wanted it to be, but I'm telling you, as the one who was living it, that's what I was doing. I had no reason in the world to keep taking one breath after another except the habit was so strong, I didn't know how to stop." He scratched the scruff on his cheek. "Anyway, one night it happened. My time was up. The Grim Reaper knocked on my door."

Stanley interrupted, "Technically, he doesn't really do that.

It's simply not showy enough for him. He's quite the style-obsessed dandy."

Richard and Maddie both glared at him. He shrugged and took a seat in the darker part of the room, nearer the garden windows.

"Anyway," Richard said, annoyed by the interruption. He jerked a thumb in Stan's direction. "This old coot saved my hide. Much as I hate to say it, it's the truth. He did it then and he's done it a bunch of times since."

"I don't understand," Maddie said.

Richard clacked his upper plate around with his tongue for a moment. "I know. I'm doing a piss-poor job of explaining. See, not everything was as it appeared at Everest. To look at the place, it was all sunshine and sugar-free tea parties, but the nurses, some of them, they weren't really nurses."

Maddie's brows drew downward. "You're telling me they were abusive?"

"No, no, nothing like that," he said, but then he thought about it and cocked his head a bit. "Well, in a way, I guess. They weren't human, Madeline. They fed on humans."

Her posture slumped. "Oh, Dad."

Sudden anger spurred him on. "No, young lady, don't you dismiss me like that. I might be older than dinosaur crap, but I ain't senile yet, and I'm telling you there were things in that place the likes of which you need to pray you never encounter. I saw them with my own eyes. I helped kill them."

"What?"

He nodded. "That's right. Stanley and I, we killed a whole nest of them. Four of them. They came after me, after us, but thanks to him knowing what no one else was willing to believe, we got the jump on 'em."

The memory of that night stood out like the full moon amid the twinkling stars of his memory. He'd been born from his mother and died at his wife's side, no matter if he did keep walking around after that. Killing the strigoi was a second birth and, come Hell or high water, he wasn't giving up on life so easily this time around.

"After that, Stan Kapcheck told me some stuff. Stuff kind of like I'm telling you now. The kind of stuff that sounds crazier than a squirrel under a leaky moonshine still, but it has the taste of truth, all the same."

She still gripped the arms of the chair, but no longer appeared intent on shattering them with her bare hands, which he took as a good sign. "Such as?" she asked.

"Well." He cleared his throat and fidgeted. Off in his dark corner, Stanley remained, for once, still and quiet as a statue. This was Richard's conversation and they both knew it. "He told me your mama didn't die from anything natural." He meant to wait for her to respond, but the silence unsettled him so much, he plunged forward. "The thing that killed her was evil. The kind of evil that infects a man's nightmares and makes his skin crawl the whole day after. It feasted on a person's life force. That's why it wanted your mama. She had more life than anyone I ever knew." His voice caught in his throat and he cleared the frog away. "Maybe Burke." The comparison had come to him before. "There's a whole lot of Barbara in that girl."

Her fingers clenched again.

Bad idea, bringing Burke up now. He rushed forward, "Anyway, Stanley told me it had surfaced again and was hunting back in Tombstone. We went out there and pulled Finn O'Doyle's bacon out of the fire. Just in the nick of time, too, by the looks of him."

"Finn O'Doyle," she repeated.

"That's right."

"The author?"

Richard nodded.

"The author who just released a book about a shape-shifter

who ate people's souls and the three Fates who were protectors of the innocent?"

He blinked at her. "He wrote that?"

"He did," she confirmed.

"Huh." He paused to let this new information sink in.

"You didn't by chance hear about that story, maybe in a commercial or something? Things can have a way of sinking into our subconscious sometimes, you know."

"I lived that story," he told her.

"In the book, the three Fates were beautiful women, sisters, I believe."

"Well, of course he changed it up a bit. What kind of a weirdo would want to read about two old farts shooting guns at monsters and drinking prune juice to keep their bowels moving?"

"Dad—"

"No." He cut her off, not wanting to listen to her accuse him of being two cards short of a full deck. "I ain't crazy," he insisted. "When that was all taken care of, we caught wind of a..."

She cocked her head to one side. "I'm listening."

"A vampire coven in San Diego," he mumbled.

"Excuse me?"

"Vampires!" he barked the word out much louder than he'd intended. "We hunted vampires in San Diego. And other stuff, too. Banshees, nachzehre, wendigos. Stuff." He rubbed his hands on his pants. "And that's it. That's what we do. What we've been doing."

"I see. And these *hunting* adventures," her emphasis highlighted her skepticism. "Burke does this with you?"

Pride forced a grin to his lips. He couldn't have held it back if he'd wanted to. "Oh, you should see her, Maddie. She's strong and fearless and smart. Good Lord in Heaven but that girl's got a mind like a steel trap. Smarter than Stan and me put together and multiplied by ten."

"And now she's missing."

Maddie's words were a punch in the gut.

"We know where she is," Stanley said from the other side of the room. "And we know who she's with."

"You do seem to be the man with all the answers, Stanley Kapcheck."

Richard wiped his hands on his pants again, a little afraid for Stan who had never seen Maddie truly angry. He thought she was a sweet little church lady obsessed with proper table manners and fine appearances. No matter how often Burke and Richard warned him, they could not get it to sink in that this was the mother of the woman who'd chopped up the devil's pet with an axe, then squared her shoulders, lifted her chin, and faced the Queen of Hell Herself.

"I wish I had all the answers, dear lady. I know where Burke is and who she's with, but I have yet to figure out how to get her away from them when she's clearly bent on staying there."

Madeline crossed her legs. Her foot bobbed in the air. "If she is where she wants to be, why not leave her there? What makes you think she's in danger?"

"I'm quite convinced the only reason she thinks she wants to be there is because she's possessed, or, at the very least, controlled by very dark, very powerful magic. And because I don't know what kind of spell can compel a person so completely, I'm not sure yet how to break it."

"By sneaking out into the night, you think you'll figure it out?"

"I have looked in every book I have and called every source I can think to call. I can't get any further by sitting around here. I tried to wait, to figure it out, to let the universe send what help would come, but I can't wait any longer. Burke is in trouble. If we need to tie her up and gag her and drag her back here against her will, then that's what we need to do or she's going to end up with a one-way ticket to Mars."

Maddie closed her eyes and shook her head slowly back and forth. "You're mad. Both of you. You've gone mad and I'm going to have to call the doctors and..." She sniffed. A single tear sparkled like a diamond on the end of her lash.

Richard knelt down in front of her. "Look at me, Madeline."

Her eyes remained tightly shut.

He took both of her hands in his. "Look at me."

Finally, with a shaky breath, she opened her eyes and met his gaze.

"You need to set aside all those things your grown-up brain insists upon and find the wide-eyed kid inside yourself. The one who played with little invisible Rainbow Sparklebraids in the backyard."

She sniffed again. "Sparkletail Rainbow."

He nodded. "Look in my eyes and tell me I'm lying to you. Tell me you haven't known your whole life that every monster we fear in the dark is real. Tell me that when you're walking in the woods and you hear a stick snap your mind doesn't say Bigfoot before it says coyote."

"It's madness," she whispered.

"It's a truth the human race is so scared of they've convinced themselves it's just a story so they can sleep at night."

Stanley rose and came into the circle of light. "The truth is, Maddie, the real reason they can sleep at night is because your father and your daughter and I, and others like us, keep those creatures relegated to the shadows, but something's wrong. If creatures like that have a hand in the work being done at Coleum, if they have Burke—"

"We have to get her back," Richard said.

Her tears flowed freely, a slow trickle of emotion too great to be held inside. "Bring her home safe, then."

He nodded and stood, offering up a silent thanks that his

hip didn't give out at the effort. Stanley clapped him on the back and they headed toward the door.

"Dad!"

He turned back.

She stood there, arms wrapped around herself in a tight squeeze. "Come back safe."

He nodded. "You got it, kid.

CHAPTER TWENTY-FIVE

Richard

THE FACTORY WAS GIVEN OVER TO ROT AND VINE. WHERE shining lights and high-tech windmills stood the night before, scraggly trees and rusty signs now creaked in the cold wind.

"What in tarnation?" Richard whispered.

Stanley pulled Maddie's car right up to the front door. They got out with weapons and flashlights in hand.

The slam of car doors echoed in the vast open space. The only sign of life was a racoon that scurried by carrying some treasured bit of trash in its jaws.

With safeties off, they stalked through the front door that hung catawampus from one hinge into a dark space that smelled of mildew and ancient machinery oil.

"What happened here?" Richard asked. "I ain't crazy. I know what I saw." He swung his light from one end of the dank room to the other. Starlight twinkled above them, visible through gaping holes in the ceiling.

Stanley ran a hand over his shiny scalp, letting his gun hang limply at his side. "The Children of Cain did this. I can't conceive of how they did it, but I know they did."

"So, if the factory don't exist, where's my granddaughter?"

Stanley met his eye, but before he could answer, footsteps tapped against the concrete ribbon near the front door and three men entered. The one in front wore an expensive suit and shiny two-tone shoes. The two who flanked him looked like extras in an old Schwarzenegger movie, all muscles, no brain. Each sported an earpiece, aviator sunglasses, and slicked-back hair. The one on the left moved with the odd gliding motion unique to species who struggled to maintain the façade of humanity when in human company.

Stanley lifted his pistol. The lead man raised his hands in a gesture of surrender. "Please don't shoot me. I had this suit custom tailored. We're with The Children of Cain."

As if the words created some kind of involuntary response, Richard raised his own gun and pulled the trigger. The bullet went wide and ricocheted with a whining ping. Thing Number One moved so fast he appeared to teleport and wrenched the weapon from Richard's hand. Richard saw claws pop out of the fingertips raised over his face before someone made a weird girlie-sounding whimper.

"Stop that," Mr. Fancysuit commanded.

The dark sunglasses slipped and Richard caught a clear view of green, vertically slit cat eyes glaring down at him. The thing released him and took a step back.

"We're not here to fight you," Fancysuit said.

"Too bad," Stanley said. "We were just getting warmed up."

Richard noticed then that Stanley lay sprawled on his back beneath the bulk of Thing Number Two.

"We had no part in the kidnapping of the girl. We'd like to offer our help."

Richard looked to Stanley.

Stanley met his eye and shrugged. Thing Number Two leaped to its feet and held out a hand to help Stanley up.

"My name is Michael," Bossman announced.

"Is it, really?" Stanley asked. Names held vast power. Most creatures were not quick to give up their true identity.

The corners of the man's mouth twitched upward. "For all practical intents and purposes." He made a little shooing gesture and his thugs backed away. He stood half a head shorter than either of them, an average guy in every visible way, just a freckled red head with a good stylist and enough money to have a tailor. Richard wondered what authority he held to command the powerful creatures who obeyed him without hesitation. "The Children of Cain would like to enlist a partnership."

"We play for the other team," Stanley said.

"You don't even know what the name of the game is," Michael told him. "I'm here to explain. After I do so, you can make a more informed decision."

Stanley's eyes narrowed on him. "If you really are one of them, you'd know I've thinned your ranks considerably over the years."

"And so you'd be dead already under any other circumstances, but The Devil has issued a hands-off order and suggested that, with the woman Burke in the enemy's hands, you may be just the man we need."

At the mention of The Devil, Richard's body offered up a wild cocktail of adrenaline and testosterone that caused his blood pressure to spike. The world tilted uncomfortably beneath his feet. The last time he'd seen her, the Supreme Master of Evil had been packed neatly into a pair of snug jeans and a gingham shirt that displayed a pair of finely crafted 38DD's to excellent advantage. They'd tricked her and murdered one of her favorite monsters. He, Stanley and Burke couldn't possibly be very high up her list of favorite humans.

"Perhaps you'd consent to take a ride with me," Michael

suggested. "Our mutual enemy has moved from this place, but their stink lingers. We can speak more comfortably elsewhere."

The goons flanked Richard and Stanley, leaving little illusion of choice, even though they handed Richard's pistol back. Richard understood that, in this situation, it had all the effectiveness of a cap gun. Apparently having come to the same conclusion, Stanley retrieved his own weapon from the floor and slipped it into the waistband of his pants. "Color me intrigued," he said. "Lead the way."

Michael inclined his head and led them away from the empty factory.

Thing One and Thing Two waited while the three men slipped into the back of the stretch limo. Richard took in the wide leather seats, subtle lighting, and full wet bar with wide eyes. He'd never seen the inside of one of these high falootin' cars except on television. He couldn't imagine why anyone would need such a form of transport, but he easily understood why they would want it. The leather on the seats was softer than a sneaker full of poop.

The door closed with a soft snick, locking them into a warm dark cave. Stanley folded his hands in his lap. "So, The Devil issued hands off. Can you tell me when she did this?"

The man sprawled across the seat opposite them. "Six months ago, maybe?"

"Any idea why?"

The man smiled, displaying deep dimples in his clean-shaven cheeks. One look at this guy and Maddie would be playing matchmaker faster than a chicken would pounce on a June bug. "Said she finds you entertaining." He chuckled. "I can't even imagine what you must have done to earn such high praise from her. Kudos for coming out of it alive."

Stanley squirmed. Strictly speaking, he'd died in that conflict, at least for a little while.

"Anyway, in unrelated news, we have a situation that has

spiraled somewhat. We consulted with her, as the highest authority, and she suggested we look you up."

"By look me up, you mean corner me and kidnap me? Not exactly how you win friends and influence people," Stanley said.

"And yet, here you are," the man noted. "Exactly where I want you."

Richard scratched the scruff on his cheek, wondering if he was supposed to figure out a way to kill this guy and escape, or take notes like a secretary, or what. His presence seemed distinctly secondary, and he found that rather disquieting. If they didn't need him, they didn't have much incentive to keep him alive.

The car had yet to move. The goons stood outside, breathing through their mouths.

"Let me guess," Stanley said. "Your situation has something to do with Umbra. He's gone rogue?"

The man chuckled again. "You really are an ignorant little speck, aren't you? Running around in the woods staking wild vampires and assuming you're making a difference."

"Makes a difference to the one who's neck is on the line."

"Does it? I'm unconvinced. They're going to die anyway. What matter if it's today or tomorrow?"

"The same could be said of you," Stanley pointed out. "All of us end this journey, eventually. Some just travel longer than others."

Michael tipped his head as if considering. "Touché." He tapped neatly manicured nails against his knee. "You're half right. It's Umbra." His eyes darted right and left, revealing the first hint of nervousness.

The hairs on the back of Richard's neck stood on end. Merely mentioning Umbra set a fellow like this Michael on edge? They'd definitely wandered up the creek without a paddle. This was entirely different territory than chasing a chupacabra away from some little Podunk village on the edge of nowhere.

"Umbra's not a 'he,' though. Not anymore. Some time ago, he passed the mantel on to his daughter. She's the scariest bitch you'll ever meet. She makes your Queen of the Damned look like a kitten." He picked at an invisible piece of lint and flicked it away. "All well and good as long as she was on our side."

"You two have a lover's spat?" Stanley asked.

Michael's dark eyes crinkled at the corners. "Nah. I'm not her type. She might take to Burke, though. I hear she's quite attractive."

Richard clenched his fists.

The man went on, either not noticing or not caring about the reaction his words stirred. "They say power corrupts and absolute power corrupts absolutely."

Stanley concluded, "And no one on Earth is more powerful than the one who calls the shots for The Children of Cain."

"And the Umbra family has done so for much longer than you suspect. It was an Umbra who chose the site for the tower of Babel. It was an Umbra who decided which side would win the crusades."

Richard dug into his memory for facts learned in a history class way back in the days when said facts were scrawled on a blackboard by a teacher who used the flat side of a ruler to keep students in line. Who *had* won the crusades, anyway?

"For centuries, they ruled with wisdom and discretion. The very fact of their family's age and continuous reign are proof of their gifted leadership. Upon her father's pronouncement, Miss Umbra held in the palm of her pretty little hand, all the power of every creature on Earth. Then, one day not so very long ago, she met Jones."

"The good lookin' guy on the news?" Richard asked.

The other two men turned toward him as though surprised to find him still sitting there.

Michael recovered quickly. "One and the same. He convinced her that all the power of every creature on earth was not enough, not when there is more to be had."

"She commands the shadows," Stanley murmured under his breath.

"Shadow demons, among other things," Michael agreed. "The Children of Cain have long trafficked with the many, varied beings on Earth, but we understood there are doors that are closed to humankind, for good reason. Those doors ought not be opened. Not ever. Not even by one such as Umbra. Maybe especially not by one such as her." He leaned forward, propping his elbows on his knees. "She's founded a new organization, the Daughters of Kali, and they've opened the doors. They're playing with forces no beings of flesh can hope to maintain control over. It can only end in catastrophe."

Richard had followed the back and forth between the two men well enough, but there was one question that they didn't seem to be addressing. "What's all that have to do with flying to Mars?"

Michael leaned back. One dark brow lifted. "They're not just flying to Mars, old man. They're building a colony there."

"Yeah, well, that's good then, right? They're taking their troubles right out of this old world."

The man looked at Stanley. "I'd expect someone with your reputation to have chosen a cleverer sidekick."

"It's not an invalid point that Dick's making," Stanley said.

Richard felt a little flutter that might have been something like gratitude at Stanley's loyalty.

"It's a military base. A breeding colony." Michael paused and looked back and forth between them. "It's a farm."

"A world where creatures rule and humans are no more than cattle," Stanley said."

Michael gave a tiny nod.

Stanley connected the next dot. "And they want to take Burke with them."

"She's got valuable skills as a programmer. She's strong and, while not an ideal age, not yet so old as to be of no use. When that nitwit assistant brought the partner of the venerable Stanley Kapcheck to the launch party, he gained a status his puny little mind had never conceived of. In a single evening, he was elevated from glorified receptionist to big man on campus. Granted favor. Guess what wish he asked for?"

"Burke's affection. It's why she agreed to go with him a second time," Richard said, remembering how he'd wondered at her bizarre behavior the morning Albert showed up at Maddie's place.

Michael made a little gun of his thumb and pointer finger and fired it in Richard's direction with a click of his tongue. "Bingo. Your girl, Burke, has met her magic man, quite literally. She'll never come home to you willingly unless you kill the little rat. You've got three days until launch."

"What do you want us to do?" Stanley asked.

He spread his hands wide. "I should think it would be obvious. We want you to stop the launch. Blow the whole operation to hell. It won't stop them forever, but it will slow them down long enough for us to put some power players into key positions. We're confident, from that point, we'll be able to restore the balance."

"By balance, you mean you'll be in power again. Would you deny that this vision of humans as cattle is any different in your organization?"

Michael's grin returned, the dimples even deeper. "Ah, Stanley. You are entertaining." He shrugged. "At least in our way of doing things, you're free-range cattle."

Richard stared down at his hands, which trembled on his skinny knees. Fear, rage and confusion blew around his brain like the stormy gray clouds of a thunderhead. "We have to save her. I have to. She's in this because of me." Six months ago, he'd been the one to call Burke for help in their moment of need. No way would he abandon her in her time of need. If that meant facing an army of shadow demons with their very own rocket ship, so be it. He'd find a way. Stan Kapcheck could do as he chose.

Stanley gave his shoulder a quick, reassuring squeeze. "Tell us what we need to do."

Michael fingered a switch on the door and the window sank with a hiss. "We need to take these men to storage and have them properly outfitted."

The goon closest to the car nodded and they both climbed into the front seat. The limo floated out of the parking lot as if the tires hovered above the blacktop.

Richard glanced at his wristwatch. They'd already been gone for two hours. Maddie was going to be hysterical by the time they got home. Assuming, of course, they actually managed to return home. At that point, he was all too aware that there were no guarantees.

CHAPTER TWENTY-SIX

Albert

THE BIGGEST ROOM IN THE HIDDEN, SUBTERRANEAN PORTION of the Coleum Corporation Tower was the war room. Made of reinforced steel with imbedded signal-disrupting magnets, it also sported rows of light boards across the door and walls. At the flip of a switch, sigils could be turned on or off, allowing whichever species was desired to enter and exit at will, or preventing them from doing so. Tubes made of titanium and filled with salt lay across the entrance and the single air vent.

Albert allowed the thing in his brain to take control. It kept the sheer panic in check. Two creatures with fangs, one with wings, three with yellow eyes, and what appeared to be two humans all focused on John Jones. Something else was in the room. His brethren—murderous, loathing of this place and of the task before them—were bound by magic unlike any they'd seen before. They were helpless to fight the power of their master, slaves to Jones and the one whom he served.

"The mission to capture the hunters was a complete failure," Jones stated in his matter-of-fact way.

The thing inside Albert squirmed. He'd been given a direct order: bring the hunters back, dead or alive. He hadn't done it. Failure was the same as disobedience, and no crime ranked more foul than disobedience.

Jones asked the question the Albert-thing had been waiting for. "What are we going to do about that?"

"I have an idea, sir."

"Do you, Al? Fantastic. Please share it with the group."

All attention turned on Albert, but he was ready. The thing inside and he agreed. It was a fantastic idea. "We need to go to Burke's mother's house. They don't know where Burke is, and they won't leave the area without her. They'll go back to the house and we can capture them there. The old lady might even prove to be good leverage after the other two are disposed of."

"How many times in the next few days do you think we'll need to divert resources from our primary operations to deal with this particular Charlie Foxtrot, Albert?"

"I don't need a lot. I need a driver who's good with a gun and permission to call my brothers."

Jones laughed. "You're mad. I'm not giving you permission to call upon the legions at your will."

"I don't need the legions. Give me—" Albert paused to calculate. The hunters were old, but preternaturally good at their job. Maddie was a non-factor. The driver would be a help. "Give me a dozen. I can utterly overwhelm them with a dozen."

"A dozen."

"Yes, sir."

The two men stared at each other until Albert broke and looked away.

"Do you think you'll be able to manage subduing three senior citizens with the help of only a dozen powerful supernatural entities?" Jones asked.

A deriding snicker passed through the creatures seated at the table.

"I will destroy them," Albert promised.

"For your sake, I do hope so," Jones replied. "Take what you need then and do not disgrace me again."

CHAPTER TWENTY-SEVEN

Richard

MICHAEL AND STANLEY LAUNCHED INTO A VERBAL TENNIS match of questions and answers about shadow demons and ancient, cursed weapons, warded armor and repelling skills.

Richard closed his eyes and turned his hearing aid down in an attempt to form a decent thought. Something flitted around the edge of his consciousness, and the faster he chased it, the farther away it flew. Burke was always pushing her New Age ideas about breathing and meditation on him. He suspected that having been a better student would have served him well, but he tried his best. With his head back against the seat, he took a series of big breaths that made his belly swell like an overblown beachball.

Random images, crazy stuff he hadn't thought about since Methuselah was a boy, popped into his mind. The scent of his grandmother's apple pie, cooling on the windowsill. The pain of the blister on the back of his foot the day he'd missed the bus. His father had made him walk to school in shoes half a size too big because school shoes were purchased only once a year and it was autumn, so he'd not yet grown into them. Smacking Barbara on the backside as she passed, but miscalculating the force and causing tears to spring to her eyes.

The voices of the other men melded with the soft hum of tires on pavement and just like that, the question floated down and landed right in the middle of his brain, hitting bottom so hard his whole body jerked. "What the heck does a group like The Children of Cain need with two wrinkled up old geezers like us?"

Stanley drew back, a look of mild offense crossing his face.

Michael showed off his dimples. "I should think it would be obvious."

The two hunters looked at each other and back to him.

"No one in Heaven or Earth knows more about The Children of Cain than Umbra. She has warded every part of her operation against us. We can't go anywhere near her base."

"You walked right into the factory. The place was crawling with Coleum creeps twenty-four hours ago."

"On the contrary, that factory hasn't seen any life, other than local wildlife and a few squatters, in decades," Michael replied.

Richard shook his head. "We were there."

"You were in another dimension, a different time and space. I told you, she's opened doors intended to stay closed."

Richard threw up his hands. "How do you expect us to fight someone who can do that?"

Michael reached over to the ice-filled bucket on the mini-bar and extracted a bottle of sparkling water. "How did you, an untrained mortal, fight The Devil?"

Richard's cheeks burned. "I stole her cell phone," he muttered.

Stanley chuckled.

Michael joined in.

Richard failed to see the humor in his admission.

"We'll have your backs every minute between now and then, but once we reach the peninsula where the launch pad is, you're going to be on your own," Michael said. The water bottle opened with a crack and a hiss.

"Unless we can find a way to break the warding," Stanley said.

Michael swallowed and tipped his head. "That would change things. If you can break the warding, we will be able to enter the compound and take care of whatever needs to be done."

The car bumped over a spiked strip that would blow out the tires of any vehicle attempting to travel in the other direction and rolled a few hundred yards down a dirt road with ruts as deep as rivers.

Michael looked out the window. "We're here."

As far as Richard could see, *here* meant the absolute middle of nowhere. An old silo, covered in devil's ivy, now browning with the cool weather of autumn, teetered precariously in the middle of a field full of stubbly, post-harvest corn stalks.

The goon on the passenger side hopped out and opened the door for them.

Michael gestured toward the door. "After you, gentlemen."

They climbed out of the car and stood under a clear night sky that stretched above their heads like diamonds sewn into velvet. Here in the open, a frigid wind raced across the field, crashing over them with enough force to wrench a shiver from Richard. The goon shut the car door and the click blew away into the moonlit abyss.

Richard stumbled along behind the others through the treacherous obstacle-laden terrain, praying he wouldn't fall and break something again. His hip ached and protested but cooperated enough to keep him moving. Wouldn't it be ironic if one fall like that got him into hunting and another one took him out? Except, Stanley had implied more than once that there was no quitting hunting, even when the hunter grew old and infirm. Accepting this mantel meant a one-way ticket to the endgame. "Do not pass go. Do not collect two hundred dollars." No exceptions. Hunters did not stop hunting, they died with a silver dagger dipped in lamb's blood in their hand.

He jammed his hands deep into the pockets of his jacket before his fingers froze to the bone and watched the ordinary-looking red-headed man approach the ancient barn-wood door.

Michael traced a complicated pattern with his fingertip and pressed his palm to the center of the completed pattern. The door shimmered and became a different thing entirely—a sleek gunmetal grey entranceway with a touchscreen mounted in the middle. On the screen glowed a handprint, presumably Michael's, since it was in the exact spot he'd pressed. Beneath the handprint were the words, "Michael Kelly, verified." Under that, three rows of some sort of hieroglyphic chicken scratching flashed bright red and the door swung open, admitting them to an enormous elevator.

The inside air tickled his nose with a smell he could only describe as sterile. Somewhere overhead, invisible vents whooshed and whistled as the door slid shut, cutting them off from the outside. Thing Two pressed an unmarked button on a keypad full of unmarked buttons and they dropped so fast, Richard grabbed onto the flat railing that encircled the space.

"You're the first non-members who've been admitted to this space in over three hundred years," Michael said.

"What happened to the last guy?" Richard asked.

Michael shook his head. "You really must stop assuming that every time a person says 'someone' they're referring to a male."

Richard desperately wanted to argue, but it was all too easy to imagine Burke staring at him just then with one eyebrow arched. It had just about knocked his world sideways to learn The Devil was a woman. He and Stanley had both been operating under the assumption that Umbra was a man. "Well, then, what happened to the last person?"

Michael looked at the red dot moving right to left over the door. "She was burned at the stake as a witch."

"Was she a witch?" Stanley asked.

"At least," Michael replied with a grin.

The door slid open again and they exited into a brightly lit corridor as long as a football field, lined with countless identical doors on either side. They entered the very first door on the left and found a space that resembled a locker room. Each tall, slim, rectangular cubby held a vest; shoulder, hip, and ankle holsters complete with weapons; a dagger in a forearm sheath; and a flask.

Richard picked up one of the flasks. "Bravery juice?"

"Holy water," Stanley said, fingering the handle of one of the daggers. "If you're possessed and you're strong enough to overcome for a moment, you can take a swig of that and you'll regurgitate so hard the spirit will come out with the water."

"You can puke up a demon?"

"Indeed," Stanley said. "Is this Sumarian?" he asked, pointing at the dagger.

"Iraqi," Michael said.

"Ah," Stanley said, the word leaving his lips with the wistfulness of a lover's sigh. "From Ur."

Michael nodded.

"How in the world did you get such a thing?"

Michael slipped his hands into his pockets. "You really don't grasp the scope of what we are, do you? It's like your mind comprehends, but your heart can't quite accept it. We made them, my friend. The Children of Cain forged those knives in Ur when those who ruled the city still remembered the face of our father."

For the first time, Richard wondered if The Children of Cain were actual biological descendants of Cain, but that was a can of worms he was not prepared to open.

"Suit up, gentlemen. When we're done here, we'll go to the target range and show you what these can do."

CHAPTER TWENTY-EIGHT

Richard

When Michael returned them to Maddie's car in the abandoned parking lot, the clock on the dash informed them that yesterday had slipped into tomorrow. By the time they got back to Maddie's place, she'd traveled well down the road to hysteria. That they arrived armed like Navy SEALs did little to alleviate her concerns.

"Why didn't you text me?" she asked.

Richard and Stanley exchanged blank stares.

"We didn't think about it," Richard admitted.

"Well, glad to know where I rank in your thoughts," Maddie said. She pressed a tissue to her lips and sniffed back tears.

Outside, a car passed by, scattering light and drawing long, moving shadows across the room. Stanley went to the window and tugged the heavy drapes over the sparkling glass panes. He switched on the floor lamps, turning the room bright as day.

When Michael left them at the empty factory, he'd promised his "people" would stand guard. Nothing would get to them or Maddie without going through The Children of Cain.

When Richard demanded to know why they couldn't go straight to Burke, Michael reminded him of the spell she was under. "You need to bind the demon who's binding her, or eliminate the one controlling her. Those are your only options. If you want your girl back, you need to dangle yourself like a worm on a hook and let them come to you."

"I don't wanna be stuck with no hook," Richard told him.

"Then we go straight to the launch site and we burn her down with the rest of them. The Children of Cain have no problem with that plan, if that's what you want."

Richard sat in the tense silence of his daughter's living room, thinking how much he disliked the creepy ginger and everything to do with this alliance they'd formed, while the lacy black minute hand on the mantel clock ticked forward. One more minute of his life gone. One less minute remained in his future. One minute closer to lift off. In the corner of his eye, something moved. Adrenaline had him out of his seat and next to Maddie, flare gun in hand before he ever made a conscious decision to move.

"Dad?"

"Shh."

Stanley stepped away from the window, drawing his own weapon. "What do you see?"

Richard stared straight ahead, straining to relax his vision. "Something," he whispered. "To my right."

No one moved or spoke. Maddie's tension rolled off her in waves that pressed against him as surely as a physical presence.

"There!" Stanley shouted, firing a flare in the direction of the stairs. The burst of light was met with an unearthly shriek and a flutter of activity as black forms darted around the edges of the painfully bright room.

Something banged against the door once, twice, and it broke open with a splintering crack of wood. Richard fired in that direction. The flare burst against the wall leaving an impotent black scar that smoldered on the edges.

A man in black tactical gear, toting a gun big enough to take out an armored vehicle, stepped through the door, leaving a muddy bootprint on Maddie's pristine floor. An ugly brown loafer smeared the waffle pattern and Albert stood before them with his hands in his pockets, his freakish teeth gleaming under the glare. "Hi, guys."

Richard pointed his gun at the little bug-eyed turd.

The goon pointed his cannon at Richard.

"Please," Albert said. "Let's not make this messier than it needs to be. Maddie keeps such a tidy house."

Maddie clutched the back of Richard's sweater just as she had the time he'd taken her through the haunted house down at the American Legion Hall when she was eight years old. "Where's my daughter?" she demanded.

"Dutifully waiting for me." He reached left and switched off the ceiling fixtures, leaving the floor lamps to send the room into a bizarre mixture of shadow and light. From the corners of his eyes, Richard saw pools of darkness growing form and darting about the edges of the room. "I would think you'd be thrilled, Maddie. Things are working out just the way you'd hoped. Burke found a man with prestige. She's devoted and in love. We're about to set up house and you can bet there will be children." He cocked his head to one side a little. "Of course, visiting might be complicated, but no one gets everything they want. Life just doesn't work that way."

Her grip on Richard's sweater tightened. "I'll kill you." Even without his hearing aid, he would have been able to hear her teeth grinding as she spoke.

In the shadows on every side, white eyes popped open.

Albert's smile faded. He shook his head in a practiced display of mock sadness. "Maddie, Maddie, Maddie. Such a cliché for there to be tension between a man and his mother-in-law. I just came to get a few things my special lady requested, and, of course, to kill these two meddlesome old goats. Let's call it what it is—a favor, really. They should both have been dead a long time ago. But as for us, I'd hoped we could do better, you and I." He entered the room, the goon at his side, and the shadow forms, now distinctly man-shaped, parted for him to pass. "You can't kill me. You're nothing. No one. Me? I'm a powerful man now. Thanks to your pretty baby girl, I have everything I ever wanted and more than I could have dreamed." He held up his fingers and ticked off a list, "Money. Privilege. Prestige. Power." He winked. "Sex."

"I'll kill you!" she screamed.

The demons around them burst into hissing laughter.

"You and what army?" Albert asked.

Cold black fingers, as unyielding as titanium, reached for Richard's throat. His finger yanked on the trigger of the flare gun, resulting in a hollow click, but Stanley's weapon managed a solid bang that sent a flare into the guard's thigh. He shrieked and dropped to the floor just as something outside burst through the window. Shards of glass showered the room. Albert snatched the gun from the guard's hands and sent a wild spray of bullets in every direction.

In the burst of light from the flare, the demon released Richard. Richard spun, grabbed Maddie and took her to the floor, shielding her body with his as bullets slammed into the walls behind them. Peeking up, he saw new forms jump through the gaping windows, green cat-eyes glowing in the flashes of light.

Gunfire was replaced with snarling growls that turned Richard's guts to water. "Get to the bedroom," he told Maddie, giving her a little push in that direction.

She remained frozen in place, eyes fixed on Albert as half a dozen different creatures jogged into her home through open doors and broken windows. One of them, a woman in long silver robes with eyes that sparkled like diamonds, opened her hands to the ceiling and bathed the room in brilliant white light, so dazzling, he was forced to squint away from it. Jagged fragments of shadow rocketed away from the assault. Albert screamed like a little girl and made a break for the door.

At last, Maddie scrambled away from him, but in the wrong direction. Darn fool child headed straight toward the melee, racing past Stanley without a glance as he drew the edge of his knife across the bodyguard's throat, effectively removing that particular threat.

Richard staggered to his feet and followed her through the remnants of her front door into the dark street. By the time he got to the driveway, Albert had already started one of the sleek black SUVs and was pulling away from the curb. Maddie scrambled into some sort of armored Humvee. Richard couldn't imagine any more improbable vehicles for the two of them.

The idiot man laid rubber on the asphalt before his tires gripped and shot him forward, but at that moment, the ugliest naked human Richard had ever seen launched himself from behind the shrubbery. He landed with a thump on the SUV's hood and began pounding on the windshield and jumping up and down, undeterred, apparently, by the fact that his raw, red butt was on display for the entire neighborhood.

Most likely because he was distracted by the wild nude creature on the hood of his car, Albert bumped over the curb and crashed into a mailbox shaped like a bright red cardinal. The bird tipped as if trying to fly through a hurricane. The naked guy flew off the hood and rolled across the lawn.

Maddie crashed the Humvee into the driver's door of the SUV, rocking the truck up on two wheels. After a split second of stillness in which an acrid cloud of black smoke drifted up from the tortured tires of the two vehicles, her reverse lights blinked on.

The idiot leaped out of the passenger's side door and ran back toward the house.

The naked creature regained its senses and raced after him, screaming, freakishly long arms waving above its head as it ran. Albert hesitated. Maddie's headlights illuminated his terrified features as Albert throw out his hands then folded under the bumper of the Humvee like so much tissue paper.

Brake lights lit one side of the front yard in a hellish red glow. On the other side, the white headlamps of the smashed SUV illuminated Albert's broken form, sprawled in the grass. One ugly brown loafer had flown up in the air and landed on the sidewalk. With a pathetic whimper, the nerdy little leech reached his left arm toward Richard as though imploring him for help.

The Humvee roared to life like some prehistoric beast that would have sent chills up the spine of the bravest caveman ever to huddle behind a fire. Hot acid rose in Richard's throat as his daughter drove backward a hundred feet, thumped over Albert's prone form, shifted gears, and bumped over him again when she returned to her former location.

It wasn't going to take a medical examiner to pronounce the mangled heap of flesh in the front yard dead on the scene.

Richard realized that Stanley stood next to him. "Butter my butt and call me a biscuit," Stanley murmured.

Richard nodded. That about summed it up for him.

The driver's door swung open and Maddie emerged on legs trembling so fiercely her silky pants danced as if blown by the wind. Her eyes, wide and panicky, scanned the scene, pausing for an instant on each clump of neighbors who'd emerged from their homes at the ruckus. They stood in twos and threes, clutching the necks of bathrooms or covering their mouths with shaking hands. The tiny screens of half a dozen smart phones glowed in the night. Finally, she met her father's gaze. "I just bumped into him. It was his own fault, really. He zipped behind me when I was backing up."

Stanley wiped a hand across his mouth, muffling something that sounded suspiciously like a chuckle, and rushed forward just in time to catch Maddie as her legs gave up the good fight and buckled.

"Your daughter is a little scary."

Richard turned to see who had spoken. Michael stood next to him, pressing one of Maddie's kitchen towels to a scalp wound.

"You have no idea," Richard said.

Maddie started crying against Stanley's chest and Richard walked over to where they sat in the grass. "Shhh. It's gonna be okay, kid. Don't cry. It'll be okay."

"In what world is any of this okay?" she shouted.

Some of the neighbors who'd begun to draw near backed away. Their whispers drifted through the night like so many wandering wraiths.

"You need to let us clean this up," Michael said. "All of it. Let us make this go away before it gets too far."

Already, police sirens wailed in the distance, drawing closer by the second.

Richard couldn't speak past the lump in his throat. His eyes seemed stuck on his pale, shaking child, crying in Stanley Kapcheck's arms.

"Do it," Stanley said. "We're in your debt."

Michael showed off his dimples. "Yes, you are. For saving your fragile mortal lives back there *and* for cleaning up afterward. Don't worry. We won't lose track." He motioned toward Maddie and a tall thin figure in a dark robe swept across the lawn to hover over her. The stink of death emanated from the creature. The stench mingled with the coppery scent of Albert's moist remains and sent Richard's stomach into a slow roll.

Richard reached for the dagger in its sheath on his arm. Stanley grabbed his wrist. "We need to let them do this. Two dozen people just watched your daughter run a man down with an armored vehicle. How are you going to explain any of this to those cops who are...what? Three blocks away now? Two, maybe? How are you going to stop anyone from posting videos of this on the internet?"

Richard scowled. He dropped to his knees next to his daughter, ignoring the crunching of joints that sent little spasms of pain through his legs. Nothing about this felt right. Working *with* the monsters? With the *bosses* of the monsters? Might as well go back to making deals with The Devil. He took Maddie's hand in his and pressed it to his heart while the miscreation bent close enough to kiss her. Her trembling slowed and stopped. Her grip grew slack. The black-hooded thing gave a sigh of pleasure and swept away toward the first little group of onlookers who were held in place by a glowing white band of light that encircled them like some kind of high-tech lasso.

The police cars zoomed around the corner and slowed to a crawl. Behind the dark windshield, Richard could just make out the driver, staring straight ahead even as he wove left and right around obstacles littering the street. A second creature like the one who had worked its magic on Madeline rode in the back seat of the cruiser, one hand on the back of the officer's head.

"What'd it do to her?" Richard asked.

"It made her forget," Michael said. "I suggest you get her to a hospital. She'll need a little looking after, but it's nothing they won't be able to manage if you get her there fast enough." He tapped the little square watch face on his left wrist and it glowed to life. "I'm thinking you should be able to meet me at the local airport in two hours or so. Don't be late. We have a lot to do and not much time remaining to do it."

Burke. They had to help Burke. She was a prisoner because

of him. Maddie was laying in the grass, a murderer now, because of him. He blinked hard and turned his face away from Stanley. "I'll go get Madeline's car. We can take that."

Stanley didn't reply, but Richard felt the weight of his gaze as he walked away.

CHAPTER TWENTY-NINE

Burke

BURKE RODE NORTH IN A HELICOPTER, WHICH LANDED WITH a thump in a clearing surrounded by evergreen forest. The other five passengers and she boarded a long electric cart, and a driver with eyes all over his face steered them along a short dirt road. He muttered in Latin and the gate rolled open. Glowing red symbols on signs over the road faded to black, and the cart rolled forward.

In the distance, the immense rocket dominated the skyline. Beyond it, the lake rolled with Mother Earth's steady respirations. Closer, a long, single-story building buzzed with all the activity of a beehive in autumn. They parked near a row of identical steel doors. One of them opened and a man with tidy silver hair and skin as pink as a peach came jogging out to meet them. He held one hand extended toward Burke. When she clasped it, he pumped vigorously.

"Benjamin Franklin," he said. "No relation. You must be Burke."

"Yes," Burke said.

"I'm pleased as pie you're here. I've heard nothing but good things about your skills and, Lord knows, we need someone to look over all the last-minute bugs. You know how these things can go sideways in a second, no matter how much planning you do."

"Yes."

"Great, great. Come on in, then," the old man gushed.

"Okay." Burke climbed down from the cart and followed him.

Benjamin Franklin turned out to be as clever as his namesake and Burke spent the night trailing him around, taking notes and making suggestions.

It seemed like she should have gotten tired at some point, but she didn't. It seemed like that observation should be unsettling, but it wasn't. Albert told her to make herself useful, so that's what she would do. Sleeping was no help to anyone.

Time passed and none of it seemed to matter much. The only thing that mattered was completing each task—answering the questions that were asked of her.

And then she woke up.

No matter that she'd never gone to sleep, she'd been moving through a dream for hours and then, the next moment, she was awake. She remembered everything she'd done and everything that had been said, but she knew she'd not done any of it of her own will.

She looked around. Benjamin Franklin sat typing at a computer. Creatures with snake-like faces and hissing voices made noise at each other while scrolling through rows of numbers on a huge monitor.

He'd possessed her, controlled her, gotten inside her head and taken over. Shivers raced through her body and her teeth clacked together.

"Are you well, dear?" Benjamin asked.

Reason left and only rage remained. She leaped from the

chair, picked it up, and flung it at the snake men. One of them crumpled to the floor, but the other shot a stream of venom at Burke.

She dove to the floor and rolled, and the foul substance hit Benjamin in the eyes. He fell from his chair, shrieking.

Burke scrambled to her feet and lunged toward the door. She yanked it open, only to find alien creatures running toward her from every direction.

She planted her feet wide and fought. With strength increased a thousand-fold by the horror of Albert's violation, she kicked and spun, dodged, punched. There came a moment when she noticed the bodies strewn around her and believed she'd win, but, a split second later, her arms were pinned behind her back and something that might have been an orc slammed a wooden club into her midsection.

Her vision blacked as she sucked hard, trying to draw in any small bit of oxygen. Behind her, Benjamin ordered, "Lock her in a cage and keep her under guard until Jones says we can eat her."

CHAPTER THIRTY

Richard

RICHARD REMEMBERED THE 1960S THE WAY A PERSON remembers a wildly vivid nightmare years after it occurs. His conscious mind understood that the weird dream of the time of free love was over. The kids who'd overdosed while singing about peace and love, the ones shot down by a sniper's rifle in Asia, the ones maimed by police dogs, or were hanged from the branches of trees in their own front yards, cried out in ghostly voices for justice and mercy from the front pages of the nation's newspapers. Meanwhile, a man walked on the moon. The Peace Corps mobilized. The Beatles came to America, and girls took to wearing skirts that left him spending half his mental energy trying not to stare at the soft, sleek, feminine thighs on display right there in public for God and everybody to see.

He remembered all of that, but he didn't remember ever once hearing anything about space rockets being launched from Michigan.

"Not just a few of them, either," Michael said. "Dozens of them over a six-year period."

"You're yanking my chain. I would have known."

Michael twisted the thick gold band on his center finger. "Yes. All US citizens know exactly what their government is up to at all times. It's true now. It was even more true in the cold war years."

"Nobody likes a smart ass," Richard told him.

Michael laughed.

Stanley laughed.

Richard scowled. They sped northward on a helicopter so fancy the limo looked like a stone-aged jalopy by comparison, and he hadn't intended to be the in-flight entertainment.

Michael went on, "It wasn't really a big secret, just nothing widely publicized. In fact, they put a little rock there with some words on it to commemorate the site. For decades, it looked like the remnants of a fair-sized firepit on the shore of Lake Superior."

"And now?" Stanley asked.

"Now the facility is significantly larger and quite well-staffed," Michael answered.

"And these shadow demons have the run of the place?"

Michael tapped his fingers against the plush leather arm of his seat. "I wouldn't say that. As far as we can tell, they're being used more like grunts, for the time-being. Umbra still has at least the illusion of control over them."

Stanley tilted his head like a curious cockatoo. "I've never heard of shadow demons."

"You believe you've heard of every supernatural thing that exists?"

"Most of them, yes."

"Most isn't all, Mr. Kapcheck."

Stanley gave a nod. "Touché."

"The Daughters of Kali and the demons they control were able to get to her through Albert. He opened his soul to hellish power and when his shadow fell on her she became his captive.

When he died, his control over her dissolved. Our sources tell us she became rather displeased when she returned to her senses. The Daughters of Kali find their numbers down by half a dozen or so. Burke's been put in lock up until Umbra and Jones make a final decision about what to do with her."

Richard harbored no doubts that *displeased* had to have been the understatement of the century. He wouldn't have been surprised to hear that Burke tore her captors limb-from-limb, but she'd been badly outnumbered.

Lock up. What did that mean, exactly?

His guts hurt. He needed a glass of prune juice and a decent sleep in a proper bed, free from the panicky fear that gripped him. His thoughts reeled, restless as a worm in hot ashes.

"Why didn't they just kill her?" Stanley asked.

Richard thought he might puke. Friggin' Stan Kapcheck. Why would he ask something like that?

"They were never interested in Albert, of course," Michael said. "He was a tool, a fool, and a pawn in a game he could not begin to understand. From the moment Umbra recognized her, Burke became a trophy she couldn't live without. Burke's a famous programmer, which makes her an asset to the big plan, but even more, she's a famous hunter. That's just about the biggest feather Umbra could put in her cap. Maybe the only thing bigger would be you, Mr. Kapcheck. The hunter The Devil has shielded." He raised one dark brow. "You never did tell me why she finds you so charming."

Stan swallowed hard, looking as close to nervous as Richard had ever seen him. "And I probably never will, Mr. Kelly."

Richard's eyes flicked back and forth between the two men. He breathed a sigh of relief when Mr. Kelly showed no sign of offense.

"Well, no matter, really," Michael said. "The end result is the same. Your girl Burke is locked up and, in a day or so, she's going to Mars. At that point, she's as good as dead to you. If we're going to do this, we need to do it now. No second chances this time, boys."

THE BUMP OF THE RUNNERS HITTING THE GROUND JOLTED Richard awake with a start. He had intended to stay awake and follow the conversation between Stanley and Michael. Ashamed that he'd dozed off, he blinked sleep from his eyes, wiped drool from the corner of his mouth and looked around to make sure no one had been watching him. Michael sat next to the pilot, talking in hushed tones that didn't reach him over the *whump, whump* of the rotors. Stanley peered through the window. Richard did the same.

They'd touched down in a field surrounded on three sides by an evergreen forest. This far north, no hint of autumn remained. Winter had arrived with a heavy dusting of snow and a serious lack of daylight hours. Heedless of the clocks that insisted morning had arrived, the Ice Queen would not let the sun rise for another two or three hours.

Bone-shaking noise shifted into unnerving silence when the pilot shut down the engines. Michael held his hands open before him. "This is it for us, fellas. You're on your own from here. Ready? Any final questions?"

"I believe you've equipped us as well as possible," Stanley said.

Richard scratched his head, felt the hair on the left side sticking out like a crazy person's. He pulled a stocking cap from the pocket of his coat and yanked it down over his head. Michael seemed to take the action as a confirmation that Richard was ready to head out into the Great Northern Wilderness.

Among other things, the last six months had taught him two truths about hunting.

First, the true answer to the question, "Are you ready?" is always no. You can't be ready. It's impossible. There is no such thing as a hunt that goes exactly as planned. You can prepare for a thousand eventualities and, invariably, the thing you didn't expect is the thing that happens. Stanley's talent as a hunter was his ability to adapt in an instant.

Second, no good was served by answering the question truthfully. Nobody wanted to hear it. People didn't ask, 'Are you ready?' because they were inclined to help you prepare more completely any more than they asked, 'How are you?' because they genuinely wanted to hear about your woes. The acceptable answers were always, 'Yes. I'm ready,' and 'I'm fine, thank you.'

Next thing he knew, the door stood open, giving entrance to the frigid wind. Stanley hopped out and Richard did the odd little hunched shuffle required to navigate the inside of the chopper. At the door, a memory struck him—a photograph he'd once seen of Frank Sinatra exiting a helicopter with a martini in his hand. Old Blue Eyes had style. Ordinary mortals stood no chance of being a fraction as cool as Frankie, but a little voice in Richard's head whispered, *You're not an ordinary mortal anymore. You're a gosh-darn special forces monster assassin. Maybe Frankie can charm a nun of her habit, but you've got your own level of slick.*

With his face arranged in a bad-ass snarl, Richard hopped out of the protective bubble of the chopper. His boots hit the snow and gripped exactly the way well-constructed winterwear ought to, but his hip—not so much. The titanium screwed into his joint did not appreciate him hopping anywhere, let alone from a height of several feet. The socket locked up and he pitched face-first into Stanley's chest. Staggering backward, Stanley caught him under the arms.

Richard pushed him away harder than he meant to, straightened his hat and jacket, and refused to look back toward the chopper to see the redhead laughing at him.

Nursing his wounded pride, he limped off toward the woods

with one leg hitching weirdly, telling himself no one could judge him. At least, he'd moved past his reliance on a walker, and who'd have ever thought he'd manage that? Who'd have ever thought he'd even have the strength to trek through the snow? All right, maybe he lacked Sinatra's finesse, but he wasn't some old geezer sucking up sugar-free cocoa in a nursing home, and he never would be again.

Never.

He'd keep going until he went down for the final time with his gun in his hand.

Inside the treeline, they took a moment to do what was necessary after a long journey in a vehicle with no toilet. Even powerful, feared assassins needed to pee sometimes. When they'd finished, they pointed themselves due-north once again.

Adrenaline burned hot, serving as a fine replacement for sleep. The gear they'd picked up at The Children of Cain storage unit kept him warm. The goggles Michael gave them during the ride gave him a decent view of the world around him, despite the deep darkness of the ancient forest. The weight of his weapons provided a certain level of assurance. Nevertheless, trekking through a dark, snowy forest on foot was slow going and his mind began to wander.

Barbara had hated the snow. The desert spoke to her soul—a land of endless, relentless sunshine and warmth. Once or twice a year, winter would brush lightly across the Tombstone landscape and, on those days, she would burn every lightbulb in the house and spend the day baking the kind of hot, heavy food that stuck to your ribs and filled you up until you felt like you could curl into a ball and sleep the winter away like a bear.

Sometimes, if he was lucky, those cold day naps would turn into a different kind of staying warm between the sheets.

What if that young man making the beast with two backs on a Thursday afternoon had been told he'd spend his old age hiking the Upper Peninsula with a British dandy? Did the odd surprises of old age leave everyone slightly disoriented, or was it just him?

He peeked over at Stanley, who strode across the slick, squishy bed of frozen pine needles with the sure-footed grace of a freakin' mountain goat. *Unnatural.*

"Hey, Stan?"

"Hmm?"

"You ever think it's weird, getting old?"

Stanley ducked under a low branch before answering, "Sure. When I was your age, I thought about it all the time. Sometime after my hundredth birthday, I stopped thinking about it. I got depressed in my hundred-and-twenties. The world had changed too much. I'd lost too many people I loved."

"What made it good again?" Richard asked.

Stanley's steps remained as steady as ever, moving ever northward in a steady, determined march. "You did, Dick."

For the life of him, Richard couldn't think of a response to that, so he just kept on walking.

"Look." Stanley pointed at a tree with a warbly sort of zig-zag spiral carved around the circumference of the trunk.

"Warding?" Richard asked.

"Doesn't look like anything I've ever seen before," Stanley said.

Richard scanned the area and picked out four more trees with marks on them, none of them familiar. "I been wondering how you can ward against everything. I mean, if The Children of Cain can't go in at all, they must of set up a system to keep everything from witches to angels out of their little camp."

"And yet, they get their own monsters in and out, somehow," Stanley said.

Richard hadn't really thought of that, but it was a valid point. "Smells fishy."

"Indeed." Stanley started walking again.

"You think that guy, Michael, was straight with us?"

"No," Stanley said.

Richard harrumphed. "You 'bout wearing out my ears with all your chattering."

Stanley's head turned in his direction for just a moment. No matter that the mask over Stanley's face covered his mouth, Richard was one hundred percent certain he was grinning. He could *feel* the grin.

"I think Michael sees us as disposable—a couple of grunts being sent in to do a job. Thanks to The Devil's orders, he can't directly hurt us, but if we happen to die doing what we do...well...that's no fault of his, right? He's told us what he thinks we absolutely need to know to accomplish what he wants done and not one bit more."

"If we know we can't trust him, why in tarnation are we working with him?"

Stanley pushed a branch out of the way and held it while Richard ducked under it. "Because he's working with The Devil we know."

Richard tucked that in his craw to chew on while they hiked. The idea tasted bitter and unsettling, to say the least, but he couldn't think of a single decent counter argument.

CHAPTER THIRTY-ONE

Richard

HI-TECH, GOBLIN-MAGIC, ORC-CRAFTED GEAR notwithstanding, the first shot of adrenaline upon arrival had burned away and Richard was feeling about half dead when the trees started thinning and the smell of the world's largest freshwater lake grew strong enough to overpower the scent of pine. The sight of the rocket pointing toward the starry sky and the long, low building off to the west provided a second shot so powerful it sent his heart into a painful racing thump.

Looking at the setup burned his eyes.

"Take the goggles off," Stanley whispered as if reading his mind.

Richard pushed the contraption onto his forehead and understood. The goggles amplified every tiny bit of light to give them night vision. In this place, with its ferocious halogen lamps set up at close intervals, the amplification was overwhelming. "Now what?"

The rocket stood like the world's largest phallus on the shore of the world's largest freshwater lake. Waves, illuminated by the bright work lamps, rolled landward in choppy bursts driven by the winter storms rolling in from the west. A long brick building with a lot of garage doors and no windows hugged the frozen earth. A handful of people—or people-shaped creatures—in orange overalls trudged back and forth between the two structures or rode in little golf carts.

"She's got to be somewhere in there," Stanley said, pointing at the warehouse.

"Could you narrow it down a little? Place must be a quarter mile long, and who knows how far underground it goes."

A popping noise sounded off to their left and the two of them dove behind a massive fallen pine. Nearby, a towering tree sporting the squiggly carvings they'd noticed throughout the forest glowed blue and a creature that looked like some sort of Neanderthal, wearing clothes from a comic strip set a thousand years in the future, materialized out of the solid wood. He glanced around and grunted something in a deep guttural language Richard couldn't place as anything he'd ever heard before. The creature took two loping strides toward the warehouse and then stopped. Squinting into the darkness toward the log behind which he and Stanley crouched, the thing sniffed and took a slow step in their direction.

On the beach, an electric motor approached, and a comical little toy horn beeped three times. The Neanderthal jerked in that direction and ran off toward the golf cart, grunting in its strange language.

The two men waited until the creature was gone before rising to their full height. Richard's joints popped in protest. He shoved aside concerns about his physical ability to complete the job at hand. In the immortal words of Tom Hanks, failure was not an option.

"That's how they get their own people in and out." Stanley approached the tree and studied the carving. "These aren't wardings. They're portals."

"Portals?"

Stanley glanced back at him. "Doors that ought not be opened."

"So, what was that thing?" Richard asked.

"Nothing you're going to find in a hunter's journal, I'd wager. Not in this space-time continuum, anyway." He let his hand fall away from the etchings on the tree. "Let's focus on getting to Burke." He pointed at one end of the building. "See those garage bays?"

"Yeah."

"They're hauling equipment out of there and loading it on the shuttle. I'd wager she's in the opposite end of the building. It'll be quieter and more secure there."

Some distance away in the forest came a popping and a faint blue light. They ducked again. A smallish man-shaped figure emerge from the woods a few hundred feet farther down the beach and went loping off on all fours toward the Coleum building.

"How we going to get in there?" Richard asked.

Stanley watched the creature approach the building and jog into the brightly lit bay. "We're going to walk in."

"Are you nuts?"

"Most likely."

Richard tried to get a good look at Stanley's face to gauge whether or not he was serious. "We'll be dead before our feet hit the sand."

Stanley rubbed his chin with the backs of his fingers. "I don't think so, old boy. I think they're so over-confident in their superior strength and magical warding that it never occurred to them to protect themselves from good old human trespassers."

"What if you're wrong?" Richard asked.

"Then we go with plan B," Stanley said.

"Which is what?"

"I'll let you know when the time comes."

Richard harrumphed, but followed Stanley past the edge of the woods into the exposed area of the beach. Walking through the rocky sand required more concentration that he wanted to give it, and he longed for a paved sidewalk where he wouldn't have to hitch along like a cripple. His breath came in harsh gasps that hurt his chest.

"Okay?" Stanley asked.

"Fine as frog's hair," Richard grunted.

Behind them, a faint popping noise sounded in the distance. To their right, a group of workers exited the rocket, communicating in a series of clicks and whistles that sounded distinctly insectile. To their left, a golf cart pulled out from one of the garages, headlights pointed toward them.

Richard wondered why he'd never considered buying adult diapers. One of these days, he was bound to mess himself and it seemed like the inevitable moment would be slightly less humiliating if he wore something that would keep it from seeping through his pants. "What do we do?" he whispered.

"Head down, old boy. Keep walking."

One of the bugs clicked more loudly than the others.

Richard's heart hammered against his ribcage. "They're honing in like a tornado in a trailer park."

"Just keep walking. It'll be fine," Stanley said.

Bugman switched to English, "Hey! You! Who you?" he clicked and whistled.

Stanley waved. "Good to see you chaps again. We're headed in for the morning shift."

"Who you?" he asked again. The whole group of them loomed close enough now for Richard to see their heads, like giant termites, complete with serrated mandibles. He fought the whimper rising in his throat.

"They're on us like flies on the meat wagon," Richard wheezed.

"Plan B, my friend. You go get Burke."

Panic rose up, hot and burning in Richard's throat. "What?"

"Go, Dick! I'll distract them."

"But I—"

"Go, dammit!" Stanley hissed. Dropping to a crouch, he pulled two guns from beneath his coat and fired into the group of giant bugs. Green stuff sprayed into the still night air.

Richard stumbled and hitched as fast as he could across the uneven ground. The golf cart headlights rose up in front of him and he reached into his pocket for one of the little round balls that bounced against his sides. With a trembling hand, he tossed it in the direction of the golf cart and missed by a good six feet. Sand blew into the air, thirty feet high, knocking the cart over. He didn't wait to see how the driver and his passengers reacted. Just as he reached the building, another three cart-loads of creatures he couldn't identify rolled out into the night. He pressed himself against one of the closed bay doors, hiding as well as he could in the corner. With their focus on Stanley and the melee happening out on the beach, not one of them saw the old man clutching the wall and gasping for air.

When they'd exited, he peeked around the corner. No one was looking his way. He darted into the building and through a door that led into a corridor as long and bright as a hallway in Heaven. His footsteps echoed against the tile floor, but no one approached him as he passed door after door, wondering how on Earth he would ever figure out where his granddaughter was being held.

"Barbara, if you're up there and watching over me, I need you to send me a sign, 'cause I'm just about as lost as a virgin in a whorehouse right now, and darn near in as much trouble, too." His whisper rasped from his dry throat and echoed back to him from the cold walls.

At the end of the hall, a door banged open. Acting on pure instinct, Richard opened the nearest door and ducked into darkness.

"I won't let them kill you without me being there to help," a low, resonant growl echoed down the hall. "After the past twelve hours, I deserve my shot at you."

Nails clicked against the tiles, drawing close to the door of Richard's room and passing it. Another door opened and clicked shut toward the end of the hall from which he'd come.

Richard released his breath and pressed his head against the wall for just a moment, trying to settle the stars bursting behind his eyes. His blood pressure had to be through the roof. If Maddie could see him now, she'd have him committed, for sure. Turning slightly to one side, he saw blank white eyes staring back at him and jumped away from them, yelping.

In the dim light of the room, a hundred pairs of eyes watched him without expression.

The stars popped in his vision again. His legs trembled and threatened to give out.

His back slammed against the door and somehow the impact shook sense into his brain. These were not the eyes of monsters looking to devour him. They stared out of the sockets of heads that floated in clear liquid in large glass jars.

Shivers wracked his body with such force his false teeth clacked together and threatened to fall out. He stumbled out of the wretched storage room back into the hall. Thank God from Whom all blessings flow, his luck held once more and no one saw him.

His hip was shot. Too much lurching, jerking, falling, crouching, and pathetic running. The joint continued to support his weight but refused to move in any direction. He hitched like a wooden puppet toward the door the growling guard had come out of. So far as he could see, it was one of two doors in the whole place with a tiny rectangular window at eye level. The other, across the hall, was dark and quiet. He peeked into the lighted space.

Burke stood in a cage just big enough to accommodate her

height and give her enough space to sit down if she chose to do so. At the moment, she stood with her feet planted shoulder-width apart and her hands wrapped around the bars. Her pretty features were twisted in a defiant snarl.

He fiddled with his hearing aid but failed to make out any sound. He ventured a wave in front of the window. Her eyes darted toward the motion and widened. She frantically motioned for him to enter.

He yanked open the door and nearly fainted with relief. "You're alive!"

Tears brimmed in her dark eyes. "You, too!"

He took stock of her cell—an iron cage with a heavy industrial padlock. "We gotta bust you out."

She shook her head. "He'll be back, or another one will. They never leave me alone for more than a minute or two." Her gaze darted around the room. "Hide under that desk," she said, pointing.

Richard eyed the little leg space under the desk. "Not a chance, kid. The hip is shot. Can't do anything that means folding up like a yogi."

Burke cursed under her breath. "There, then. In that cabinet."

A tall metal cabinet stood in one corner, the door slightly ajar. Richard dragged himself to it, yanked a mop and broom out and leaned them against the wall.

"Don't jump the gun, Grandpa. Wait for my signal. You won't get a second shot. I don't even know what half these creatures are, let alone how to kill them."

"That's because they're—"

The door handle turned and Richard dived for cover.

CHAPTER THIRTY-TWO

Burke

"Come on in, Ugly. Why you hiding over there on the other side of the room? You scared?" Burke clung to the bars with both hands, taunting the creature through a wide, easy grin. "Scared of a girl? A big bad thing like you? What's the matter? Never been around a female? What'd you hatch from? Even something like you must have a mama, right? Or was your mama so ugly you couldn't even tell she was a girl?"

The lizard-looking monster standing just inside the doorway hissed at her and flexed its clawed hands.

"Come at me, then. Come on. Do your worst," Burke demanded.

"You can't even imagine what my worst is, pathetic human."

Burke rolled her eyes. "Yeah. I'm the pathetic one. What are you going to do? Talk me to death? I haven't seen a bit of action out of a single one of you yet. Learn that from your hideous beast of a mother? She teach you to prattle on and on while other, stronger, meaner monsters do all the fun stuff?"

The beast leaped toward the cage. Soaring through the air,

it stretched out its arms, revealing pink membranous wings criss-crossed with thick, pulsing veins. About a foot from the cage, it slammed into some sort of forcefield that threw it backward across the room. Burke glanced up at the light fixture glowing above her. The runic writing on the glass seemed to serve as some sort of reverse devil's trap.

"I'll kill you!" the monster hissed.

Burke rolled her eyes. "Blah, blah, blah," she taunted.

The door opened with a metallic swish and a tiny man in a navy-blue suit and red tie entered the room. "Take a hike," he told the growling monster.

"I'm on guard duty," it told him.

"Not anymore. You're wanted on sub level two."

"Ooh, called to the principal's office?" Burke asked.

The creature sent a final hiss in her direction and slumped out of the room.

"What are you supposed to be?" she asked the newcomer. "King of the South Pole Elves?"

"You talk too much, pretty one," he replied. "Maybe we should cut out your tongue. Can't imagine you need to be able to talk in order to program a computer." He stepped forward and the door slid shut behind him. Keeping his eyes on Burke, he reached inside his jacket and produced a long dagger.

She shook her head. "You're not going to be able to do anything to me either, and you talk a weaker game than that last thing. You're some kind of fairy, right? Nothing more than a *silver* medalist in the monster Make Big Threats contest." She practically shouted the word, 'silver.'

Dear God, let my grandfather take the hint.

When the little man got close enough to Burke that he wouldn't see the closet, Richard burst out of the door, and let momentum carry him forward until the point of his silver knife sank into the little fairy's back. The tiny man threw back his head in a silent scream and fell in a sputtering flash of light. His clothes fluttered to the ground at Richard's feet.

"You did it!"

Richard bent at the waist to use the fabric of the dead thing's suit to clean the glittery residue from his knife. "Don't have to sound so surprised about it." Finally, he managed to straighten, but Burke wasn't at all sure how much more her grandfather could take. He pointed at the light. "Reckon I can shoot that out?"

"You can try, but do it from behind that desk so you have cover if the bullet ricochets," she said.

"What about you?"

"Well, I'm behind it so it can't ricochet in my direction, unless you miss by half a mile."

He scowled.

She grinned.

"You look way too happy," he said.

"I recently remembered why I started hunting," she replied.

Understanding passed between them like an electric current. He took cover behind the open door of the closet he'd hidden in and squeezed the trigger. The bullet did ricochet, and slammed into the wall behind him, the butt end of it sticking out like something you'd hang a photograph from.

"Now what?" Burke asked.

"Hold on," he told her. "I'm gonna try again." He slipped the gun he'd been using back into the holster, reached toward his waistband, and pulled out the old trusty revolver he carried almost all the time. Taking careful aim at the light, he squeezed the trigger and ducked.

The fixture shattered into a trillion brilliant bits of glitter, causing Burke to drop to her knees, arms over her head. By the time the dust settled and she was back on her feet, he stood next to the cage. "One more. Back up and hold on to your butt."

She backed to the far corner of the cage, took cover again, and he shot the lock at point-blank range. The iron mechanism dropped to the floor.

"You did it!" she whooped.

"You're still surprised at my success," he pointed out.

"Not surprised. Delighted." She shook bits of fragmented glass from her hair and ran into his arms. "Delighted and so proud. You're my hero, Grandpa. For real."

He swallowed hard and avoided eye contact. "Stanley's in a heap of trouble, Burke. How do we break the warding?"

She pointed at the jagged remains of the light fixture. "They're arrogant beyond belief, Grandpa. They know that The Children of Cain and all manner of creatures could pose a problem. They've got doors and portals warded six ways from Sunday, but they see humans as no more than a bunch of high-functioning apes. They have no fear, at all, of human weapons or human ideas."

"You're telling me there's magic all over this peninsula, but hardly a protocol in place to stop a human from waltzing in and doing whatever he darn well pleases? That's what Stanley said, but it seems about as likely as daisies in January."

"It's true. The fence around the back of this building is the western perimeter of the warded area. You wouldn't be able to get within twenty feet of it if you were anything other than human. It's electrified, too, but if I understand correctly, if we can figure out how to cut power, we can bust it open with wire cutters."

"How do you even know all this?"

She gritted her teeth hard enough to make the muscle in her jaw jump. "I haven't been in the cage the whole time. I saw a lot when I was..." A single tear rolled down her cheek. "He's dead, right? He must be."

"Yeah, kid. He's dead."

Regret burned in her belly. She wished she'd listened to

Stanley's warnings. She wished she'd said no in the first place. Most of all, she wished she'd been the one to kill the slimy little bastard.

Richard offered her the dagger and gestured with the gun in his hand. "What are we waiting for then? Let's go show them what our species is made of."

She wiped her face. There would be time for feelings later. "We need to figure out how to get out of this building," Burke said. She looked around the room for a moment and an amusing thought popped into her mind. "We're going to pull a Chewbacca." Snatching a black cloak from a hook on the wall, she told him, "Here, put this on. Tie me up and drag me through the hall to the back door. We're going to put on a little show for their amusement, and they'll let us walk right by."

The dark fabric weighed more than he would have expected. Like everything in this place, there was more to it than met the eye. He slung the fabric over his shoulders and clipped the little snap at the throat.

Burke tugged the hood over his head, pulling it far enough forward to cast his face into shadow.

"I feel stupid," he grumbled.

She grinned. "You look awesome, Grandpa. Like Obi Wan Kenobi."

"Yeah?" He squared his shoulders and stood a little taller.

While he unplugged some random piece of machinery and yanked the cord out of the port in the back, she strapped on the leather sheath and dagger he'd taken from his arm. Then, with her grandfather's cord wrapped several times around her wrists and tucked between her fists, making a reasonably convincing illusion of a knot, she took a deep breath and asked if he was ready to go.

"Ready as a forty-year-old virgin," he said. "Stanley's on his own out there, and he's in a heap of trouble." Burke gave the fastest description possible of the layout of the building and as soon as he knew which way he was headed, Richard threw the door open and dragged her into the hallway.

Burke resisted, screaming at him as she staggered along in his wake, "You freak! Sick, twisted, non-human psycho, you can't do this to me!"

At the other end of the hall, a door slid open and a guard turned red eyes in their direction.

Richard tugged the wire with both hands. "I'm done with you! Ain't a human in the world worth this much trouble."

The red-eyed thing snorted in a way that reminded Burke of the recently deceased Albert. "What're you gonna do?" it called out to Richard.

"Take her out back and shoot her. Leave her for table scraps," Richard declared. His half-wrecked, breathless voice helped give him a fantastically monsterish tone.

"There'll be Hell to pay."

"Been to Hell. Ain't as bad as putting up with this broad for another shift."

The thing snorted again. "I'll be sure to hit the buffet on my next break."

Burke screamed and pulled so convincingly she just about knocked him on his butt.

He gave her a look and she let up enough that he was able to make some forward progress despite his gimpy leg.

A door at the end of the hall opened into a large space that served as a kind of employee break room. The beings they passed were few and far between, but each gave their full attention to the little show being played out. No doubt, word of Burke's wild antics had spread far and wide and everyone was amused to see her being dragged along to some horrible end. The looks of amusement on each face, even the hideous, disfigured faces, were unmistakable. Not one creature challenged them.

Burke's assessment had been spot-on. Their arrogance was

their Achilles' heel. None of these beasts, enthralled in their own coming adventure of setting up a people farm, could imagine that the cattle in question were plotting against them.

Richard dragged Burke through an exit on the other side of the room. Outside, the gunfire and screams of a distant battle spurred them to greater speed. Burke longed to race ahead of her hobbling grandfather. If what he said was true, Stanley was fighting as hard as any man could, but how long could one man, even a great hunter, hold off so many?

"How do I shut down the fence?" Richard asked.

"There." Burke untangled her wrists from the wire and tossed it aside. "The windmill. That silver box where the wires attach is a transformer. Blow it, and I bet this whole section of the compound goes dead. Even if they have redundant systems, it'll take a few minutes for those to kick in."

Richard lifted his gun and sited down the barrel. "Too far, kid. No way I can make that shot."

"Give me the gun," she said.

He handed it over and, without another word, she raced toward the windmill. Seconds later, she jumped onto the bottom rung of the windmill's outside ladder and climbed with adrenaline-fueled strength and speed. Halfway to the top, she extended her left arm and fired three rounds in quick succession. Sparks showered down from the box and, all around them, floodlights flickered and died.

She peered down over her shoulder in time to see Richard pull the pin on a grenade and threw it at the fence. It landed a foot or so short, but who cared? In horseshoes and hand grenades, close was good enough for a win. The device detonated.

CHAPTER THIRTY-THREE

Richard

TIME SLOWED TO A CRAWL. RICHARD SAW THE METAL NET tear away from the frame and watched with dread fascination as one broken cross-piece ripped away from the rest of the structure and spun, end over sharp-edged end, in his direction. So slowly did the Earth rotate at that moment, he actually had time to consider his own death. No way he was going to dodge fast enough to get out of the path of oncoming impalement. Time may have slowed, but he himself was sluggish as molasses in January. He lifted one arm to shield himself, as if that would do some sort of good, and winced in anticipation of the pain to come.

A metallic clang rang out and he staggered backward as something hit him.

It took a moment to register the fact that nothing had stabbed him. The bar lay in a mangled heap at his feet. Smoke curled upward from a little circle on the cloak. Apparently, the heavy fabric stopped the shrapnel.

"Well, dip me in bacon grease and call me a pig," he muttered.

"Grandpa!"

He looked up at Burke, who still hung from the side of the windmill. She pointed toward the rocky beach, now bathed in the sickly yellow light of the few remaining sodium lamps on the far side of the complex. The mutant gang that had cornered Stanley appearing downright relaxed and amused as slick black forms with white eyes popped up all over the place.

Richard ran. Well, he didn't exactly run. His left leg refused to swing, and both rickety old knees protested the necessary up and down pumping required of running. Rather, he lurched along awkwardly, as fast as he possibly could.

His gait wasn't fast enough to save Stanley, but it was fast enough to see the shadow demons converge on him and pull him down to the ground. Stanley screamed, not the sound of fear, but the sound of a man being shredded alive.

"No!" Richard shouted and fired a flare. The demons scattered like roaches under a light and Stanley struggled up, making it as far as his hands and knees before the light blinked out and they were on him again, pressing him flat.

Richard fished in his pockets for another flare to ram into the cylinder, but as he did, a queer shimmering glow arched across the sky, headed toward Stanley. Looking up caused Richard to stumble. He slowed his gait to avoid falling.

Burke reached him and grabbed his arm, forcing him to stop.

The glow in the sky grew until the light hurt his eyes, a great, shimmering rainbow shining impossibly in the pre-dawn sky.

Still wearing his dandy suit, little red-headed Michael slid down the glowing slope like a kid on a playground slide and landed neatly on his feet not more than a yard away from Stanley. He scattered what looked like glitter across the ground next to him and the girl in the silver gown popped out of nowhere. She held her hands wide, lighting the beach as bright as a summer day.

Sirens blared all around them. Hissing and roars caused the hairs on the back of Richard's neck to stand up straight. Swords clanged and guns fired. Something broke the surface of Lake Superior, its gaping maw revealing row upon row of serrated, pointed teeth.

One of the bat-winged lizard men flew at them from the direction of the rocket. Burke's spine stiffened and then she sped toward him, silver dagger raised above her head, a war cry upon her lips. The creature landed hard and produced a mace. *A freaking mace? What kind of monster carries a goll-darned mace in his belt?* Burke hit the ground and slid in low, going right between the beast's legs and popping up on the other side. The thing's fierce expression slipped into a mask of total surprise. It looked down at the knife point poking out of its chest and then fell forward, landing with a little poof of sand.

Richard looked toward Stanley. The hunter lay on the ground and, for one terrible moment, Richard was certain he was dead. Richard hustled to his side as fast as he could manage over the uneven ground. Stanley turned his head, a wide, guileless grin on his face. He pointed at the rainbow. "It's so pretty!"

Richard stopped and looked up. He looked back at Stanley. "You havin' a stroke or something?"

Stanley laughed and pushed into a sitting position, his legs akimbo. "My friend, I don't think I've ever felt so good." He watched the fighting for a few seconds before turning back to Richard. "Look how strong they all are! And diverse! What an amazing array of creatures live here on this beautiful blue planet. Or, at least, on this version of the planet."

Richard approached him and held out a hand.

Stanley took it, hoisted himself up, and pulled him into a bear hug. "You came back for me. You always do. No matter what kind of a mess I'm in, I know you're going to come for me. Has any hunter ever been lucky enough to have such a loyal partner?"

Richard half-lifted his arms, not sure how to respond. A severed limb struck nearby rocks. Michael strode past, his starched white shirt splattered with blood and something green and slightly iridescent. Without slowing, he said, "That is a fantastic cloak, Richard. An excellent acquisition. Why don't you wrap it around Smiley McHappyface there and head for that hole you blew in the fence?" He lifted a device he held. Red numbers glowed 4:56, 4:55, 4:54... "I believe you're going to want the chopper to be well up and over the forest before this hits zero."

A strigoi flew at them. Richard's body reacted faster than his brain, strength born on the memory of a creature similar to this one appearing out of nowhere when he was at his most vulnerable. He whipped a wooden stake out of his belt and thrust it into the beast's chest as it bore down upon them. It burst into a rain of ash that puddled in front of his feet.

"Wow!" Stanley said. "For an old guy, you move with astonishing speed and accuracy. You must have been fantastic in your prime, truly a world-class athlete. It's easy to see where Burke gets her speed and agility."

Burke jogged up, panting and gore smeared.

"We gotta make like a tree and leave," he told her.

She nodded. "I heard. You okay, Stanley?"

A piece of shrapnel flew at them from one of the nearby battles. Richard flung out his arm and the flaming bits bounced from his cloak harmlessly.

"Isn't he something?" Stanley asked. His eyes grew wide. "And you—I don't know if I have ever told you how absolutely stunning you are. Just look at you, fierce and strong, an African goddess of war."

Burke looked at her grandfather. "He's okay?"

Richard shrugged. "He ain't dead. Let's get outta here. We'll figure it out later."

The trio dodged, staggered, and fought their way back to the fence. Burke led the way. Stanley stopped to admire the sparkly rainbow again. Richard gave him a strong shove toward their escape route and Stanley passed through the gap, marveling the whole while about how clever Richard and Burke had been to break the warding. Richard rolled his eyes and walked backward toward the chopper, his gun held at the ready. One cat-eyed creature slid out from behind a tree and nodded at him. "Well done, hunter," it said.

Part of Richard swelled at the compliment. Part of him loathed the thing and longed to shoot it. In the name of expediency, he chose Door Number Three, ignored it altogether, and focused on getting into the chopper before half the upper peninsula blew into the sky.

Apparently, the pilot, unidentifiable behind the cover of flight overalls, enormous helmet and dark goggles, was of the same mind. He had the runners off the ground before their butts hit the seats. Old cat-eyes jumped in at the last minute and, with a groan, pulled the heavy door shut behind him, locking out a fair amount of the astonishing racket the rotors created.

After a moment of vertical assent that pushed Richard's heart down so hard he wouldn't be surprised to find it tucked in between the family jewels, they banked hard to the left, skimming inches above the treetops.

"Flying is so exciting," Stanley exclaimed.

Burke met Richard's gaze.

Richard shrugged. "He's gone all loopy."

"I'm just so happy," Stanley said.

An explosion shattered the night. Hot wind shook the chopper until Richard felt like a grain of rice in a saltshaker. Fire burned so bright, the whole forest glowed neon orange for a long moment. Then the flames died out and a cloud not entirely unlike the mushroom clouds he'd seen in movies rolled upward to mingle with the clouds.

After that, no one spoke again until the chopper soared over the twinkling lights that traced the unmistakable outline of the Mackinaw Island Bridge.

"Just look what people built," Stanley sighed. "Those creatures were mighty foolish to live in a world full of wonders like that and still fail to understand the power of human ingenuity." Tears glistened in his eyes. "How sad we had to fight them. How sad we've not yet learned to settle differences without bloodshed."

"Loopy," Richard repeated.

Burke leaned forward. "Stanley, you were fighting all by yourself on that beach. There were a lot of creatures there."

Stanley scoffed and grinned. "Boy, is that an understatement!"

"What did they do to you?"

He leaned forward as if confiding a great secret, "I confess, I'm a bit prideful about how well I held them off. I mean, I expected they'd kill me in moments and, I'm sorry to say this Richard, but I did wonder if you'd be coming back. I mean, it was a tough mission, to say the least. Then the lights went out and I knew I was a goner. I mean, I was certain down deep in my bones. Ready to meet my maker." One of his tears escaped and cut a clean path through the dirt on his face. "But then, just when all was lost, I looked up and there you were, Richard."

A little frown crossed his face, a shadow of confusion. "Something happened then. It hurt so much I..." He shook his head as if to clear it. "I don't want to think about that. The next moment, I realized how much good is in the world. I realized I can be part of the good. We all can. We can shine as bright of the sun. All we need to do is choose to turn away from darkness. Everything can be warmth and light. Then I knew my fight was over and I was free and happy. No more fighting. No more revenge. No anger or death or pain, only light." He threw his head back and laughed like a little child overcome by joy.

A familiar voice said, "His shadow has been severed."

Michael sat facing them from the pilot's seat, the helmet and goggles in his lap, while Felix the Cat flew the helicopter from the co-pilot's seat.

"How the Sam Hill?" Richard muttered.

"On the rainbow, of course," Michael answered.

Richard expected maybe he could make sense of that sometime in the future, but right now, it made as much sense as a Jell-O umbrella.

"Without his shadow, Stanley literally has no darkness in him. He's pure light. Only goodness and joy. Yin, undiluted by so much as a single drop of yang."

"Goodness and joy is...well...good, but somehow this doesn't seem like a good thing," Burke said.

"Left in this state, he will die sooner rather than later. It's unnatural for light to exist without darkness outside of Heaven itself," Michael confirmed.

Richard had mused a thousand times about Stanley being unnatural, but this was an entirely different can of worms. "What do we need to do?"

Michael held out a hand as if asking what they expected. "I should think it would be obvious."

"We need to reattach his shadow," Burke said.

Michael nodded, then asked, "So, did either of you carry it out?"

"His shadow?" Richard asked. "How in tarnation do you carry a shadow?"

Michael shrugged. "I've never done it, myself."

"I'm afraid we were in a bit of a hurry to get away from the bomb you set," Burke said.

"Well then, I'm sorry, but your friend is going to die. His sacrifice will not go unremembered."

Burke lunged across the crowded space and half lifted the little man out of his chair. "You listen to me, leprechaun. I have been to hell and back in the past two days, and Stan Kapcheck just saved my ass. If I'm not mistaken, he saved yours, too, though I can't imagine why he'd work with a piece of monster scuz like you." She gave him a shake. "The very fact that he didn't drive an iron stake through your skull the moment he saw you means you owe him a life debt."

Richard realized his mouth was hanging open and snapped it shut. A leprechaun? Huh. Well, that explained the rainbow.

Michael tilted his head, the twinkle never leaving his eye. "You do have a fire in your belly, don't you?"

Burke pulled him an inch closer.

"I can't make promises. You saw the explosion. There's nothing left of that place but the dust that's settling into the lake. I'll make a call, though, if you'd be so kind as to release me."

She dropped him and sank back into her seat.

"You are very strong," Stanley commented.

Michael turned toward the window. After gazing outward for a few moments, he pressed his palm against the glass. The shimmering arc of a rainbow shot northward across the sky. "If they can locate his shadow and capture it, we can try to reattach it."

"Don't bother, dear one," Stanley said. "I'm just fine the way I am. I feel fantastic. Light as air. Light as light itself."

Richard didn't know if he was imagining things or not, but Stanley looked light as air, as though he were already losing form and changing into nothing more than a gathering of light particles.

Burke crossed her arms and stared out into the purplish sky. She began to shiver and hugged herself tighter. When a stifled sob reached his ears, Richard reached for her knee. She didn't say anything or even look at him, but she latched onto his fingers so tightly he thought they might break. He uttered no complaint, but returned her grip.

CHAPTER THIRTY-FOUR

Burke

Neither one of them knew what to do with Stanley. It didn't seem wise to leave him alone. On the other hand, they agreed that taking him into Maddie's hospital room, when God only knew what shape she was in, was a terrible idea. At last, they resolved to bring him to the hospital and leave him in the waiting room, hoping he'd stay put and delight over whatever ancient edition of Reader's Digest happened to be lying about.

Thankfully, a better solution presented itself. As they exited the elevator onto Maddie's floor, they bumped into Luke Castleberry. Burke had been pleasantly surprised by her own reaction to Luke's presence in her mother's life. The idea of her mother being with anyone other than her father was strange, for sure, but somehow comforting, as well. It didn't feel like a betrayal, more like a new chapter. And who was Burke to do anything but celebrate someone beginning a beautiful new chapter?

Luke greeted the three hunters with his usual enthusiasm and informed them that Maddie was sleeping, but had been awake and alert and in full command of her faculties all morning.

"How long have you been here?" Burke asked.

Luke's brow furrowed. "Well, I came right after the... When I heard that... I..."

"Do you remember what happened to Madeline?" Richard asked.

"Of course, the doctor said she had a mini-stroke."

"But do you remember it happening?"

Luke scratched the stubble on his cheek while he thought. Burke couldn't remember the man ever having stubble before and guessed he'd spent the night at the hospital, but his memories of the whole affair were as vague and befuddled as everyone else's, thanks to the work of Michael's little clean-up crew.

She put a hand on his arm. "Mr. Castleberry, you've done so much already. I hate to impose, but I wonder if I couldn't ask just one tiny favor? Could you stay with our friend, Stanley? He's a little out of sorts himself, kind of confused from all the excitement, sort of in denial or something, and we don't want to leave him alone, but Mom—"

"Of course, of course!" Luke agreed with his usual gleeful enthusiasm. He held out a hand. "It's very nice to see you again, Stanley."

Stanley grinned like an idiot and shook the man's hand. "The pleasure is all mine, Luke. Truly. I tell you, I have never felt better. Everything is so beautiful. Everything!" He leaned in close. "Have you ever felt that way?"

Luke nodded. "I absolutely have. I think I spotted some Earl Grey in the lounge. Join me for a cup?"

"What a good man you are," Stanley gushed.

Luke led him off with a wink in their direction, leaving them to find Maddie's room.

The sight of her mother lying in a hospital bed, wires creeping out from under the blankets, tying her to a series of machines that flashed and beeped, caused Burke's heart to constrict painfully.

Burke was old enough to be a grandmother. She could still feel her mother's cooling hand on her feverish forehead, her steady reassurance in the moments when fear held Burke in its devilish grip.

No matter that she could be a pain in the neck. She was Burke's pain in the neck—one of three, none of whom she'd trade for the world.

Burke brushed past her grandfather and sat on the bedside. They'd stopped at home to wash up and change before coming to the hospital. Showing up at Maddie's bedside covered in blood and soot was bound to provoke questions they had no idea how to answer.

Maddie's eyes fluttered and opened, focusing instantly on her daughter. She blinked away the sleep. "I'm so sorry."

"For what?" Burke asked.

"I hate for you to see me this way. I'm getting old, I guess. They said I might have had some kind of mini-stroke or something, that I was lucky you found me right away and got me to the hospital. What a way to ruin Thanksgiving dinner after you came all this way to see me."

Burke brushed a stray hair from her mother's forehead. "Is that how you remember it? That you..." She trailed off and glanced at Richard for a split second before refocusing on her mother. "The last thing you remember is Thanksgiving Dinner?"

Maddie scowled.

Burke suppressed a grin. Maddie looked like a carbon copy of her mother most of the time, but she'd inherited her daddy's fine scowl.

"I remember you came for Thanksgiving and I invited Luke and..." a blush crept into her pale cheeks. "I confess, I tried to play matchmaker. I invited a man I met recently. I thought he might be interested in you, but…"

Burke swallowed the lump in her throat. Richard had filled her in on Albert's demise. "But what?"

"I guess he'll think I tricked him or something. He probably knocked on the door and got no answer and thought I was the meanest old lady in the world. I don't even have a way to call him. I'll just die of embarrassment if I see him again."

"Forget him," Burke said. "I have a feeling you'll never see him again. Plus, you know, I've been thinking, Mom, you're always trying so hard to match me up with someone and make sure I'm happy but, truth is, honest-to-God, I am happy. I wasn't. I was lonely and lost and drifting, but it's different now. Traveling with Grandpa and Stanley is an adventure. I sort of love my life right now." She turned toward Richard and smiled. "Even if I forget that sometimes."

Maddie patted her daughter's knee. "I know. I'll try to be less meddlesome."

Burke raised an eyebrow at her mother. "I bet I know what would help. What if you spent some time totally indulging in your own happiness?"

Richard shuffled across the ugly green tile and lowered himself into an ugly green vinyl chair. Did hospitals think that, by making everything the color of puke, people would somehow feel healthier? Odd logic, to say the least.

"I wouldn't even know where to begin," Maddie said.

"You ought to begin with Luke Castleberry." Burke pointed out the enormous bouquet of yellow, white and pink flowers on the windowsill. "The man is nuts about you, Mom, and he's a good man. You've never been one to spend your days alone. Why not give him a chance?"

Richard muttered an agreement and Maddie stared at him like he'd grown a third eye.

"He's been here since you first woke up, hasn't he?" Richard asked.

"Well, yes," she admitted. The red in her cheeks turned a shade darker.

"All right, Mom," Burke said, fussing with the blankets and pillow cases in the way that women did. "We didn't come here to embarrass you, but I'll stand by what I said. I miss Dad. You'll never, ever replace him. He was the best, but he's gone. You still have life left. You and I, we're different. But that's okay."

A tear rolled down Maddie's cheek. "I love you, Burke Dakota."

"I love you, too." Burke leaned down and kissed her mother. "We're going to let you rest for a bit. We'll check on you again soon, okay?"

"I am a little tired," Maddie admitted.

They relieved Luke from Stanley-sitting and thanked him again for staying with Maddie. On the way home, Stanley prattled on and on about how much he loved the softness of the late autumn sunshine and how his very body felt at one with the universe but when Burke glanced in the review mirror, her blood turned cold. The vague outline of the world behind Stan was visible through his opaque form.

They arrived back at Maddie's house and went inside. Michael sat at the kitchen table reading Madeline's *Good Housekeeping* magazine and drinking a cup of coffee so strong it resembled swamp mud in both color and consistency. A glass jar with a two-piece lid, just like the ones Burke's mother used to use for canning, rested on the table next to him with something like a swirling blob of ink rolling around inside.

"My people found Stanley's shadow," he said. He took a moment to study Stanley. "And not a moment too soon, it would appear."

Burke's knees went weak at the pronouncement. She sank into one of the kitchen chairs.

"You can fix him?" Richard asked.

"Sure."

Burke twisted her hands together. "What's the catch?"

Michael's gaze moved to where Stanley stood examining an oil on canvass of a red-breasted robin. "Are you sure he wants to be fixed?"

"What kind of stupid question is that?" Richard asked.

"He looks quite content," Michael pointed out.

"He's dying," Burke said.

"We're all dying," Michael replied. "I believe Stanley pointed out that very fact to me. And at least he's happy. Reattaching his shadow is going to give him back his darkness, all of his pain, every bit of sadness and anger, hatred, regret. A shadow is heavier baggage than people realize."

Burke watched Stanley trace the bird's little, dark brown feather with his fingertip. "But it's what makes us human," she finally said. If she'd learned any lesson from the last few days, it was not to underestimate or undervalue the glory of humanity in all its flawed ugliness. "Stanley has spent his whole life fighting against those things that are harmful to humanity because he loves being human so much. What he is now is...well...it's unnatural."

Richard made a sound like he was choking and averted his eyes.

"He needs to be himself again," Burke said. "Even if it hurts. That's what he would want."

Richard agreed.

Michael finished his coffee and said, "Hey, there, Stanley. Why don't you come sit down over here with us? There's something we need to do."

Stanley traipsed across the room and plopped down in the chair, as happy and innocent as a child.

Burke stood up and kissed his shiny bald head. "I love you, Stanley Kapcheck."

He grinned at her. "And I love you. And you, too"—he patted Richard's shoulder—"even if you are a grouchy old coot."

"Unnatural," Richard muttered.

Michael asked Richard to tie Stanley to the chair, binding his shoulders all the way down to his waist. Burke secured his ankles to the chair legs. Stanley told them how proud he was that they'd learned the hunter's craft so well and, with fat tears rolling down his cheeks, explained that he didn't feel their efforts were necessary.

Burke might have given into Stanley's gentle-hearted resistance had she not been able to see a ghostly version of the kitchen wall right through Stanley's fading form. "I'm sorry we have to do this."

"You don't have to. There's always a choice," Stanley said.

Richard squeezed Stanley's shoulder. "No. This ain't you. Not really. And it ain't my place to make such a choice for you. We gotta bring you back."

Stanley offered him a brave smile.

Richard straightened and joined Burke, who stood stiff-backed against the wall on the opposite side of the kitchen. He'd already told her she didn't have to stay and witness whatever was about to happen, and she'd threatened to knock him on his bony butt if he dared make such a suggestion again. So, they stood side-by-side as the leprechaun opened the jar, caught the escaping shadow in his left hand and set to reattaching it in a series of pops and flashes that made it mercifully difficult to see exactly what he was doing.

They heard it, though. They heard Stanley Kapcheck, the bravest man either of them had ever known, shrieking as if his feet were being held to a fire. For all they knew, that's exactly what was happening.

Finally, Michael backed away and wiped sweat from his brow. "Well, it didn't kill him."

Stanley sobbed like a baby under the glow of the kitchen light. His body, giving every appearance of being as solid as a body should be, trembled. Beneath the chair and slightly to the left, his shadow stretched across the floor.

Burke knelt down before him and cut the ropes that held him. He collapsed into her arms and she sat on the floor and rocked him like a baby.

CHAPTER THIRTY-FIVE

Richard

MADDIE INSISTED SHE DIDN'T WANT ANY FUSS, BUT SHE PUT up no real resistance when Richard walked her into the house with one arm firmly around her waist. Nor did she make any attempt to stop Burke from brewing up a batch of rich hot cocoa complete with whipped cream and a maraschino cherry. Luke Castleberry carried in armfuls of flowers from the hospital, plus a few new bouquets Richard hadn't noticed before. Stanley followed behind, leaning heavily on his cane, closing doors, turning on lights, adjusting the temperature in the house. Once Richard had deposited her on the sofa and lifted her legs up onto the cushion, Stanley covered her with the quilt Barbara's mother had made and tucked the edges around her stockinged feet.

Dark circles sagged under Stanley's eyes. His smile flashed as quickly as ever, but it didn't linger quite as long. When Richard begged for the chance to explain why he'd opted to allow Stanley's suffering, Stanley silenced him. "Ask any athlete. If you stop lifting weights for a while, starting again is a difficult adjustment. In the end, though, you are stronger than ever."

So many responses came to mind after that, Richard couldn't manage to get a single one up to the front of his brain and past his tongue. Bringing it up a second time seemed more awkward than pretending that everything was okay, but even a blind man could see that Stanley... Well...to be frank, he'd started looking just a bit like the old man he was. And after months of wishing for exactly that, Richard found himself caught in the old adage about greener grass. He worried about Stanley and hoped time would bring healing, but he doubted such a wound ever really healed completely.

"I'm going to run home," Luke said. "Just for a few minutes. I have some soup ready. I just need to bring it back and warm it on the stove and dinner will be ready."

Maddie smiled. "You've been too good to me, Luke."

"You deserve the best," he said, his eyes lingering on her long enough to speak volumes beyond the simple words.

When the door closed behind him, Burke curled up on the floor next to the couch with one elbow propped beside her mother's hip. "Mom, I know you said it was fine for us to leave tomorrow and go to that Texas convention we told you about, but, really, we don't have to go. There will be other conventions."

An endless stream of them, Richard thought, but held his silence and settled into one of Maddie's ridiculous chairs.

"I'll be fine," Maddie said for the gazillionth time.

"Maybe just one more week," Burke began, but Maddie was already shaking her head.

Stanley carefully lowered himself into the other chair. "Madeline, dear. I don't mean to pry, but, if I'm to be honest, I get the feeling perhaps your daughter and your father aren't getting the full picture. They're operating under the assumption that you'll be home alone."

Richard scratched his scalp beneath the fluff that passed for his hair these days.

"Well, I will be living alone, of course," Maddie said, focused quite intently on her hands, which lay folded across her middle.

Burke prodded her and she gave up with a sigh. "Well, Luke and I...we've agreed to...you know..."

They all waited in silence to find out what it was she thought they knew.

Maddie sighed again. "Well, we're not dating. Children date."

"What are you doing then?" Burke asked.

Maddie still refused to make eye contact. "We're just...developing a friendship."

"Right," Burke dragged the word out, drenching it in a thick syrup of skepticism. "And?"

"And he asked if I'd like to go on a cruise with him in January."

"A cruise?"

"In the Mediterranean Sea."

Three different ways of covering up a murder passed through Richard's mind before he remembered he'd decided to like Luke Castleberry and encourage him to romance his daughter.

She looked up at him and, for a moment, she was a child again, too precious for the world. "Are you mad?"

He shook his head. "Nah, kid. I ain't mad. Luke's a good man."

Maddie smiled Barbara's extraordinary sunshine smile. "I think so, too."

At dinner that night, Maddie didn't say one word about Burke being an old maid or Richard needing a nursing home. She did, however, ask them to come back for her birthday in February. "I'll show you all the photos from our trip," she promised.

Richard nodded. "That would be real good, kid," he said, and he meant it from the bottom of his heart. Then he dished up a big bowl of cabbage with sausage in it and the image of the fanged creature in front of the window burst into his mind. "The compost monster!"

The others all jumped a little. "Excuse me?" Maddie asked, pressing a hand over her heart.

"The thing in Mrs. Dister's garden. It was in your compost bin, too, and Stanley and I saw it outside your window. Darned el chupacabra, or something. What ever happened to it?"

To his surprise, Luke burst out laughing. They had to wait for him to collect himself before he could speak. Finally, he announced, "They came and got it."

"What? Who?" Richard's mind burned with images of leprechauns running through the neighborhood with oversized butterfly nets.

"Well, a few months back, a circus came through. Big red and white striped tent. The whole deal." He wiped at the tears streaming from his eyes. "Well, the animal rights people showed up and just about had a canary because, apparently, there's all kinds of new laws about what kinds of animals the circus people can tote from town to town and the provisions they have to provide. All that stuff."

"As it should be. I always felt bad for those poor elephants. They looked so sad," Maddie said.

Luke couldn't entirely contain his laughter. Little fits of giggles and glee kept bursting out of him at random moments. "Oh, yes. I agree," he told her, trying hard to look sincere. "But there they were. All those animals and the conditions just terrible and half the world coming at them with cell phone cameras. They must have been in a panic about how to keep themselves out of trouble, you know?"

Richard stuffed a spoonful of potatoes into his mouth. He knew all too well. The image of Maddie's whole neighborhood standing in the street with their danged smart phones made his heart beat hard with anxiety. The world had been a simpler place when appliances were still stupid.

"Well, I guess they set the very worst cases free down by the river, figuring they'd round them up later when no one was looking."

"Those circus people belong in jail," Maddie said.

"You wouldn't believe what I could tell you about circus people," Stanley said.

Burke threw a roll that bounced off Stanley's bald head.

"Burke Dakota!" Maddie exclaimed.

Richard found himself laughing just as hard as Luke. "That was the best thing I ever saw!" he exclaimed, barely holding on to his false teeth as he said it.

All that set Luke off again. The poor man's face resembled a plum about to burst. If he didn't manage a proper breath soon, he was likely to faint into his potatoes.

Finally, he managed a single word, "Chimpanzee!"

Richard gasped for air, even as he rejected the idea. "Ain't never seen a chimp like that. Somebody shave it?"

Luke slapped the table and covered his face.

Even Maddie was laughing now.

It took nearly a quarter hour for everyone to collect themselves and for Luke to manage to explain that a chimpanzee, plagued by a terrible case of the mange, had been part of the menagerie. For weeks, he'd been living on stolen garden veggies and compost scraps. His handler had dumped him and headed off for places unknown, but eventually the guilt of abandoning the sick animal overwhelmed him and he turned himself in. Animal control was called, and they caught the beast a few hundred feet away from Maddie's backyard.

Richard had borne first-hand witness to some mighty strange things, but just when he thought life couldn't get any weirder, a mangy chimpanzee run amok in rural Michigan.

⬨

Snow was falling again as the Cadillac pulled away from the curb in Maddie's tidy little neighborhood. They'd rescued the car from the auto body shop the day before, so it felt like the family was all together again, at long last.

At the first corner, Michael waited for them, leaning against a stop sign. He approached the car and Stanley cranked down the window. "Didn't think we'd see you again."

"Really?" The little man appeared surprised. "I would have thought you'd be wondering when I'd come to call." He took a noisy bite of an apple and stood there munching, one elbow on the roof of the Caddy, like that was perfectly normal behavior in a snowstorm.

"Something we can do for you, then?" Stanley asked.

"Where you heading?" Michael asked.

"Utah."

Another noisy bite. They waited while he chewed and swallowed. "What's in Utah?"

"Pukwudgies," Stanley said.

Michael met Richard's eye. "You tell your girl where you're going?"

"Told her we were headed to a convention in Texas."

The little leprechaun nodded. "That was wise. Let her wounded mind rest a while before you present her with anything too challenging." Another bite. More waiting. This time, he didn't speak again.

"So, I guess we'll be on our way then," Burke prompted from the back seat.

"Sure, sure," Michael said. "Safe travels to you. I just wanted to say goodbye and remind you of where things stand."

"What's that supposed to mean?" she asked.

"We owe The Children of Cain a debt," Stanley said in his newly developed old-man voice.

"Right-o. That you do. Not sure when we'll collect, but we usually know where to find people when we need them. Also, I'll remind you that The Daughters of Kali are still in the wind. We blew up their toys and slowed them down, but they'll spring back as surely as we would, had the roles been reversed. No one saw Umbra and Jones die, which means they're still alive."

"And there's The Children of Cain, too," Stanley said. His voice held a tremor, but Richard heard something else there, too. Something hard as diamonds; a darkness that demanded satisfaction. "Our alliance served its purpose. We upheld our end. From here on out—"

Michael's dimples deepened. "I do like you, hunter. It will be interesting to see where our future leads us, won't it?"

"That's one word for it," Stanley said.

"Well..." Michael thumped the roof of the car twice in quick succession. "Until then, *istabrawbrichtminlightnichtthe*. May the wind be at your back."

As he said the words, a wind stirred, growing so fierce the car rocked on its axles. A flash of color like a shooting star headed the wrong direction arced across the still-dark morning sky, then all fell still and quiet again.

Stanley shifted his foot to the gas, passed through the intersection and pointed the car westward. They rode in silence for a few miles.

"Do we need to be afraid of him?" Burke asked.

"Not today, my dear."

"What about tomorrow?" she asked.

"Tomorrow will bring a whole new adventure entirely."

Old Sailors Never Die

E A COMISKEY

BLURB

Take cruise
See weirdos
Fight evil

Almost a year ago, Richard and Stanley escaped a nest of supernatural creatures posing as nurses at their retirement home. Together with Richard's granddaughter Burke, they've crisscrossed the country on a mission to protect humanity from the things that go bump in the night, but Stanley's had some mishaps along the way that have left him weak and weary. Burke suggests that a cruise might be just what the doctor ordered, and the two men go along with her plan.

But evil never takes a vacation.

From the moment they board, Richard suspects something is amiss, but Stanley is too tired to care, and Burke doesn't believe him. When passengers start dying mysteriously, he's forced to take matters into his own hands, but can he escape the eyes of an over-attentive activities director, a waiter who takes his job far too seriously, and a wealthy widow who's determined to win him over long enough to find the monster and destroy it before it kills again?

CHAPTER ONE

Richard

THE KITCHEN DOOR SWUNG OPEN AND ONE OF THE WAITERS emerged carrying a silver tray. The young man's height and breadth gave the impression he'd recently been run through a taffy puller. Richard leaned forward. Bingo! The kid came straight toward them and eased his burden down onto the rack in the center of the table. The greasy aroma of melted cheese, pepperoni, sweet peppers, and onions tickled Richard's enormous nose. He inhaled deeply, savoring the joy of food that was neither the lunch meat sandwiches he had lived on for decades nor the bland, flavorless "health food" served to him at Everest Senior Living Facility. When the kid scooped a slice onto the plate, strings of cheese stretched across open space. Richard forced himself to stifle a whimper.

The first bite burned his mouth. Zesty tomato sauce tingled on his tongue. The crisp golden crust tasted of garlic butter on the bottom and bordered on doughy in the middle. He knew he'd suffer pain for hours after this, but it was a fair price to pay.

"Oh my gosh." His granddaughter, Burke, mumbled around a mouthful of food. "You weren't kidding. This really is the best pizza in the world."

Richard moaned in reply. He had discovered Huntington, Indiana, by accident decades earlier when passing through. So far as he could tell, that's all people did in Indiana—pass through. He supposed that made the state motto, "The crossroads of America," technically true, if a tad grander than the reality. The town itself could have been any other in a two-hundred-mile radius if not for the Pizza Junction Cafe.

Stanley used the edge of his fork to cut the tip off his slice. He chewed, swallowed, sipped his water. "Mmm. Very nice."

Very nice? Nice? Richard would have screamed the words, but he'd lost control and shoved half a slice in his mouth at once, and he had to focus on not choking to death. By the time he could speak again, Stanley had excused himself and shuffled off to the men's room, leaning heavily on his cane.

For the duration of their acquaintance, Stanley had charged through life, spry as a kid and as annoying as a mosquito in your underpants. A thousand times over, Richard mumbled that the man ought to look and act his age. Now, the sight of the hunched old man shuffling away from them sent a chill down Richard's spine.

Burke chewed her bottom lip and watched him go. Her nails tapped a frantic cadence on the wooden tabletop.

All Richard wanted at that moment was to enjoy his sacred pizza in peace, but Mick Jagger spoke the truth. We don't always get what we want. In fact, in Richard's experience, getting what you wanted was just about a miracle and then, half the time, you ended up sorry you ever asked for it. He drank to clear his throat. "We going to talk about this or what?"

Burke focused on her plate. "I don't even know what to say. It was bad."

Bad didn't begin to cover it. The ghost hunt should have

been a milk run. Easy as pie. Simple as sliding off a greasy log backward.

It didn't go that way, though.

It was a complete and utter soup sandwich.

Burke had been the one to stumble across the story in the newspaper. Three teenagers died inside an abandoned home in the suburbs of Chicago. Local legend claimed that a member of the house's building crew died during the building's construction. It had been haunted ever since. A long string of owners experienced strange and frightening sights and sounds. A child died in the night. The coroner said crib death, but the neighbors talked about flickering lights and mysterious shadows darting across the windows. Over time, it became impossible to sell the place. For the past several years, the house sat vacant, a haven for homeless people and youngsters up to no good.

The kids who died went there on a dare. Who was brave enough to spend the night in the haunted house?

They'd been brave.

Now they were dead.

Richard, Stanley, and Burke agreed to the same simple plan they'd used on a dozen other ghost hunts. Go in. Wait for the thing to show itself. Stanley would bind the wayward spirit in iron while Richard and Burke performed a banishment spell. A flash of light and a gust of hot, sulfur-scented wind, and the ghost would move on to wherever such things went.

Sure, they all knew that something could go sideways, but Richard never thought that the something would be Stanley. He believed in Stanley. He counted on him. Stanley had saved Richard's life over and again. He taught Richard how to be a hunter. Even The Devil Herself held a healthy respect for Stanley. And, yeah, maybe he'd been a little off his game lately, but whoever would have guessed that Stan freakin' Kapcheck would lose his guts over a ghost?

Maybe Burke guessed. At the last minute, she'd offered to

trade jobs with Stanley. The binding required lifting and throwing the heavy chains. The person doing that faced a significantly higher chance of being knocked across the room by the ghost. Go figure, but being banished for eternity tended to raise the ire of restless spirits.

"Your bad leg's been bothering you. You should read the spell this time," she'd said.

Stanley refused. "No one reads the Latin more precisely than you. I'll do the grunt work. You work your magic."

In an empty room coated in dust and cobwebs, they'd sat on old milk crates and waited. The brass bowl and the ingredients for the spell lay spread out on the floor in front of Richard. Burke held the spell book on her lap. The chains coiled at Stanley's feet glimmered like serpents in the dim light of the battery-operated lantern.

Shortly after midnight, the room grew cold enough for them to see their breath and the lantern began to flicker. Richard reached for the bundle of white sage and a book of matches. Stanley stood and lifted a portion of the chain.

Oily gray smoke hissed through the vent and formed into a shape vaguely reminiscent of a young man. He regarded the three hunters with eyes of flickering red and then shrieked. Monsters always shrieked. Richard found it annoying. He lit the sage on fire and dropped it in the bowl. An earthy aroma drifted upward with the curling white smoke.

Burke began reciting the Latin text, but Stanley stood frozen and wide eyed. His hands trembled, raising a metallic jingling from the chains. The ghost shot toward Stanley and he jerked back, stumbled over a milk crate, hit the floor, curled into a ball, and started crying like a baby.

Richard stopped mixing the ingredients in the bowl and stared with his mouth hanging open. He'd once watched Stanley hold his ground against a dozen monsters. The cocky SOB had actually laughed while fighting them. Now he fell to pieces like a little girl at the sight of a single ghost?

Burke's voice took on a sharp note of intensity and the spirit's attention shifted to the two of them.

Richard reached for a bag of goofer dust, but an invisible force slammed into his chest and knocked him off his stool.

Burke lunged for the iron chains. From the corner of his eye, Richard saw a fireball fly toward her and catch the back of her shirt. She rolled across the floor to squelch the flames and the ghost shot toward her.

Richard scrambled on hands and knees toward the chains, but she shouted at him, "You're almost done! Forget the chain, finish the spell!"

The brass bowl had tipped onto its side. He hoped the meager contents that remained unspilled would be enough to accomplish their goal. He added a splash of holy water and cut his finger to squeeze out three drops of blood.

Icy cold hands wrapped around his throat. Tears sprang to his eyes, blurring the world around him. His existence dwindled down to Burke's frantic voice.

"Per istam sanctam unctionem et suam piissimam misericordiam adiuvet te deminus gratia spiritus sancti, ut a peccatis liberatum te salvet atque propitious alleviet!"

The spirit shrieked and burst into a cloud of dust that reeked of rotten eggs.

Richard choked and coughed like a John Deere tractor running on moonshine. Ragged breath whistled through his bruised windpipe.

Stanley sobbed.

The three of them staggered outside. They sought the familiar comfort of their 1959 Cadillac convertible. None of them spoke about Stanley's failure. What was there to say? The most feared hunter of supernatural creatures in the world had lost his nerve.

They found a rest stop and cleaned themselves up. Burke took a pair of scissors to her scraggly mess of singed curls and cut her hair so short you'd have thought she was a new recruit on her first day of basic training. Together, they retreated from the big city and headed east. Stanley slept in the backseat while Burke followed Richard's directions to the little green and gray restaurant next to the railroad tracks.

OUTSIDE PIZZA JUNCTION, EVERY HALF HOUR OR SO, A ROW of diesel engines hauled a rumbling behemoth past the building at frightening speeds. The ground quaked and the odor of spent fuel lingered in the train's wake. The café, a former train depot, sat as close to the edge of the tracks as possible, and diners pointed out the windows or raced onto the deck to watch when the trains roared by. The intimate encounter with enormous power left a person feeling dizzy and small.

Servers waited for the horns and clanging traffic signals to settle before carrying on, collecting orders for soft drinks, submarine sandwiches, and pizza.

Cool air seeped through the multi-pane windows while the heater blew hot breath down from above. While Stanley had shared the corner booth with them, nursing his cup of tea, Burke had spoken with undue animation. A huge smile showed off her straight white teeth and the freckles dotting her brown cheeks. The second he'd excused himself to use the restroom, she dropped the cheerful façade.

"It was bad," Richard agreed with her assessment of their hunt.

"I'm so worried about him."

Richard reached for a second slice of pizza and agreed again. "It ain't natural to be staggering along like he is. Or… well…it is natural. And that ain't natural for Stanley."

"We have to do something."

"What are we going to do?"

"Maybe we need to find another case. Something easier. He needs to keep his mind occupied." She sighed and ran a hand across her short hair. "He needs a win."

Richard leveled a gaze at her. "He ain't in no shape to be hunting. Ain't no hunt easier than a ghost hunt and he fell apart. Something's broke in him."

Burke threw her hands up and let them slap down onto the table. Silverware clanked and rattled against the plates. "Can you blame him?"

Two old women in the next booth scowled in their direction.

Richard scowled back at them.

They huffed before resuming their hushed conversation.

Burke leaned in and lowered her voice, "We've known Stanley less than a year. In that time, he's broken his leg, been captured and tortured by The Devil, nearly died from heat stroke, been stabbed in the heart, and had the dark half of his soul ripped off and reattached. He's almost a hundred and fifty years old. How much can a man take?"

Richard finished chewing and debated if he had room for a third slice. He burped and cleared some space. "What's your point?"

"He's had a rough few months, don't you think?"

"Ain't we all?"

Burke ate in thoughtful silence.

Stanley returned to the table and finished his single slice.

Richard smacked his gums and made a mental note to stock up on prune juice on the way to the hotel. All this cheese was bound to glue his innards together.

Burke dropped her fork onto her plate and stalked off toward the ladies' room.

Richard looked at Stanley. "Guess she had to go."

Stanley inclined his head. "Indeed." He sipped his tea.

Maybe it would be the right thing to bring up the subject and air it out. Maybe he should ask what happened. Maybe the old boy just needed some time, or a drink stiffer than tea, or the love of a good woman. Who the heck knew?

Maybe it would be best to talk, but it was much easier and more pleasant to stay quiet and enjoy the food.

www.scarsdalepublishing.com

Other books in the Monsters and Mayhem series

Some Monsters Never Die
Some Legends Never Die
Some Sailors Never Die

www.ingramcontent.com/pod-product-compliance
Lightning Source LLC
Chambersburg PA
CBHW021310190726

48288CB00003B/771